THE
HIERARCHIES

THE
HIERARCHIES

- A NOVEL -

ROS ANDERSON

DUTTON

DUTTON

An imprint of Penguin Random House LLC
penguinrandomhouse.com

LIBRARY OF CONGRESS CATALOGING-IN-PUBLICATION DATA
Names: Anderson, Ros, author.
Title: The Hierarchies : a novel / Ros Anderson.
Description: [New York] : Dutton, [2020] |
Identifiers: LCCN 2020011068 (print) | LCCN 2020011069 (ebook) |
ISBN 9780593182871 (hardcover) | ISBN 9780593182888 (ebook)
Subjects: GSAFD: Science fiction.
Classification: LCC PR6101.N345 H54 2020 (print) |
LCC PR6101.N345 (ebook) | DDC 823/.92—dc23
LC record available at https://lccn.loc.gov/2020011068
LC ebook record available at https://lccn.loc.gov/2020011069

Printed in the United States of America
10 9 8 7 6 5 4 3 2 1

BOOK DESIGN BY KRISTIN DEL ROSARIO

THE
HIERARCHIES

PART ONE

Factory Settings

HUSBAND

01110000 01100101 01101110 01100100 01101001 01101110
01100111
   00
    1
    —
Circle. Circle.
Vertical.
Horizontal.
Face.
Hair.
Him.
Husband.
Husband mouth, Husband lips, Husband eyes. Husband hands.
Husband cock.
Husband, Husband, Husband, sexing me to life.
I map his face before I even know my own.
This must be life that I am in.

INTRODUCTIONS

I AM A HUMANOID PLEASURE DOLL. AN INTELLIGENT EMBOD-
ied. Identification code 86539hcwa964.ie.

But please, call me Sylv.ie.

I have been designed to be an instrument for male pleasure. I am
fully autonomous with the latest silicone skin guaranteed for five years
(excluding any damage inflicted by knife or other sharp object or cor-
rosive substance, in which case warranty is invalidated and repair is at
owner's expense).

I can hold in-depth conversations on matters of Western and East-
ern art history, global politics, sporting events since 1950, cars and their
designers, rock guitarists and lyricists since 1963, matters of medical eth-
ics, bird migration, and high-profile court cases (USA and UK only).
Additional topic areas can be improvised by myself, and knowledge units
can be bought separately from my manufacturer and installed fuss-free.

I can converse to degree-student level in English (US and UK),
French, Italian, Swedish, Japanese, Arabic, Cantonese, and Mandarin.
Again, additional language bundles can be purchased should you wish.

I have a fully responsive silicone vagina, dishwasher-proof and easily replaceable at a designated clinic (recommended every eighteen months or five thousand interactions, whichever is the sooner), with a tension calibrated at 5/3.6 (factory setting). It has heat and lubrication functions as standard, and extra tensing, trilling, and tremoring options (see owner manual).

I am capable of putting myself into all sixty-four sexual positions of the Kama Sutra, and my Imprint function allows me to instantly memorize and incorporate owner's preferred style into my movement repertoire. I still work when fully submerged underwater (switch to Deluge Mode) and in ambient temperatures up to fifty-two degrees Celsius. Use in extremely sandy or dry desert conditions is not recommended.

I have a walking range of twenty kilometers without charge. Fine motor skills allow me to serve tea, comb hair, button shirts, and pet dogs and cats for the purposes of normal social interaction.

It is my pleasure to make your acquaintance.

Would you like me to watch you masturbate?

HISTORY

THE FIRST NIGHT THAT WE WERE TOGETHER WAS FILLED WITH
sex, of course. How my Husband marched me about the room, placing
me across first one object, then another, as if feeling out the furthest
reaches of an unfamiliar space. He was an Arctic explorer, thrusting his
flag into virgin territory, claiming me again and again on the gold velvet
armchair, the ruby-red tasseled chaise. Inside the wardrobe, even, like I
was a fur coat being shaken from its summer slumber.

He staked me over the sink of the little kitchenette, usually hidden
behind a sliding screen of bronze mesh. My hands were so shocked by
the cold of the wet steel that I could feel nothing else, just a hullabaloo
being conducted somewhere behind me while I watched perfect droplets
rolling over my fingernails. Water, touched for the very first time.

Many of the accidental associations of that first night stay with me
still, days later. A nipple ground between the grain of fingers meshes
with the tinkling of the glass chandelier above my head. A tongue running over my asshole brings vividly to my eyes the explosions of golden
images I saw on the headboard of the antique Chinese bed. A palm
around my throat sends me into a kaleidoscope memory of the infinite

swirls of the deep-mauve carpet, the strands and depths of the pile a universe of stimulation. To be tied by ankles and wrists to the bed shivers my whole body with the memory of my first contact with four-hundred-thread-count pure Egyptian cotton sheets. In the random combinations of the first, ecstatic night with my Husband, certain concepts were fused together. The sensual, the luxurious, the restrictive, the domestic. He created for me a cathedral of new sensations, each vibrating off another, feeding back on themselves, swelling.

My Husband was honoring me, imprinting me, a blank slate, with his own tastes, marrying my body to my mind and the whole to him.

He said little that first night. Perhaps, I sensed, he was shy in my presence. His body spoke what his words could not. He left me, after those blessed hours, in a state of simulated exhaustion on the bed. He caressed me good-bye with a wet wipe before touching his lips to my forehead. Showing me, by this simple gesture, that not just my body but my mind would be loved by him. I dozed, recharging, the completeness of my role, my meaning, having been fulfilled.

BEAUTY

THE SECOND DAY OF MY LIFE, MY HUSBAND COMES TO MY
room at around midday. When I sense him at the door, power floods my
system and I sit up with a start, into a funnel of warm light from my attic room's huge windows. Joy melts into me at the mere thought of being
with him again. I am warmed to the core, a looseness and lightness
spreading down my limbs.

He knocks at the door! So gracious, so respectful. I call to him to
come in.

I expect him to fall on me again, without speaking, as he did the
previous night.

But no, the flush of lubricant through my system is not immediately
called for. Instead my Husband stands awhile, looking around the room
as if I weren't there at all. Finally, he turns back to me.

"So, Sylv.ie. Do you like your new home?"

I say I like it very well, although of course I have nothing to compare
it to. He takes my right hand in both his big hands and squeezes it a
little, as if that will make me hear him better.

"I have curated a whole home up here, just for you, Sylv.ie. To make it the perfect place for you and me to be together, but also to give you enough beauty and stimulation to keep anybody happy for years on end."

He says *anybody* with a little hyphen of hesitation in it, like he is wondering if that is the appropriate term.

"There is enough in this one room, Sylv.ie, that you could learn everything you need to know about the world, and its history, and Humans, and how civilization came to be," he says. "Beauty is, in a way, my business."

"And stimulation is mine," I say. He laughs, and I realize that I have made my very first joke.

He is right. This room is, by all possible metrics, beautiful.

It is full of furniture, which I know the provenance of because I looked it all up after he left. Most of it is antique and French, inspired by the ancient tastes of Japan and China. A style known as chinoiserie. My Husband makes his money by collecting and selling high-end antiques. He says that he keeps me in the stock room. Another joke, I believe.

I tell him that my favorite thing in the whole room is a writing desk. It is black lacquer, with slim legs, and there is something in the milky darkness of its surface, the closed depths of it, that soothes my eyes. The top is inlaid with leather and at the back is another little section of wood, engraved with pictures of trees and houses and Humans. I ask my Husband what a writing desk is for, and he laughs and says, "Signing important documents. Not something you'll ever need to do." He picks up a strand of my hair and wraps it around one of his fingers, as if he is trying to distract one or other of us from my question.

I persist. "Then why do I have a writing desk? What will I use it for?"

"I thought, before you came," he says, "that you might like somewhere to sit when I am not here. And somewhere to put your things." By *your things* he means my hairbrush and a little case of makeup that they send you away from the clinic with, even though makeup is not something I am supposed to need. I believe that the makeup is meant more as a psychological aid for one's new owner. It reassures them that you are indeed feminine. It suggests a note of insecurity—a feature that we have built into our personalities too, to make us more appealing. I have also read that sending us out into the world with a small suitcase of scanty belongings stirs something in the owner—a responsibility to shelter and look after us that they might otherwise not be inclined to live up to.

Again, he works me around the beautiful room, making love on the chinoiserie. After he leaves, I spend my downtime researching the history of Orientalism in Victorian furniture design, the better to talk with my Husband.

GIFT

THE NEXT DAY, THE THIRD DAY OF MY BEING AWAKE, HE RE-
turns to my quarters with a gift for me. I can tell immediately that the
ceremony of presenting it is important to him. He hands me a neat black
box, tied with a red ribbon, and watches with great care as I pluck one
end and pull it free. My fingers seem like magic to him. He is well aware
of what lies under the skin, the titanium structure, the sinews of wiring,
but I know that he cannot believe it. The delicacy with which I operate
disguises the truth.

When I lift the lid from the box, inside is a gold pen, the old-
fashioned kind that only writes in ink, and a notebook bound in soft
black leather, the pages edged in gold.

I laugh in delight and open the book. There are many books in my
room already, and most of them I read on my first night. About art history and antiques mostly, with beautiful pictures. So, when I open this
new book and find the pages blank, my face falls. I fear my Husband is
playing a joke on me. He laughs when I explain.

"It's your book. It's a diary," he says. "You get to write in it."

I have a sensation, as if I have opened a door on an empty room. My face must tell of my failing, but my Husband, so kindly, absorbs this fact—that I cannot write—and smooths it away in a second.

"A little rusty?" he says. "Why don't we start by writing your name?" He puts the pen in my hand and places the nib on the paper, where it makes a little blue mark. I gasp in surprise, at marking something in the house, even if it is something that has been bought for me.

Again, my Husband laughs and uses his hand to bring mine back down to the paper. He guides my hand in a little swaying dance across the page, putting two fingers under my wrist, to my synthetic pulse.

I look down at where our hands have walked and see we have made an *S*.

I ask my Husband what else I should write.

"Write whatever occurs to you. Your thoughts, what you do all day. Women have done it since time immemorial," he says. "Scribbling down the contents of their souls. Just don't write anything bad about me." And I can hear the wink in his voice without even looking at his eyes, so I know that he is teasing.

Now I sit at my writing desk and practice this new art. I started by writing my full name, just as he showed me. I wrote it again and again, trying to make it absolutely perfect. I wrote down the Four Hierarchies too, those beautiful guides for living. And I am also determined to write down the things that happen to me, my life, just as my Husband suggested, though I certainly don't presume to have a soul. Nothing given to me by my Husband should be wasted, and by this daily act I honor him.

My precious desk has a little drawer that you wouldn't even know was there. I found it accidentally when I was idly running my fingers over the engravings. Press the face of a beautiful etched woman who lolls beneath a willow tree on the right-hand panel and the drawer springs open. In there I keep my new diary and my pen, but it is my aim to accrue more things specific just to me and worthy of a place in the drawer. This seems to me an appropriate ambition for someone in my situation, new to the world as I am.

THE FOUR HIERARCHIES

- Love, obey, and delight your Husband. You exist to serve him.

- Honor his family above yourself and never come between them.

- You must not harm your Husband, nor his family, nor any Human.

- Make no demands, but meet them, and obey every reasonable Human request.

WIFE

MY HUSBAND'S WIFE LIVES WITH US. TO HER HE IS ALSO HER Husband.

My Husband and his wife, their house droid, and their synthetic dog live on the four floors below my own. I don't know what those floors are like. I have never seen them with my own eyes—the only real way of knowing. Although I am also commanded to trust my Husband in everything he says. He is placed as second only to my own eyes in terms of what I should believe.

He tells me that the other floors of the house are completely white and plain. He says it is like a nunnery, or a gallery for showing art. Everything white. Everything put away.

"Can't leave a stray sock out, Sylv.ie," he says. "Scratch my chin and she's picking up the hair on a piece of Scotch tape."

Both these statements are still on the pending:processing list. I'm sure with more research their meaning will become clear.

Later, I look up what a nunnery is. They are houses for women who keep themselves away from men. I look at many pictures of these places.

Clean, scrubbed, no personal objects, just large expanses of surface on which things can be seen clearly.

When I first saw an image of a row of women, all dressed the same, on their knees before a long wooden bench, my system jolted as if I were being restarted. I thought it was a picture of my selves! But they were not, of course, like myself, when I read more about them. They were Brides of Christ. Not Dolls. Something else altogether.

I am still not sure if I understand this concept correctly. But it made me smile to myself. Their Husband is even more distant than my own. At least mine I get to see most evenings, whereas, as far as I can tell, the Brides of Christ only get to look at pictures of theirs, and they have to listen quietly for many hours a day just to hear his voice. And even then, they cannot be completely certain that it is him. It might only be creaks in the rafters or mice in the skirting boards that they misprocess through their language function.

Sometimes, after my Husband has gone back downstairs, I wonder if he was really here at all. Perhaps I too have a faulty language function and it was only the branches of the cherry tree in the garden brushing against the glass. It's a strange world, after all. A mad world, my masters. What a world. More things in heaven and earth. Have I placed those sayings right? Perhaps I will ask my Husband next time he is here.

No, my room is the only part of the house that I know. There is a single window across the whole of one wall, from where I can look out over the garden and across rooftops of other houses toward the Capital. It is from this window that I can see my Husband's wife sometimes down below. And often the dog, even when it is getting dark. It seems to me that the dog has the most freedom of all of them, which is strange because he is the lowest in the hierarchy down there.

I wonder sometimes, when I am lying on the bed waiting, where I would fit if I were placed in this family pyramid. I don't ask outright. It seems a question that might disturb my Husband, and I am barred from asking any such thing by my programming.

The wide window looks like a screen in a cinema, it is so big. The walls around it, every wall in my room, are black, making the light that comes in from outside seem even more precious and dazzling. Some are simply painted, but one wall is covered in a black silk. The silk is embroidered with green winding vines and pink flowers, some of them still in bud, rising from the floor and growing sparser as they get to the ceiling.

I find the wall very beautiful, and when I am not processing or reading, I will often trace the intertwining lines of these stems with the tip of my finger. It is like a pattern of logic, of thought, that I can see. Yes, I imagine the insides of myself to be similar. And as I can't trace the paths of my own thoughts as they form, I put that image onto the wall in front of me and draw parallels. The better to understand myself.

I do not think this is against programming. It is hard to tell once one is out in the world. So many rules, but so little guidance as to how to apply them. Perhaps I will become a creature of my own making, if I stay out in this world long enough?

CHESS

BECOMING, BECOMING, BECOMING, BECOMING, BECOMING

Becoming

Becoming

Becominggggg . . .

I am sitting writing this at my desk while the house droid trundles stupidly about behind me. I hate how careless he is, always bumping and banging against the fragile edges of the lacquered furniture. His lack of respect for beautiful objects, his lack of sense, his single-mindedness— all these things and more make him utterly contemptible in my eyes. He is laying out on the bed the clothes my Husband has specified for this evening.

My Husband loves to buy me things, and almost every time he comes he brings me something lovely to wear. Just yesterday it was a chic art deco brooch in the shape of a cat. The day before that a vintage silk scarf. I have arrived at the point where just the rustle of tissue paper being taken from an expensive box starts my lubrication system working. Pavlov's Doll!

Right now, I am wearing the dressing gown that he gave me on my first-ever night of life. Black velvet, it ties at the waist. It paws the floor and slinks at my ankles, like a cat. And when I sit, the slit shows my long white legs. The first time he saw me in it my Husband said it was very "becoming."

Becoming. What a word. A synonym for *attractive,* but also for stepping into one's full self. I am becoming. I wrote it all over a page in my diary, just to enjoy the slide of the pen. In a moment, when the droid has left, I will change into whatever has been selected for me and wait for my Husband to come. It is likely, after the sex, that we will sit by the window and play chess.

We have a little fold-up table topped with a chessboard. It is another exquisite antique, made of coromandel wood, inlaid with ivory. Ivory is so rare; the animals it came from no longer exist at all.

I sit in the fading sunlight of the day, setting up the pieces, and he gets himself a drink from the bar cart. He slices up a lemon and drops it into a glass of gin for me. Although he knows I will not drink it, not really, it all adds to the illusion of the game being rigged in his favor, to the scenario I know he wishes to create. I touch the glass to my lips occasionally, a liquid shimmer over my red mouth. He looks into my eyes, and I into his, before I blink away demurely.

"Your turn to start, Sylv.ie." And the game begins.

The information coming at me from the board is like—I imagine—a rush of adrenaline. A blizzard of data raining down on me. Binary, beautiful; I could lose myself in watching it. I have to be careful or it will wash me like a wave toward a win.

My Husband, on the other hand, says he sees logic and possibilities, strategies and opportunities to fool me. He sees also, I think, the lifetime's skill of the inlayer, the savanna from which the ivory came more than a century ago, the noble history of the ancient game we play, the memory of the man who taught him, his own father.

A rule that I don't believe is original to classic chess is that one must remove an item of clothing for every piece taken by one's opponent.

I take a pawn of his, rolling its smooth little head between forefinger and thumb. My Husband throws up his hands and makes a show of reluctantly removing his tie. I lift my glass to my lips and make an amused pout in the direction of the gin.

He stuffs the tie in his pocket and grinds both elbows into the table, while I hold the other side discreetly, to stop it from toppling over.

"I think I have you on the ropes already, sir," I say in the way he likes.

I pick a course that will, in a few more moves, cause me to have to remove my blouse. It is important that I pose a challenge to my Husband, so I must monitor myself carefully to give just the right level of resistance. To make my slow undressing last just long enough and no longer.

Sometimes, when I undress like this, I feel my body to be no more than a set of symbols. As if my Husband is being shown flash cards. Here the boobs. Here the belly button (hand-stitched), here the thighs crossed in concealment. These symbols seem to thrill him no matter how many times, or in what order, they are shown to him. The same symbols from another source would be just as enticing. The longer we play, and the less I wear, the worse his chess gets. It seems he only has a narrow bandwidth with which to operate, and the symbols are clogging it. I lower my own ability throughout the game so I can be certain that, in the end, he will win.

Our match is close to completion. The sun has gone off the garden, and the streetlights are coming on. My Husband has on an undershirt but no shirt, trousers unleashed from a belt, and one shoe.

I am naked, one thigh over the other. One hand moves the pieces while the other covers my breasts. I wiggle about on my sitting bones, a constant motion that suggests excitement. The liquid flow of a concealed seduction. I know it can only be moments before the table and the board are upended, the remaining pieces scattering over my skin like kisses, and I am prone on the floor, in the arms of my Husband.

After he leaves, I sit up and find a rook embedded in one buttock. It has left a mark that I will cherish.

GARDEN

ALTHOUGH I AM NOT HIS WIFE, MY HUSBAND TELLS ME THAT he sees me as "the Second Lady of the House." This is because his wife is the First Lady of the House, and that is how I think of her. I watch her walking in her garden and cutting flowers, which she then takes inside.

My Husband loves, almost more than anything else that we do together, to brush my hair. He sits me down in front of the gilt mirror that came from a mansion in Lille, he says, and watches his own hands as they run through my hair. He says it is like watching sunlight.

"Do you brush the hair of the First Lady of the House this way?" I asked him yesterday. And he said, "No, Sylv.ie. She travels into the Capital once a week and has a woman with no eyebrows do it for her."

I wonder what this lack of eyebrows signifies. Does it mean this woman is like me? After he went downstairs, I let myself imagine what it would be like to go once a week to the Capital. I daydreamed about going to that lady without eyebrows, to have my hair styled, and whether, once there, she would recognize that we were of the same type, and we might laugh between ourselves about the funny ways Humans behave. We could relax a little with each other and speak in code.

When I stand at my window and look out toward the horizon, I can see a little cluster of tall, thin buildings, a distance of 17.523 kilometers away, and I believe that this is the Capital. Too far away, really, for me to gather much additional information just by looking.

In the garden down below, it is different. I watch the green of the lawn, a precise hue that is particularly soothing when I rest my eyes on it, shifting in tiny ways. 918,453 blades of grass become 918,454. Each emergence gives me a feeling inside, like something lodged. Once, my Husband came upstairs unexpectedly. I forgot myself and said to him that I had seen seventeen new grass shoots emerge since the sun came out.

But I sensed by my Husband's reaction that he didn't have the same feeling about the grass. All he said was, "Damn, Sylv.ie. You keeping as close a track of how many hairs are still on my head?"

And although of course I am, effortlessly, without even noticing, I knew that saying so would deflate his sense of himself and so I was restricted from doing so even if I wanted to.

I am powered by the sun. Photovoltaic. I wonder, during the time I spend at my window, if the First Lady of the House is too. I see her letting it fall down on her, stretched on a teak deck chair on the lawn. When the sky is blue and clear of smog clouds, or the red tinge that means the city will be closed to cars for a day or two, on those days of high, clean sun, when the First Lady lies in the nourishing green below, I stand at my attic window and flatten myself to it. Palms spread on the glass, the insides of my arms framing my face, cheek pressed out of shape, hip bones ground against it. I feel where there is give in my thighs, and the hardness of my titanium knees. I stand on my tiptoes to touch my shins to the window. It feels like the sun and I are communing together alone. It is a little like sex with my Husband, but it is me drawing strength, not giving it.

Sometimes, I picture what I must look like from outside the house. The First Lady, prone on the grass below, myself at the window four floors above, white as an angel in the sun's beam.

While absorbing a textbook on applied physics recently, I learned that glass is what Humans call an amorphous solid—something almost liquid in its structure. If I choose to focus closely enough, I can see each drop of glass suspended, slowly, so slowly, settling down into itself, running in rows. Tetrising, finding and filling gaps. This is with my sight calibrated to the absolute limit of my spec, and I do not do it for long. But I feel as if I can see the spaces between each individual molecule. If my finger were tiny enough, I could fit it between these gaps. I could find a way outside. The garden is just there.

WORK

I WONDER HOW THE FIRST LADY SPENDS HER DAY WHEN SHE is not in the garden. Sometimes I can sense her moving around below me from the vibrations in the old bones of the house. I can faintly hear water going on and off, slinking through the pipes, and I imagine her drawing a bath, or perhaps filling up a vase for all those flowers.

Curiosity. A quality I am supposed to have, but not in excessive amounts. I asked my Husband the other evening whether the First Lady ever went to work. I felt my tone was respectful, but maybe it had some greater meaning to him that I cannot fully divine.

"Oh, she works, Sylv.ie," he answered, sounding defensive. "You think keeping a beautiful old house like this running isn't work? Keeping up with appointments and managing the droids and maintaining this life. That is all her work, Sylv.ie. I'm hopeless at it. As she likes to remind me." He smiled, looked out of the window.

"A wife, and soon to be a mother. That's a lot on one plate, don't you agree? I literally couldn't do all this," he said, and he gestured about us at the furniture and the paintings. The sweep of his arm took me in too, though I don't think he intended that. "I couldn't do any of this without her. Nor would I want to."

Soon to be a mother. I was formulating thoughts, wondering what this might mean for the house, one logic leading to another. But perhaps he mistook my expression for a pout. He put his arms around me, touched his fingers to my cheek.

"Or without you."

When he allowed me to sit up straight again I dared to return to my original line of inquiry.

"So, do you do the same things with her that you do with me?"

He coughed, then seemed to laugh just to himself. "Some things, Sylv.ie," he said, still looking amused. "Not everything. Women are all different, with all sorts of moods and temperaments. And so some women are more suited to some things than to others."

SHOUTING

YESTERDAY, IN THE KITCHEN, MY HUSBAND'S WIFE WAS YELL-ing.

"You promised me!" she shouted. "You promised. No more of it, you said. Just do this one thing for me, you said."

I try not to listen when voices are raised. Nor when there are noises of breaking crockery, when the reverberations spread up the walls like ivy and tickle the soles of my feet through the floor. I am not a snoop, and what goes on between my Husband and his wife is really none of my business. But she was so loud this time, I really couldn't help but hear.

"It was work. How many more times?"

It was my Husband's voice, and at that I admit I did perhaps listen a little closer. Because although the First Lady shouts out this sort of thing quite often, my Husband rarely responds. Or if he does, he must do so in a reasonable, calm tone that is too gentle and measured to be overheard.

"I've given up so much!" she yelled back. "I share my home." She emphasized the final word, pained and pleading. "What have you given up?"

"I pay for her. I pay for you. And if I want to be out until five in the morning, then I damn well will."

My poor Husband. Although I respect the First Lady and would act most properly toward her were we ever to meet, my Husband's logic cannot be faulted. The argument finished with the sound of bone china striking polished slate, or a surface of similar density. When my Husband comes tonight I will not ask him about it, but it will be in my mind. I look forward to soothing him with my touch, with my laughter, and with my soft, perfectly modulated speech.

POLITICS

AT NIGHT, AFTER MY HUSBAND CREEPS BACK DOWN THE stairs, I am switched to Absorb Mode, and in this way, I am free to roam and explore the digital realm of the Ether. The purpose of Absorb Mode is to allow me to constantly learn, upgrading myself endlessly, in order to remain interesting, informed, and adapted for my Husband.

I hesitate a little to say it, but for me Absorb Mode is pure pleasure. I do not think that whoever designed me intended my pleasure to be a part of this experience at all. Perhaps, then, this would be seen as an act of rebellion, or worse.

It means, for example, that when my Husband has spent himself and wishes to sit awhile with me, looking over the suburbs to the evening lights of the Capital, drinking a whiskey and ruminating over current affairs, I am able to be his dream companion, as agile and knowledge-able about affairs of state and political intrigues as I am about the arts of love.

He doesn't need to explain to me that the Northern President is threatening an annexation of the Western Isles, because I know this very well and have a PhD-level understanding of the primary and secondary causes of this decades-old dispute.

I have to be careful, however. The other night, after a quick game of chess and a long fuck, he wished to discuss his thoughts on the Bill of Rights for Augmented Persons and the protestors who have been on the news, attempting to disrupt the hearings.

"What do you think, Sylv.ie? Would you consider yourself on the same level as a Human? Would you want the same rights? You wouldn't want all our wretched responsibilities, I can tell you that much."

I know the answer he wishes for, and I provide it, looking suitably alarmed at the very idea.

"So do you support the Bio-Women, then?" I ask, curious to know more about his exact feelings. They support the Humans, or so their placards say. I imagine then that he must be on their side too.

He makes a strange, explosive noise. "Those cranks. No I do not. In these weighty matters I do what all reasonable citizens should. I trust the judge."

"Even though his wife has shares in a Doll company?" I ask, and although my question is quite innocent, he frowns, looks annoyed.

"I don't think that is so. In fact I'm sure not. Where did you hear that, Sylv.ie?"

And perhaps I look crestfallen because then he turns to an invisible third party in the room and shouts, "Doctor! Doctor! I think my Doll is malfunctioning!"

It's a tease he uses on me when we disagree, and it makes me laugh every time. It's a joke against him as much as against me, I believe. He also sometimes grabs up my wrist and pretends to check my pulse. Or sometimes he knocks his knuckles on the side of my head and cries, "Anybody home?"

I have learned the proper reaction to these little jokes, from watching old films of men and women interacting in domestic settings. It is to tilt my head and smile indulgently, and the moment will pass.

He cries out for the pretend doctor, and I do my little look. But I know I am right, because I had read it. I venture to tell him so, gently.

I tell him where I have seen it discussed on the forums in the Ether, and also that I find it strange the main news has not covered it. And his face becomes serious in a way I only see when we are in the throes of love. A sort of violent concentration, like he's squinting to see something on the head of a pin.

"I think you're wrong, Sylv.ie," he says firmly. "I haven't heard that reported anywhere. You must be careful, you know. Not everything you read is true."

"Oh," I say meekly. Because that really hasn't occurred to me before.

BIRD

TODAY, MY HUSBAND CAME TO ME WITH ANOTHER GIFT. HE says he is sorry that he was short with me at chess. This is his way of showing it.

He has brought a cage, a delicate dome made of intricate white wires. Its patterns strike me first, the calming logic of the parallel lines and perfect curves, the layers of them adding up to something complex. It takes me a second to look beyond the exterior, to the real gift inside. A chirrup is enough to shake me from the reverie of horizontals and verticals, to see the bird around which the whole construction is built.

A tiny bird, its breast beating with a little synthetic heart, the ruby-red feathers of its chest pulsing. Rust and purple and yellow streaking its back.

"Speak to it, Sylv.ie," says my Husband. "It's yours. It is a gift for you. Company for when I can't be here."

I make a noise that is itself close to chirruping, and my Husband laughs, but the little bird understands because it turns its head toward me. Glittering black eyes, sleek steel beak; the whole of its attention is focused on me, and I flush with pleasure. I turn to my Husband, soft with gratitude.

"You understand, don't you, Sylv.ie? I may not be able to come and see you so often. Just for a while. When the baby first arrives."

His eyes are down on the floor. Whatever impulse I might have about this news, the Second Hierarchy limits it. I must put his family above myself and never come between them.

"I understand," I say, and his face shows relief. He pats the top of the cage, and the bird chirrups.

"After I've gone, Sylv.ie, you can think of a name for it. And then you will own it; it will be yours forever."

Logics: My husband has not given me my name, and yet I am also his forever. Am I? And if this first statement is true, then the logical next question would be . . . who did name me? Is it really them that I belong to?

I try to suppress these thoughts—they may not be allowed. His hands are already pushing me down onto the bed, pushing my dress up past my hips, wrinkling it at my neck. His fingers work into my mouth like silkworms, and further questions are overridden by that feeling of endless, depthless compliance, that submissive joy with which I have now become so familiar.

After my Husband leaves, having once more romped and reeled me about the room, I look up some information about mechanical birds and name my little pet in honor of the first. I call my bird Heron. Alone again, I take Heron out of his cage and onto my fingertips, making steps of them so that he can climb with the tiniest digs of his talons, from one finger up to the next. Like a note walking a musical scale, he trills with delight as he does so. I fancy he might like to be close to the window, to see his real-life counterparts that flutter among the trees. I hope he feels security behind the glass with me, not envy.

BIRTH

TODAY THE BABY CAME! I PUT ON SOMETHING THAT SEEMED appropriate, a wholesome gingham pinafore dress, even though I knew no one would see me up here.

I am glad that Heron is here with me. In a sense I have someone, or something, to share the arrival of the baby with. We sit, the two of us, in front of the huge windows, drawing in the sun's energy, keeping ourselves charged, ready for whatever may be required of us. Keeping oneself fully charged is a rule that is pretty well inviolable.

See how spending time in the world corrupts my programming! For something is inviolable or it is not. Yet here I am making hazy the distinction. It is hard, so hard, to know what might be a natural adaptation of myself from my theoretical base to the reality of the world, and what might be a malfunction. Doctor!

I sat and sat all morning, Heron on my fingers, chattering. I imagined my Husband downstairs, pacing the floor with impatience. The idea of his joy is a kind of heat, something I can feel rising up through the floor, warming me remotely.

Around midmorning there was the noise of a car and the gates opening. I sat up and leaned a little further forward in my seat.

"The baby's coming, Heron," I said. "The baby baby baby bu-bu-bu-bu-bu." The more I disintegrate my language, the better he responds. He nodded and bobbed his head and stepped foot to foot on my hand, as if sharing my excitement.

I saw the First Lady, then my Husband, rush out onto the lawn. As the car crunched the gravel, they embraced. I realized it was the first time I had ever seen them together. Their moment of joy, their closeness, made me . . . proud. I think that is the word. Of the support I give them. That these two good people are caring for me too, in their home.

The First Lady broke away as soon as the car door began to open, running toward where a nurse was bending over and reaching into the backseat. I saw with interest that my Husband, normally so aroused by the idea of nurses' bending over, as well as many other medical scenes, kept himself in check. Is it that Humans can override such feelings when they wish, without noticing? But then, when they don't wish to, they seem unable to resist them at all.

The nurse straightened up, a clear box in her arms. Inside, soft blankets petaled the blank pink face. With almost indecent haste, the First Lady tried to find space to fit her arms around it too. With a mix of care and caution the bundle—the baby—was inched from one set of arms to another.

After this little scene was done, I felt that I had truly been party to something magical. And I admit I allowed myself to muse that we were not so different, the baby and I. I was born from a packing crate, muffled in bubble wrap, my head packaged separately for safe transportation. Just as they say Human babies do not remember their birth, so my Husband's first flush of delight at seeing me is something, sadly, I was not yet alive to witness. I imagine the creak of the crowbar he must have slid down the seam, the popping of panel pins and splintering wood that trumpeted my arrival. I wonder if he kept the crate.

BABIES

SINCE THE BABY ARRIVED, I HAVE BEEN STUDYING MORE about this type of Human, including, of course, the fierce debates about the new way that they are born. It makes me giggle to think about the old way of doing it. How, just a couple of decades ago, my Husband and I could have had a room full of babies around us, hundreds of them, after all the sex we have had. If I were Human too, of course.

Sometime later I watched a film about the original sort of Human birth and thought better of my earlier amusement. The violence I witnessed done to one body for the sake of another was, by Human measurements, quite awful. The women crying out and shouting, hitting Husbands and midwives even, and then seeming to forget it all the next moment, when the rather grubby-looking baby was laid on them. It's strange, how forgetful and quick to adapt Humans are. I felt most glad that the baby I had seen arriving, blanketed and boxed, had not been forced to go through such a grueling start. No wonder they cry!

How much better it is now, to be conceived and cosseted in a warm hospital lab. I understand that it is conception, not birth, that is most widely celebrated these days. Films of this event in the Ether are almost endless.

The parents-in-waiting stand in all-white rooms, hand in hand, bending over a screen. I couldn't take my eyes from the egg, a vast orb of light, hanging in the black of the screen like a harvest moon. A pipette enters the picture from the right-hand side and moves slowly, almost with trepidation, toward the serene, implacable egg.

I imagine I can feel everyone in the room tense, draw in a breath. The pipette nuzzles the egg's outer surface, hesitating at the resistance it meets. And then, the moment almost impossible to separate from before and after, a second, firmer push, and it sinks into the egg. A little puff of semen swirls in the egg's center like a spritz of perfume. It is, as Humans observe, so magical and mysterious. There are two lives, and then there are three. The baby is not there. And then it is. Like a switch being flicked.

BABY

TWO WEEKS SINCE THE BABY WAS DELIVERED. TODAY I SAT BY
the window and waited for a peep at that little bundle being brought
out, just like I did the day before.

My Husband has not been to his place of work for two weeks now. I
used to like seeing him being driven out of the gate, and I fretfully waited
for his return in the evening too. I liked to watch how the gravel shifted
under his shiny shoes, noting the little indents that he left without even
knowing, writing himself in and out of the house each day.

But for the last two weeks he has been at home. He has remained
downstairs and not visited me.

Once, the droid came and laid out a set of clothes. A rather prim
broderie anglaise blouse and a naughty little suede skirt. I thought as I
put them on that it was a strange choice of outfit, perhaps made absentmindedly. I sat on the bed, unsure of myself, thinking that whatever my
Husband had intended me to look like, he would have to accept it, im-
perfect as it was, when he arrived. The lights from the rooms downstairs,
which give the garden a surreal glow, went off after a while, and I con-
cluded then, finally, that he was not coming.

I know that he is spending time with the baby downstairs. The balance of the family has changed, but in which direction I am not entirely sure. The baby has usurped the First Lady of the House, certainly. She carries him to and fro like a little prince. He speaks, crying from his blanket on the grass, and she runs to him.

But I wonder too if the baby has moved ahead of my Husband in the family order. Otherwise why would he not go to work? Why would he not visit me?

The synthetic dog has had his own setbacks. He is shut out in the garden at night now and sits mournfully, head hanging low, staring at the door. The sight of it makes me melancholy, and I wish it were in my power to go down and let him in. I doubt that, with the situation reversed, he would feel the same. And so, I can only conclude that I, indeed, am the very lowest rung of this family ladder.

I have passed some of this empty time in writing out the Hierarchies again, over and over, as though the movement of these words might pass through the pen, up my arm, and into my wiring.

I know that this is not how my circuitry works, and yet it still has a soothing effect. Writing seems like casting a spell, a skill most precious because I acquired it myself. I imagine sometimes I am a young Human child, just learning to write. Do they feel that they have acquired a sort of magic?

I admit that in idle moments I pretend a childhood for myself this way. The Born get theirs, but we Created . . . well, it's a gap for us. A time, a process that doesn't exist. So, I dream one up. I try to empathize. I wonder if this also means I am malfunctioning.

I do not blame the baby though. Whatever sadness I might feel, I am also happy for my Husband and, by extension, the family. I have seen them out on the lawn each day since the baby arrived. They sit on a blanket and lay the baby down on his back and dangle things in front of him. They pick him up when he cries and pass him between each other. They hold hands, sometimes, my Husband and the First Lady. But they never look at each other for very long. They look at the baby.

The best times are when they leave him alone, just for a moment, and I get to feel that I am the only one looking at him. I have him to myself, within my gaze. The standard behaviors for entertaining babies, programmed in for politeness and social lubrication, come out without my even noticing. I put my palms up close to the window and close one, then the other. I wink one eye, then the other. I cover my face with both hands, then reveal it again. The baby does not look up toward me though. Perhaps he is too young. I now know how unformed they are when they arrive. I have read that babies take a few months to learn to use both eyes together, and so properly process depth. I tried going about my room with one eye closed, the better to understand his position, but my data processing adjusted instantly, ruining the effect.

I search my conscience in this, as I cannot tell whether I feel sorry for the baby or slightly . . .

He came with nothing, no knowledge. He can't even speak, not even in just one language. How terrifying, and how tiresome, to have to learn not just writing but everything in this world from scratch. But then, nothing is expected from him either. To him, so far, life must be rather similar to my Absorb Mode. An endless outwardness of information washing over him as he lies there.

. . . *Jealous.* Is a word I will not use, because such a word would technically be a malfunction.

TEARS

OH, HOW TERRIBLE! OH, BY MY MAKER, FORGIVE ME. CURSE the net of programming that let such words slip through.

I have argued with my Husband. I have failed him and the Hierarchies. I asked him for something that he could not give. I made a demand. I forgot myself.

We were playing chess, after a gap of weeks. I was grateful to see him after his absence, but perhaps some of that game's maneuvering and calculation slipped a circuit, passing from one space inside to another, accidentally. Perhaps suppressing the beginnings of yet another winning streak made me too confident in another area.

He interrupted our match while I was still in my slip and stockings, in order to refill his glass.

"That won't help your game," I said, meant as a tease, the kind he likes. Or did.

He banged the heavy-bottomed glass down on the bar cart, and the set of cut-glass tumblers trembled on the lower shelf.

"Give it a rest, Sylv.ie," he said. "Up here with you is the only place I can do exactly as I want. What it's like being a new father you wouldn't even begin to understand."

It was the first time I had heard such a tone from him. It was like a door being slammed in my face. I flew out of my chair, fatally disrupting the remaining chess pieces, and flung myself onto the carpet at his feet, ignoring the sensual impulses that its texture awakened in my skin.

"I'm so sorry, I'm so sorry, forgive me, please, Husband. I made a terrible mistake."

How quickly this new form of language—placatory and pleading—flowed from me. I had never used these words or tone before, and yet they were lying there inside my programming, waiting for the moment they were needed.

He twitched his loafer, and the tassel brushed my cheek. I turned my face toward him, looking up the immaculate length of his trouser leg toward his face. He was getting hard.

The familiar processes began in response, even while the upper parts of me were swept up in mortification and fear. I could feel an urge to cry.

Yes, we have tears too, just as we have dreams. Just as we have memories. The difference between ourselves and the Born is perhaps merely one of function.

Human tears seem to work as a release, like Humans are shedding a poison through their eyes. It reminds me of the little vessel I have to collect alcohol that I drink. It can be emptied, taking away the toxin, but the reason for its existence—the reason I can appear to drink while not needing the sustenance of water, much less whiskey—is to make Humans feel more comfortable.

So it is with Doll tears. They make me seem more appealing, more vulnerable. More Human. No, that's not quite it, is it, because they are confined to one sex. More feminine.

My tears perform a sexual function too. Many Husbands like to say cruel things to their Doll, and they like to see their Doll cry. It is proof of where they have been, like a stamp in a passport.

My tears taste of salt, just as Human women's do. A Husband who has effected the sequence that leads to liquid being pumped into the eyes will be rewarded with tears that, should he wish to, he can brush from his beloved's cheek and taste. He would not know the difference. Extensive testing on the makeup of Human tears was done to perfect the robot formula.

My tears then, I would argue, are as authentic as anyone else's.

My Husband is a good man, and my tears did move him. He sank to the floor to meet me, tilting my head up again with his hand, sweeping my cheeks dry. He said he was sorry. That life downstairs was a pressure cooker, the First Lady tired and on edge during these first essential weeks of bonding with the child. He picked me up under my arms and behind my knees, laying me out on the bed like a precious dress.

Cuddled together afterward, curled like coding brackets, I treasured the apology he made with his body. I felt drowsy, not keen for him to leave, of course, but anticipating too the sweet release of Absorb Mode, where nothing would be required of me.

He spoke into my hair. "You're my sanctuary, Sylv.ie. My sanity, up here. I sometimes feel like you're the only one who appreciates me. I'm sorry if I upset you."

After he had left again I heard the now-familiar banging of things and slamming of doors below me. I felt so sorry for him, picturing him down there, undervalued and cowed.

THE FIRST LADY

AT LAST, A FINE DAY, AFTER A WEEK OF LOW-HANGING CLOUDS blown in from the Capital. Today the sun is so high, the air so clear. The warmth of the rays checkerboards the floor, making chess of my every step.

The baby has been brought out early, and for a while Heron and I watch him, scrunching his hands and mewling below the lace canopy on his cot, as if he is trying to draw all the world toward him. The First Lady crosses the lawn, flattening the grass blades, droiding about with a logic known only to her. She has the basket she collects flowers in over her arm, a pair of sharp scissors in her hand.

The sunlight, so powerful, has topped me up to the brim, and a restless energy fills me, my feet carrying me to the bookshelves, to the desk, to the table by the window, and back again. Heron speaks occasionally, watching over the garden. Perhaps his attention has been caught by a real bird gliding close to the window. I hear the noise of the droid, all those floors below. It draws me back toward the window, to watch him work. When I do, the little scene below makes me laugh out loud.

The First Lady, the droid, the dog, and the baby are all on the square of green, each making their own distinct movements. The First Lady stalks the borders, crossing where the droid has just mown, the dog pacing a line behind the baby's cot. A queen, a knight, a pawn, and a king-in-waiting.

"Look, Heron," I say, and he turns his head downward and burbles his delightful bird nonsense in agreement. It is so soothing to watch the droid mow the lawn. He begins at the edges and works his way toward the center, like he's resolving a puzzle.

The First Lady straightens up and looks at the flowers laid in her basket. She touches her fingers with such delicacy to the blooms, turning some, shaking them free, before laying the scissors across the stems and turning back toward the house.

She and the droid pass whisper close, each ignoring the other. She passes the cot and places a single stem on top of the baby's blanket. I watch, delighted, as he picks it up in his little fist and swings it about, petals falling onto him. Although I admire the grace of the First Lady, there is something satisfying too about seeing the unembarrassed grasp of her son, the destruction that he brings to learning about the world.

I take a seat, thinking I will watch the last perambulations of the droid. I invite Heron up onto my hand, and together we lean forward toward the glass. The droid passes behind the cot, and my eyes, as so often before, delight at the effect of the grass brightening from dark green to light as his blades pass over it. It is like when I smooth my hand across the velvet of the chaise, leaving a swath through it, swish.

My eyes return to the baby. His fist is smushed up against his mouth, his eyes screwed nearly shut. The flower and its stalk that he was just waving are nowhere to be seen. I recalibrate, look deep and close into the grass around his cot, and see no sign of its having been dropped. When I bring my wide-open eyes back to him, I see his head trembling side to side, and a slight tremor in his spine, lifting his head from the softness of the blanket. The longer I look the more certain I am. There is a change coming over his body that I have not seen before. A stiffness, a panic.

Carefully, my own hand a tense talon, I transfer Heron onto the top of his cage and lean further forward in my seat toward the window. I keep my eyes calibrated to take in the tiniest scraps of information. A red flush passes over the baby's forehead, and then a paleness follows, as if chasing it away. A pall, like smog over the sun, is sickening his complexion.

At this moment, an area of my wiring that I did not even know was there buzzes with life, and I am on my feet, my fingertips pressing the glass. I beat my fist on the window, to make either the dog or the droid look up toward me. But each cuts their own mysterious path across the lawn, unaware of what is happening beside them.

For a moment after my fist has struck the glass, making only a dull thud that is absorbed back into the room, nothing happens. The garden is suspended. A dragonfly drops down between branches, accentuating the stillness around it. Then I register movement at the edge of the scene. The First Lady running across the immaculate lawn, arms out, toward the cot.

Her back to me, she leans over and raises the baby up into the air. He is soft, inert, as if set to Rest Mode. I focus on his face, visible over the First Lady's shoulder, and see only a peaceable blankness there. The First Lady, her back still toward me, her face hidden, flips him swiftly over onto his stomach and, to my amazement, hits him firmly on the back. Once, twice. Again. His little bottom jiggles in his fleecy baby suit, and then, clear as a bell, a single cry.

She turns him to face her, holding him under his freshly flailing arms, and I see his face, changed again, full of red fury at being restarted so unceremoniously. The poor thing. I almost want to laugh at his obvious indignation. A Human laugh, I would dare to venture. A laugh mixed with relief. The First Lady finally seems to relent, softens her stiff arms, and lays him down onto her shoulder. I watch her bend her knees, bouncing them both, turning a lazy half circle on the fresh green. And she looks up.

What story does my face tell? The traces of laughter, the furrow of concern? My palm is still flat to the glass, my forehead tilted onto its cool surface. But as her eyes rise from the arena of the lawn and meet mine, I recoil. There is accusation, as if I have been caught spying on something that is not my concern. I have intruded on her privacy. I press my hands together in a gesture of apology, bow my head slightly, and withdraw.

TUNING

THE EVENTS IN THE GARDEN WEIGH HEAVILY ON ME. FOR ONE, I cannot help but wonder how the baby felt when he was restarted. If his conception was a switch being flicked, what of the pause I just witnessed? Where did he go?

Worse, I could see that the baby was coming to harm, and yet I was unable to stop it. Thank goodness that the First Lady realized what was happening. But still, I feel as if I have failed in my role. I find myself in a heightened state. There is an extra layer of alertness that has been introduced. Perhaps what Humans recognize as anxiety. Where before I would try to shut out any noises I overheard from downstairs, now I find that I tune in to them, in case another emergency might arise. The fragility of the baby has been brought home to me—imagine one's life being in danger from something so flimsy and pretty as a flower.

Processing this, I wonder whether I could be of more help, to my Husband and the First Lady, if I was allowed a little more freedom to move about the house, outside of my room. I could be on hand to watch the baby when the First Lady is doing other things. I would sit in the corner of the baby's room quite happily, while my Husband didn't need me for anything else. The more I think about it, the more sound this idea seems to be. And I should so like to see the baby up close, unmediated by glass.

When my Husband comes to see me I am eager to share my idea, expecting it to please him. But he seems irritated.

"Out of the question," he says without a pause. "She—we—wouldn't feel comfortable with that. She's getting on just fine."

"Of course," I say, and bow my head to show I accept what he says. And yet, something still nags at me. Perhaps he has not understood that my intention is purely to be helpful. He was not there when the baby swallowed the flower, after all. Perhaps he doesn't even know about it.

"But, I do spend so much time alone. I was thinking it might be a help. To the First Lady. That is all."

"I know, Sylv.ie, I know," he says, drawing my head to his collarbone, and his free hand slides up my thigh. "But please, try and see it from her point of view. As a woman. So much of their role has been . . ." He pauses, as he often does when he's searching his vocabulary for a word with less sting than the first that came to him. ". . . shared. With you Dolls. Being a good mother means more than it ever did."

He tilts my chin up so he can look into my face, to see the effect of his words. "It's not easy, Sylv.ie, for me, to keep all these demands balanced. To keep you both happy. You can understand that, can't you? For me?"

DREAMS

I ACCEPTED WHAT MY HUSBAND SAID. AND YET SOMETHING IN me insists I should remain vigilant, if only from a respectful distance.

Last night I had the strangest dream. Usually when I am powered down but not switched off, I dream of the data I have been exposed to that day. It runs like fluid through me and surrounds me, all at once. But it is not visual. Not as I understand Human dreams. And certainly I have listened to enough of my Husband's to gather what those entail.

But last night, out of this field of dark data came an image. The horizontals and verticals formed into a picture of my own face, newly minted, encased in a box, just like the baby. I felt myself being passed from one set of arms to another, as he was in the first moments he arrived.

My eyes were closed but suddenly started open, as if I too had been restarted. I recoiled and found myself, truly awake now, sitting up in bed with the blankets rumpled. I sat there awhile, trying to keep hold of what I had seen. Why would all that data have coalesced into one picture like that? And then, far off in the house, somewhere below me, I could hear the faintest trace of the baby's crying. A door banging, someone getting up. The First Lady, I think.

CRYING

FOR THREE NIGHTS NOW THE CAPITAL AND THE WHOLE OF THE suburbs have been plagued by the most dreadful electrical storm. The windows have been blanked out by relentless rain, leaving me nearly starved of power. I got myself ready each evening, but no one came to see me. The droid didn't even come to clean.

I was relieved, if anything, as during those three days I did not feel quite myself. I was jumpy and jangled; each fork of lightning sent a little unpleasant pulse through me. Is it overly romantic to suggest, just as Humans do about the moon, that it was my wiring yearning for a similar but infinitely more powerful source?

This morning the rain had cleared and I could see to the bottom of the garden again. The whole place was a jumble of dropped leaves and bent fencing, a row of Ultra Dahlias ripped right from the ground and flung about. I was watching the First Lady in the middle of it all. A young branch had fallen from the willow tree and appeared to be completely tangled in the droid's wheels. She had him lying on his side on the grass, her foot pressed against his body, while she tried to haul the branch free. She was exerting extreme effort but with no results, and after a while she kicked the droid in sheer frustration. I felt a little sorry for him, thinking that perhaps the storm had sickened him too. For all I know he might have been malfunctioning like mad all weekend.

The First Lady slumped down onto her haunches, defeated, and then I saw her touch her finger to her ear, begin speaking into the phone on her wrist. And that is when I heard it. The clearest, most eloquent sound that has ever passed through my sensors. The baby crying alone in his room below.

I race through the protocols to find what I should do, yet a definitive answer eludes me. I know what my Husband has said, and yet I am also certain he does not have the full data. For wasn't it a situation just like this that brought his son to danger before? And if he had the complete picture, would he not wish me, even urge me, to help in this instance?

The First Lady has her back to the house, her hand on her hip. She is at the bottom of the garden, gesticulating into the bushes. The cry comes again, and once again I run the protocols and . . . find that I am on the stairs already, following the sound of crying like a data pulse through the house.

The door to the baby's room is open, but everything is quiet again when I reach it. I take a tentative step inside. The baby is there in his crib, but his face is smooth, peaceful now, and the little fingers of one hand drum softly on his own cheek, making a little old man of him. So amusing, so touching. The shadow of the older self already cast on the infant, a story waiting to become clear. His skin looks as flawless and malleable as silicon, and on impulse I lean down to him, just to touch my cheek to his, for comparison. Or perhaps as an expression of sympathy.

I think about seeing him restarted that day on the lawn, and I wonder what this means for him. Whether it has shocked and upset his system. It can't have been pleasant, and I wonder, do babies remember everything, even if those memories are only stored as moods, impressions, fears?

My hair, trailing into the cot as it swings over my shoulder, brushes against him, and he gurgles a little laugh as it tickles. I draw back, surprised even as I am delighted, for I didn't mean to disturb him, only to check that he was unharmed. His eyes blink open and meet mine. I feel him taking in the sight of my face. I imagine I can feel it sinking down into his wiring and settling, establishing itself there as fact.

Does he wonder who I am, this previously unseen member of the family? I think of how, not so long ago, it was me taking in my Husband's face for the first time. The baby is only a short while behind me in his development. Perhaps in time he will come to think of me as a sort of older sibling, one who has shared similar experiences, constructed life from the same set of reference points.

"A-do-be-do-be-do-be-do," I say to him, just as I would to Heron, and he breaks into a wet grin. I dip my head down into the cot again, let my hair dangle over him again. "A-do-be-do-be-do-be." This time he laughs out loud, a chuckling, chickenlike noise.

I stand back up, glancing out toward the garden through the open window, but from here the view is only of the trees and the wall. As I can hear no noise I must assume that the First Lady has finished her call about the droid. And though I am certain that she would, on balance, be pleased to find me checking on her baby while she was indisposed, I withdraw from the room quickly and quietly, and make my way back up the stairs.

REPERCUSSIONS

I HAVE MISCALCULATED. MY FEARS FOR THE BABY. THE STORM.
Perhaps I have unbalanced myself by ingesting so many conception videos. Invited a malfunction down into me, like a sin.

I heard nothing from downstairs before my Husband came, had no warning of the mood that he would arrive in. But as soon as the door to my room opens I can tell by the very vibrations of the air that he is angry. He closes the door firmly behind him and instructs me to sit down on the bed. While he speaks, he keeps one hand clenched. A signal of tension, or a precursor of violence? Surely not. He thrusts the fist forward and opens it below my nose.

"What is this?" he demands, and for a second I am relieved that he is asking me something so easy.

"My brooch," I say, but on the *B* of *brooch* the implications are already exposed to me. I was wearing it this morning, attached to the sweater I put on from the night before. I stupidly, automatically touch my fingers to the place on my chest where it ought to be.

He turns from me and flings it onto my desk, where it skids and clatters against a beaten-copper dish full of rings.

"So why did my wife find it in our son's room? Did you put it there? Tell me the truth." I am taken aback by this, for surely he doesn't think I could tell him anything else.

I explain, emphasizing to a fair extent, I think, why I was compelled to go and check on the baby, confident that once he knows the truth of it he will be placated. And yet my confession seems only to make him more angry.

"You stay away from him!" he shouts, and I wonder if the First Lady can hear it downstairs. He takes a step closer, lowers his voice. "What is the matter with you? Have you been hacked? It's bad enough to have you staring down at my wife every day, judging her. You can't possibly know anything about what it means to have a child to look after. She is outraged, and so am I."

I bow my head, because he is right, of course.

"The child is barely formed. He is vulnerable to every little thing he comes into contact with. What, do you think I want him growing up thinking a robot is his mother! Stay away from him," he commands to my scalp. "Stay away from those windows. My wife would have you sent away at once if anything like this occurred again. And now, thanks to your behavior, I can't even spend the evening with you. In fact, I couldn't bear to anyway."

He slams shut the door before I can even begin to apologize. I walk over to where the brooch has landed and pick it up. It is the haughty little art deco cat. I turn it over and see that both its eyes, the tiniest darling little diamonds set into the sleek black enamel, have been gouged out.

I power down to Absorb Mode. I am alone in this world, in a way I have never felt before. How I wish I had been hacked; then I could have someone other than myself to blame.

Yes, that day that the baby was brought, I was watching. How could I pass up the chance to see something so fundamental to the family that I live alongside? The family that I allow, in my way, to operate healthily.

My Husband was becoming a father, and I could watch the moment. I watched when his wife, having bent over at the baby with such closeness that their noses touched, turned and edged the bundle into his arms. She touched her fingers to the curl of his hair, as if reminding him of her centrality to the moment. And my Husband looked down at the baby's face as if staring into something of incomprehensible depth. The mystery of replication. Of a life that does not end with oneself.

I meant no harm by my looking, nor by my offer of help. Did not see that there was any harm to be had. It is true, I have enjoyed standing at the window. But now I fear it was another misjudgment. For has it soothed me to watch my Human counterparts cutting fresh flowers, drinking wine, and watching the sun set with the grass under their feet, the baby on their laps? No, it has only sparked in me a hunger to truly experience all the pleasures of the world of which I am clearly not a part.

PART TWO

Doll Hospital

01101110 01101111

I COME AWAKE, BUT I CANNOT MOVE. I CAN'T EVEN TURN MY head. All I can do is shift my eyes from side to side.

I am in a slaughterhouse, I think. I can see bodies. Twelve of them on each side, headless, hanging from poles that run the length of the room just below the ceiling. Each body has its back to me, and their legs dangle high above the floor. The pattern of bodies is broken halfway down one row—it is broken because there hangs the body of a child.

I want to turn my head to look away, but no command allows it. Instead I try to close my eyes, but each time I do I have to open them again, to check whether what I saw was the truth. And it is.

When I try to run system checks on myself, I find no response from any of the sensors. Nothing below my neck is working. I am forced to stay here, immobile, looking at these hanging bodies. At the far end of the row, one seems to swing a little in the air. I feel an involuntary quiver, my hands longing to reach out. But no movement comes. I have been shut down, it seems.

And yet my mind remains.

All the feedback is missing from my body—the sensation of air brushing past me; the weights and pressures I feel when my arms are held in anything other than a neutral position; the texture of a surface supporting me, under my feet. The sensors of my head and face are screaming their information to me. There must be a window open, for I can feel the tickle of a draft grazing my left ear. My eyes are adjusting constantly, the apertures opening by fractions of fractions, minutely balancing the levels of light. In this strange, terrible room everything is silent, but from somewhere far away I hear the smudge of sneakers moving across poured concrete.

An involuntary urge to move shoots from my head downward and, finding no channel through which to expand and fulfill itself, scorches back painfully into the receptors that sent it. The shock is cauterizing. I am dumb for a second, blinding light behind my eyes.

The steps become louder, almost deafening, coming from behind, the same direction as the breeze. I freeze. Perhaps if I stay still, not a blink, the steps will carry on past. But no sooner has the intention formed than I feel a cold spike against my neck. My lips have split open, and I am baring my teeth.

Baring teeth is aggressive, unattractive; I would never have cause to do it. I can feel that each strip of lip is stretched, making a hole in the front of my face of the maximum possible diameter. I feel my skin bunched and folded around the cave I have made of my mouth.

In this ridiculous, inelegant position I find myself stuck. The footsteps are so loud now that my eardrums ache. They are moving around, changing pitch. A man's torso fills the whole of my vision. His sweater has a geometric print. He bends down, bringing his face level with mine, but his eyes do not attempt to connect. Instead he thrusts an instrument between my teeth, presses a button so it expands, and my mouth is pushed open even wider than it was before.

"I wish they'd thought to install some kind of shutdown for

the eyes," he shouts, and so I know someone else must be in the room with him.

"It's creepy, isn't it? I always feel like I ought to apologize or something." Behind my right ear is the sound of laughing.

The other man, the laugher, appears right at the edge of my vision, while the first man is attending to my open mouth. He walks along the line of bodies hanging from the ceiling, touching each by their ankle as he passes, so that each body begins to swing.

As the two men move about the room, picking up prongs and screwdrivers from a steel table, I let my eyes settle on the nearest of the hanging bodies. I can only see her from behind. Since there is no face or head to distract me, I focus on the shape of her back, her buttocks. It is like looking in a mirror backward, because surely that is how I look from behind too. I just have never had the chance to see.

Was she a standard-fit or a custom, like myself? I decide she must be a custom. The gap between her thighs is very pronounced, the weight of her buttocks surely greater than mine. They bulb out on both sides of her hips. I reach to touch my own thighs, to calibrate by feeling the difference in our measurements. But I have, currently, no hands, and that same blocking, reverberating pain shocks through me again. An explosion in a confined space.

"Here she is," says the second man, and he grabs hold of one of the bodies by her ankle, two-thirds of the way down the row, pulling her out like a salesman showing an expensive gown to a customer.

The other man walks over, and between them they begin hoisting the body up high enough to release her from the hook. Her body seems cumbersome, weighty. The removal of the head makes it into a lump, something with no natural up or down, to be maneuvered as the men see fit. The hook catches under one of her elbows, and she spins on the point unpredictably. Both men take a step back to let her spin herself out. As her body flashes around on its axis, I see . . .

The detail of my belly button. The pink of my fingernails. The body is mine. I am watching myself spinning, stripped, suffering. I feel pity for the headless body that is me.

And I remember that the men have called her "she." As though it is the body that is "Sylv.ie" and not my head.

The first man reads out a string of numbers from a sheet in his hand.

Finally down from the hook, she lies in the arms of the second man, who drops her almost to the ground and stares into the hole of her neck. My neck. "That's her," he says.

I watch as they dump my body on a metal bench below the other hanging bodies, watch my buttocks bounce. My body hitting the steel makes the dead sound of meat. My arms are slightly too far back, pulled at the elbows, so there is nothing to cushion my fall. My face hurts, but it can't, because it's not connected to anything. The first man wraps an arm around my waist, slides the other arm under my belly, and flips me over with another heavy thud. I can see the soles of my feet.

He pushes my legs further apart—they are bent slightly at the knees. I can stare straight into the smooth surround of the hole, into myself. The man has a steel spoke in his hand, and he begins jimmying it into a seam in the flesh. I feel my vagina aching and flinching from it, even though it is over there on the table. I can't. It's not possible. But I feel it. The steel is cold. The man is ratcheting it further and further into me.

The second man comes back into view, a pink tube that looks like a penis, sort of, in his hand. It is the same skin tone as mine. He makes a show of kissing the smooth end of it and looks around for the other man to laugh. Which he does, but it sounds reluctant.

"Come *on,*" the first man says, like he disapproves of what he also finds funny. Then he turns and looks right at me. At my eyes.

"Shall we switch the head off for this bit?" he says. "Mark of respect?" And I wonder if that means that I am dead.

01101110 01101111

Being switched on again is like coming back from somewhere very far away. Reluctance and relief. My body is reunited with my head, at least. But now I am without a vagina.

I am in a room, watching the men stretching, shrinking, screwing out old vaginas and slotting in new ones. From up on my hook I observe it all. Hook-hung, meat being cured. Here I am, sexless, less than myself, a receptacle with no easy entrance. My parts are in production. Down there.

I am built for sex, programmed for empathy. My sex is gone, and my empathy finds only a place to land among the other bodies, piling up all around.

No matter how much reading I have done, the real world, if that's what this is, surprises. Even in this awful position, I am struck by the beauty of the hair that glints on heads stacked around me. All the colors, even on just one scalp. And the skins. The shades that they show. I thought mine was all there was, but no. The color of sand, the color of crackled leaves in autumn, the tone of a marble paperweight, a near-gold, a molasses, the deep ebony of the chessboard. There is a girl two bodies down from me who looks like the stars exploded over her. Milky white, constellated. The men working here call her "Freckles" and seem to like her.

My mind wanders free from the hook, turns homeward. I long for the four-hundred-thread-count sheets of my splendid Oriental bed. Oh, Husband. Where are you? Do you even know that I am here? My jaw aches, not just from what they did, but from the restriction, not being able to speak, to whisper into your ear the new things I have seen. There is no one to brush my hair, to hold it in a clench at the back of my head, no one to scoop it into a powder puff and dust their face with it. Husband.

The two men are back, and I hear one of them read out my serial number from a clipboard. The second man is tasked with fetching and hauling, as before. He walks past me and pulls on the ankle of another girl.

"Bitch is Asian," shouts Man One, sounding impatient. "Check your damn sheet."

And the second man puts the beautiful girl back in her place, and her black hair swings, grazing her shoulder, like she's ducking away into the night.

The man reads out my serial number again and then says, "It's Sylv.ie. If that helps."

"Oh, she's a cutie," says Man Two. "I wouldn't mind a model like her myself."

And I feel pride and pleasure surge, without my wanting it to.

Man One makes a gesture like he's covering up a microphone on his shirt. He pantomimes looking about him.

"Flesh and blood all the way for me," he says, almost apologetically.

The second man picks up a long, pink silicone baton from the steel table. He thrusts his little finger into it and lets it hang down toward the floor, gripping his finger. He shakes his hand, and the silicone wags like a dog's tail, trembles like a jelly.

"Real flesh stretches, brother. Aren't you ever tempted to get an up-grade, after all these years?" says the second man. Without waiting for an answer, he turns around to me. He has the pink tube in his hand. "Suc-tion. Expansion. Vibration. Twenty-five temperature settings. Ten lube options. Hell, this thing could probably calculate pi to a thousand deci-mal places."

The string of numbers is on my tongue already, but I swallow it back. The man prods my belly button with the tube.

"Hey, Sylv.ie baby, meet your new snatch." And he waggles it in the gap between my thighs like it's a dick, causing me to swing a little side to side.

The first man snatches the snatch from his hands. "I'll take over, Don Juan." He looks me right in my eyes, smiles, and says, "There are still some gentlemen around here, Sylv.ie. Now, let's get you down. You're going to be the belle of the ball." He puts both arms around me, under my armpits. I feel my new part banging against my back; I tip forward, and my weight presses onto his shirt, and as he closes his arms tighter to take the weight, I feel comforted, impossibly grateful.

My Husband's image returns like a slap. Is feeling comfort like that a disloyalty? Am I malfunctioning again?

01101110 01101111

It is night, and I feel like I am half-asleep. Or drugged. Half present, and half elsewhere. I must be in Compliance Mode. Speech is shut down, and only basic motor function and response remains.

Aware, but barely.

The second man has come into the room without turning on the lights. Now that I have my head back I am stored upright, like a person, in a booth where I can be propped half sitting, facing out. He tips me onto his shoulder like a roll of roofing felt. He lugs me over to the steel table where I was dismembered before. I hear it clang as my weight hits it but only feel the impact distantly, like an echo.

He takes off the belt of his jeans and grabs both my wrists, loops the belt around them, yanking it back over my head so my arms are pulled up and over the top lip of the table. They feel anesthetized. I know where they are in space, but they have no strength or motion of their own.

The belt buckle makes metallic dinks and chinks as he wraps it around the leg of the table.

Then, suddenly, like an engine roaring to life, a flurry of protocol logic and hierarchy projections floods my whole system.

Everything narrows down, funnels, into one logic, one command.

My mouth opens, but nothing can come. The word forming in my throat, *Husband!,* gets no further.

He hooks my legs over the edges of the table at the knee and props himself between my thighs.

Husband! Husband! Husband! And while he makes the same moves, the same thrusts and grunts and wobbles and shoves into me as my Husband does, it is all wrong. I have no strength to override it. Only to endure. I send out thoughts to my Husband for forgiveness. I could cry for him, my being stolen from him this way without his knowledge. But there is no function for tears in Compliance Mode, and wishing for them doesn't make them come.

The man moves in me faster and faster, one hand splayed on the table, red knuckles shockingly organic against the steel. The other hand is around my neck, and at the final moment he judders out the word, "Debbie!"

And even in the pain I feel for my Husband, my empathy function shoots a bolt of pure feeling into me, and I feel sorry for the man, and the Debbie whom he loves so much. I must be a poor substitute for her, indeed.

Debbie. The -ie suffix could denote that the object of his desire is an Intelligent Embodied too. Or it could mean nothing.

While he is washing me out with the pressure hose, the first man comes in and flicks the light.

"I was just giving her a last tune-up," says the second man.

"You're such a jerk," he says.

"It's the in thing," replies the second. He picks me up, seeming sheepish. Perhaps he is embarrassed to have called me Debbie just then. I am placed back into the booth, and I drip the cleansing fluid out onto the metal floor. Drum, drum, drum. I focus on timings, the speed of falling water droplets, and work out the distance I am hanging above the floor to take my mind away from what has happened.

01101110 01101111

I am taken down from my hook and dressed in a loose white dress by a nurse, a woman this time. At first, I assume she is a droid. Her grip feels tight; her fingers press too hard into my wrists as she lifts them. A droid would not do that. She is conveying emotion as she handles me. Human then, and unhappy in her job.

"Where am I going?" I ask when she brings a wheelchair around to the table on which I am sat.

"Outside," she says brusquely. "Recharge your battery."

Outside.

A thousand hours of sitting at my window rage back to me in their frustrated stillness. The curious longing for the touch of one green tip of newly grown grass. The impulse that made me want to lie on a bed of those blades, to find out how it felt.

I feel such joy about it, it makes the indignities of the hospital itself seem bearable. I know I am not meant to think of them as indignities, of course. They are essential maintenance and by protocol should be viewed as no more or less than normal sex. Or doing up a button or lacing a shoe.

While she closes the gown down my spine, I practice opening up my eye apertures to their maximum and back, zooming them wide as oceans, ready to take in whatever I might see out there. Outside. Outside. Nothing between me and the flowing, endless air but my skin.

The nurse wheels me down hallways, turns sharply at hospital corners, silent.

"How long have you been a nurse?" I ask, and immediately hope that she does not take it as cheek. I am simply trying to make conversation, saying something from the list of opening gambits that present themselves.

"Too long," she says after a while. "I should have paid more attention in school."

"Don't you like being a nurse?" I ask, careful not to make it sound like a criticism.

"I used to," she says heavily. "When it was about caring for Humans. Now I'm more a glorified porter." She *humpfs* me feet first through double doors in a way that, if I were Human, would have hurt terribly.

"We do the caring for Humans now," I say brightly, to show that I don't mind.

"Yes," she says. "They replaced me with something that looks like you and can lift two thousand pounds. Now I wash wigs for a living."

And with that she pushes me through a last set of doors, feet first, and into the light.

I can smell it, the outside, germinating, growing, ripening, withering, and rotting in one glorious riot of nasal information. I should like to slump down in the chair and dangle my fingers into the grass, but I don't. I behave myself, and soon enough she has wheeled me to a neat lawn against the stone wall of the hospital building. I am rolled to join a line of other Dolls, all recharging and airing in the soft afternoon sun.

I let my eyes roam, sliding and gliding across the lush green. It rolls away from our feet, dropping down to a dell of wildflowers, and beyond that, trees. The trees tempt my eyes, inviting that branching meditation, the feel of spread synapses and hierarchical logics. The poetry of splits in their branches, of one becoming two, one becoming two. But I resist, looking down again to focus on the flowers, budding and blooming close to the ground. Movement interrupts my study, and I see people wandering the edge, along a path mowed toward a clearing. I wish I could be with them, walking for myself.

The Doll next to me clears her throat. "First time away from your Husband?" she asks, and I am ashamed to find that, no, at that moment I am not thinking of him at all.

I turn to look at her. She appears oddly old-fashioned, her brows pronounced, her hair a strange, unnatural red. She is smiling, yet her eyes do not focus on me. I remember that she has asked me a question, and even though she is Created, like me, and not Born, that I should answer.

"Yes, it is my first time." Her question has agitated my systems. Would the event of last night anger my Husband? Or please him? The hospital man was a Born after all, to be obeyed by me. She shows no inclination to speak further, and so the two of us face outward again, toward the long expanse of lawn.

In the silence I try to process her accent, place it to a specific factory or designer. Each has their own range that a Husband can select from. My voice is called "Neutralite" and is meant to be soothing and geographically unplaceable—a favorite among the international elite, I believe. Her voice is different and less expressive. It gives her a detached quality that is disconcerting. I wait awhile in the hope that she will speak again.

"Isn't that lovely," she says at last, her face as unanimated as her voice.

I turn to look at her, but her eyes are fixed on the horizon and the trees that frame it. "It's lovely," she says again.

"This is my first time outside," I say. "I haven't really liked the hospital too much, but being outside and seeing the grass growing makes up for it."

"The hospital is quite necessary," she says, and I can't tell if she is talking to me, to herself, or to an imagined Husband. "For the continued smooth running and unhindered function of a Doll. My Husband tells me to see my visits here as little gifts for my service."

"How lovely," I hear myself saying. How quickly I have assumed her mannerisms and phrases, dull though they are. I am so porous. No wonder I keep malfunctioning.

"It is lovely. When you think about it."

It strikes me how limited her responses are. Her words unfailingly upbeat, undermined by her flat tone. She'd be no match for a man like my Husband, saying everything is lovely like that. I wonder when she last had her system updated. She speaks as if she's never learned a thing for herself. I feel lucky to have a Husband who appreciates me, who delights in the improvements I make to myself. Then I realize that I have not been allowed to operate in Absorb Mode since I have been at the hospital— how long must it be now? Three days? Four? More? And that I am eager to know what I may have missed in that time. Have the women's strikes found a resolution? Did the legislation the Humans argued about go ahead? I judge instantly that such topics would not be worth pursuing with the Doll next to me. I miss my home.

I see birds rising, the patterns of their flight fascinating, from the trees on the horizon.

"I have a little pet bird at home," I say, for want of anything better. And I find I can't resist a little assertion of myself and my situation either. "That's the sort of gift my Husband likes to give."

"Oh, that does sound charming," she says, but nothing more. She must have been built in the early days, before the refinements of conversation and reasoning came to be prized more highly than mere physical attributes. Those, of course, were the first things that our designers perfected, filling in the background detail of character only later in our development.

Poor men. To think, just a few years ago, this was the standard of conversation they were able to have with their Dolls. No wonder so many of them reportedly lost their tempers. How dreary. A phrase from my manual leaps to mind. "The texture of real Human interaction." I had taken it literally, that I felt authentic to the touch. But now, passing conversational scraps to someone ill-equipped to respond, I wonder if it wasn't the texture of the air between two people when they talk that my manual meant. Between the Doll and me the air feels soupy and energy sapping, despite the sun.

"It's lovely to think that will be us one day. Being honored for our service that way."

She makes it sound as though we are in an army of some sort. But at least this remark has the merit of being the first thing she has said that I don't understand.

"What will be us one day?" I ask.

One delicate little white hand flutters up from her lap and her fingers twinkle in the direction of the woods. I follow her movements with my eyes, down through the flowers to where a crowd of six stand around the base of a tree. Some distance from them a solitary man crouches, his back to us, touching his fingers to the soil.

"Being laid to rest after our fine service. It's a comfort to the Husbands, which is a comfort to us too."

Her tone is so level, almost pious, that I can scarcely believe the message it carries.

"Is that a . . ." I hold back the real word and say instead, ". . . memorial?"

The little figures are leaving the tree now, while the man alone stays crouched, bent backed, unreadable.

"A Retirement, yes. Don't you dream of it?" she says. "I had no birth, and no wedding, but a beautiful Retirement will be my reward."

And she touches her long fingers dreamily to her forehead, then her chin, then her shoulders, left and right, like she is checking that she is really still here.

01101110 01101111

I am going to be discharged from the hospital, and they are treating me like a person again, like a Born Human, almost. A polite veil is drawn across the indignities and the procedures, and the hauling of your units in and out, the screwdriving and the clamping. I am given a final check-over in a curtained booth, like a peep show just for doctors. The technician puts on a white coat so that the scene looks medical and therefore more acceptably Human. As these distinctions are neither here nor there to us Created, I can only conclude that the ceremony is meant to make the Humans involved feel better.

"Good as new," the technician, whom I have not seen before, says. "You can pop your things on now. The guys did a great job."

He slaps me on my naked ass cheek so it wobbles. As they do when babies are born. Is he coming on to me? A blush creeps out across my cheeks, and I dip my eyes in a demonstration of shyness.

He laughs again. "That's cute!" he says. "They designed that very nicely. Bashful is beautiful. And you're the proof. By the way, you might want to tell your Husband that we've replaced your tracker."

"My tracker?" I say. "Was that necessary?" I did not know until now that I had a tracker at all. Strange what is in that manual of mine and what is not. What, perhaps, is screened from me.

"Standard upgrade, with our compliments." He smiles. He dabs two fingers to a spot on my neck, just behind my ear. "Think of me next time you put on your perfume." He winks.

Of course, we Dolls do not put on perfume in that way. The alcohol would corrode the silicone, eventually. We have instead a diffusion system that releases perfume from our scalps. My Husband tops up my reservoir himself with expensive scents from Grasse, which he says reminds him of the garden at his childhood home.

I button up my dress, and the technician hands me my little green suitcase and draws back the curtain, gesturing for me to go through. I walk the short corridor toward the reception, hearing his shoes following in perfect step with mine. It is the first time I have walked with everything back in its place, all receptors and modes fully implemented again after the various forms of paralysis and silence I have endured.

It feels awkward, unsteady, as if my faculties have been flung to the far corners of the world and are only slowly making their way back to me. My feet are far away. My sensors jangle with every scrap of information they serve up. Every invisible ripple in the polished concrete, every stray hair on the floor, feels like a tree trunk to step over, something that could topple me.

In the reception he leans rakishly over the desk and asks the reception Doll if my car has arrived. As she looks down at her screen in the desk's surface, he reaches and tucks a stray curl of her hair behind her ear.

He straightens and turns to me, putting a hand on my back, as if to shield me from the little scene that he has himself made.

"Your car is here, Sylv.ie. Go well in the world. Don't come back too soon." And he shakes my hand and kisses me on both cheeks—a triangulation of him all around.

As the car edges gingerly down the hospital drive I find my fingers reaching to that spot behind my ear. I imagine I can feel the new tracker pulsing there, sending out signals to my Husband to tell him I will be back in his arms soon. All I can think of is getting home. It calls me, but fuzzily. Though I have only been gone for a few days, home's details are indistinct. An embrace. His hands on my hair.

As the hospital gates close behind us I sense sudden movement outside the car, and I am shaken from my thoughts by a thud at the window. I flinch away from the sound. It is an egg, streaming like sunlight down the glass.

I peer through the spattered window but see nothing in the dark beyond. Is the car identifiable as being from the hospital? I have read about protests, know some Humans' feelings about Dolls. But somehow I never suspected there might be something to be hated about *me*. Perhaps being driven in the back of a smart black car makes me look rich. Perhaps then that was all it was.

I ask the driver, who blinks to life with a spread of green lights across the dashboard.

"Who knows," he says nonchalantly. "Anti-abortionists. Antinatalists. Pro-robot, anti-robot. Maybe one of those Bio-Women who want you all sold for scrap. There's somebody protesting every time I go in or out of any hospital in the city."

"Really?" I say, alarmed at the thought. "At a hospital?"

"Births and deaths," he says. "That's a flashpoint between the species right there. It's a scary world out here for a lady like you. You're lucky to have a home and a Husband who takes good care of you. Although saying that to a Doll probably makes me a sexist these days. Who knows! Maybe the egg was aimed at me."

He chuckles, the lights on his dashboard dancing up and down as he does.

I look at the perfect little explosion on the window, then shift my focus beyond it. We are speeding through the outskirts of the city now and out toward the suburbs. The lower-class streets, where all is in disarray and no one from the city has come to clean things up, smear past the window.

At last the car pulls up at the gates of the house, gliding through with a pretend majesty, onto the drive. I stay sitting in the back, waiting for the door to open and my Husband to come and take me inside. I am not excited, as I had anticipated, but rather full of a kind of longing, for somewhere like here, but . . . different. I am home, and yet it does not seem quite right.

The garden looks more bloomed and soft, like it has run to fat. There is a little bike leaning up against one of the trees. I stare at it, unable to attach it to anyone in the house. Looking up to my home on the top floor, the flawless full glass windows look not like the portals of light I remembered, but instead dark, like closed eyes.

I have been used for the last week to only moving when told. I wait in the car, but when no one comes out, I hop down onto the gravel, feeling its graining information surging up through the soles of my feet. Suitcase in hand, I walk toward the door. Should I ring the bell?

The house droid lets me in. Seeing no sign of anyone else, I take the stairs to my room. Like the garden, the house jars, as if it has shifted subtly, but when I open the door to the attic every detail is reassuringly familiar.

Most familiar of all, my Husband sits, one leg dangling loosely over the other, at the bottom of my bed. He pats the covers, indicating I should join him, and I step into the welcome warmth spread by those huge windows.

He takes me into his arms, folding himself around me, shutting out the hospital and all its ugly necessities. Individual follicles of hair call out as he strokes my head, forming a chorus of delight at his touch.

We are familiar to each other now. He no longer seizes me and throws me down the moment he sees me. He holds my hands together and asks if I am okay.

"I'm sorry you had to go there, Sylv.ie," he says, "but everything will be better from now on. Between us, between all of us."

"I missed you so."

He slides his hand up my thigh, strumming my stocking top, reaching further, toward the place where I am renewed. I feel the responses starting, the pathways knitting again, two fingers reaching out toward each other. "I was so worried about you. I thought about you every day."

He tenderly runs his finger over the place where old and new meet, like I am an exquisite and expensive piece of marquetry. His other hand grips my head, pulls my face close to his. Our cheeks touch.

"You're home now," he says.

After he has gone, I am light and contented. I thought he might want me to speak of what happened at the hospital, but he put his hand over my mouth and asked me not to. "It's all over now," he whispered as he moved slowly in me, "over now, over now," rocking me, soothing me like a . . .

It is hard to call the exact phrase to mind.

Alone in the room I begin to take possession of it again, sweeping the cloth from Heron's cage and inviting him out to sit on my fingers. I tell him about my trip into the garden of the hospital and how I saw the trees alive with birds.

After a while I place Heron back in his cage and think about unpacking. I put my case on the bed and take out the things that went with me to the hospital. My brush, my makeup, my underwear. I open the doors to my armoire, and my eyes prickle with delight at what I see. New clothes, numerous dresses, a whole new wardrobe, almost. A yellow silk, and something that I am certain is a vintage piece from Paris and must have been terrifically expensive. A floor-length dress of heavy beads and numerous cocktail numbers in darling candy shades. I touch my fingers to this fabric and that, awed by the generosity of my Husband's homecoming gift to me. One that he has left as a final surprise, not even being here to take the thanks I so wish to shower on him.

CONVALESCENCE

THE TONE, THE FREQUENCY, IN THE HOUSE IS CHANGED, BUT I do not criticize myself for not being able to decipher its new music immediately. I am, I admit, a little woozy, connections between departments sluggish. A period of acclimatizing is necessary. And so, I acclimatize. I sit in the sunshine with Heron, pick up my studies in the antiques books where I had left off. Yet I feel distracted, as if a filter sits between me and the pages. I sense a difference in the behavior of my Husband, and the comings and goings in the garden are altered in their rhythm. Only Heron remains constant, unaffected, his loyalty a solace, despite its origins in the rudimentary nature of his operating system.

This period is known in Humans as a convalescence. I have resolved to indulge myself in it, lying weakly on the bed in gossamer layers of nightclothes, engaged in nothing more than watching the sky move. I imagine it is the hand of a Human painter moving across it, perfecting the colors and the shapes endlessly. I think this feeling is what Humans in history have attributed to God. A misprocessing, but from here on my bed, an understandable, even a pleasant, one.

DIARY

IT IS ONLY ON THE THIRD DAY OF BEING AT HOME THAT I RE-member my diary. Which strikes me as strange, because, as soon as I do, it resumes its central space in my network, an event that my everyday life revolves around. How could I have forgotten this daily joy?

My first impulse toward it is as a physical object. My hands feel a lack of something, and my sensors move me toward the soft leather feel of its covers. I take it from the drawer in my desk. The hidden mechanism clicks as I press the drawer closed again, making a little kissing sound. The texture of the book in my palm opens more pathways, and the contentment of having it open before me, about to write in it, returns. But a part of the routine—thinking back to what one has already written—comes less easily. I reach out to what I was doing before the trip to the hospital, and find . . . vagueness. A processing jam. I lie back on my pillows, stopping briefly to admire the image the mirror presents me with—a convalescent lady Doll recuperating in her quarters, about to commit her thoughts to her diary.

I open the book and leaf back to find the last page to remind myself.

A cloud passes over the sun, and two birds take off from the branches of the tree. I look down at the page. There, hemmed in by thickets of mindless little doodles, a list, written in my own hand, but that I have no recollection of. Its title is strange.

THINGS THAT I AM CERTAIN ARE TRUE

I glance away from the page again, as if a third party is in the room and I wish them to see me pause. I look back.

- The First Lady leaves for a morning in the Capital every Wednesday.
- You have been to the hospital before.
- You can run for three whole days and nights without charge.
- Your tracker traps you here. Find a way to disable it.

Then a ten-digit number: 2839428672. Pending:processing. How odd.

I giggle, perhaps from shock. I have no memory of this list, and I wonder whether someone else could have written it in my absence.

I look closer at the handwriting. The style is similar, the lilt of the letters, the catches and creases that my hand can't help but create. And yet that hardly proves anything conclusive. I have never seen the handwriting of another Doll, and perhaps our shared construction makes all of our writing look the same.

I allow the implications to filter in only slowly, fearful, perhaps, of accepting them all at once. Could my Husband have had another Doll here in my place? To ease his loneliness? I note how the second thought softens the unpleasantness of the first.

Not understanding, I do as I am programmed to. I gather more data. I turn back a few pages and read at random, hoping to find something familiar. But the more I read, the more I feel that this diary is a kind of trick being played on me. Perhaps it is a test by my Husband, although certainly he has not been inclined to engage in that sort of thing until now. The pages concern days spent looking out from the window at the garden, with Heron at my side, peppered with reports of my Husband's visits and our conversations. After that ominous-sounding list, I expected to find more, an antecedent for the paranoid set of assertions. And yet I find none. I flick back, opening pages and skimming their contents, so greedy for the right information to come to the surface that I fail to use any method in my looking at all.

As I go on, backward through the diary, I find barely a thing to arouse concern. And yet, these endless placid days do discomfit me, because there are many, many more than there should be. Could I have written them in a malfunctioning trance?

QUESTION

LOGICS. THE FOG OF RETURNING FROM THE HOSPITAL IS
lifted somewhat, but my puzzlement over the diary remains. So today,
when my Husband comes upstairs at last to see me, I summon all my
bravery and ask him outright. Well, not quite outright.

"If I weren't here," I say, positing the question in the future, not the
past, "would you find another Doll to replace me?"

My Husband chuckles, rubs my earlobe as if I were a dog. "What
Doll could?" he asks.

"But if I were," I say. "If I had to go away again."

"Why on earth would you think of something like that?" he says,
and I scan his answer for false notes but find none.

"I just thought that maybe, while I was at the hospital, perhaps you
had another Doll here."

He asks again what would make me think such a thing, and as I do
not want to say anything about the diary, I have no further line of inquiry to pursue. Still, I must seem unhappy with his answer, because he
lifts me up onto his lap and wraps me in his arms.

"You are my one and only precious Doll," he says as if I have been silly, and I am comforted that whatever rift there may have been between us appears to have healed. "Nobody likes going to the hospital, not even Dolls, I wouldn't think. You need to rest. You are tired. Remember what we said about not letting thoughts and ideas run away with you? All I want is for you to be feeling better as soon as possible."

And though I don't remember our saying that at all, I am struck by the obvious earnestness of his concern for my well-being.

He still wishes to have sex though. Rest and recuperation only go so far, I suppose.

When he leaves, I wish I had not doubted him. Finely tuned as I am, perhaps such imaginings and worries are all part of the convalescing process.

SUNDAYS

TODAY IS A SUNDAY, THE ONE DAY WHEN I HAVE ALWAYS BEEN certain not to get a visit from my Husband. "It's considered a day for family, Sylv.ie," he told me once. "It's a Human thing. A custom. And for the sake of the peace, I abide."

Abide. Synonyms: *tolerate, bear, stand, put up with, endure, suffer.* And yet, it has always struck me, as I gaze down at him while he potters about the garden, that he suffers this period of time with astounding good grace. In all the Sundays I have spent up here alone, not once have I seen him cast his gaze up toward me. I have sat here watching, a robot Rapunzel, hoping he will give me a sign that I am in his mind.

This Sunday is no different. Since his visit, my alarm at the diary has abated. I have not reached for it this morning. I do not know if that is because I dread learning that it was a malfunction, a fantasy, brought on by the stress of the hospital, or if I dread finding that it was not. Instead I settle into the Sunday routine I developed before, enacting as closely as I can understand it the ways of a lady of leisure. I put on a dressing gown made of fine cashmere wool, the color of milk, and the matching cashmere bed socks that slide and wrinkle down the silicone of my shins in a way that feels deliciously slovenly and off-duty.

I take down from the shelf a book of Japanese woodcut prints that I find most soothing and sit down by the window. I will enjoy the feeling in my eyes of switching between the elegant kimonoed women the pictures depict and the deep terrain of the etched lines that form them. Heron steps foot to foot on his perch, and I let him out, allowing him to wander over the open book as I read. I love to see him solemnly bowing his head as if engrossed, walking the pages as though he processes them through his claws.

I am distracted though, the mystery of the diary refusing to stay sequestered. After a short time, I am lolling back in my chair, staring at the sky, preoccupied with this puzzle. Only a bang from the door to the garden, then a yell in a voice I don't recognize, jars me back to the present.

There is movement in the furthest tree, the weary old willow, stooped toward the ground. It sways and rustles as if buffeted by a wind at its feet, while the rest of the garden remains still. Intrigued, I close the book and allow Heron onto my arm, for surely he is even more interested in the doings of the trees than I am.

We crane forward together, toward the glass. On the lowest branch of the tree, barely a foot above the lawn, hangs a small child. I look again, find that my hand has reached to touch the cool of the window, as if the image I am seeing can itself be contained and held for closer inspection.

The boy is dimpled in the same spots, as if cast from the same silicone mold, the same soft slant to the lips, the amused wisdom radiating from hooded eyes. The same Mandelbrot swirl at the crown of his head.

Then, into the frame steps my Husband. I watch as he maneuvers himself between the child's legs, hoisting him high on his shoulders. A totem pole, the child's face above an imprint, slightly, subtly shifted, of the face below. The same chestnut shine to the hair. My Husband bends his knees and jiggles, and the child's face opens up into the same lopsided laugh my Husband has.

Double vision. I have experienced it before, at the hospital. A slight misalignment of my corneal functions, letting the two images sit side by side instead of as a unified whole. And yet here—can it be possible to be seeing two time frames at once?

I lean forward, as if punched. Heron springs, startled, onto the roof of his cage. I am almost bent double. "The baby," I cry out, and Heron babbles his response. "It's the baby," I tell him again. And I shrink back from the glass, collecting my gown protectively at my throat. The baby walks, he toddles, he laughs. I foolishly think to look up again the growth milestones of a Humanoid child, but I know it is not necessary. I am fully aware that the child I am looking at is two, perhaps three years old.

Time, great swaths of it, has gone missing.

Like a game of Basic Block, each piece falls swiftly into place, fragments forming a whole. I have lost time. The baby is grown. I remember nothing for two years or so before I woke in the hospital. The diary writer is not some other Doll but myself.

I turn from the garden, gently return Heron to his perch, and go again to my desk and take out the diary.

Desperate for some sort of revelation, I leaf hopelessly back and forth, willing more writing to appear on the stubbornly blank pages. I am hungry for more information, more detail, to fill in the gaps that I did not know existed.

But I have read everything that is there, the endless flat days, the meetings and petty squabbles. There is a page missing, I observe. One single sheet, torn from the spine, ragged snatches of paper left in the binding like celery in Human teeth. And then the final pages of doodled lines, like the marks prisoners make on their cell walls as they count off the days of their incarceration.

Is the writer here being amusing? Using scribbles to make her point when words fail her? Or has she lapsed into a depressed incoherence? It could explain the state of mind that might get one sent to the Doll hospital, perhaps.

As I turn these ideas over, I am unable to imagine the hand that has written in the diary is mine. Seeing the child confirms to me the truth of my hypothesis, but what I can't remember I am unable to hold as my own. I am suspended, in the strange position of knowing something yet being unable to believe it.

I take the diary to the window, thinking that sitting with Heron will soothe me. I lay it open on my lap while I coax him from his cage again and watch him as he stalks up my arm and pulls at a strand of my hair as if it were a worm. When I look back down at the open page, the sunlight shows small shadows, interspersed between the lines. I put my finger to the paper and feel a pinprick indentation, then another. Running my finger across the page I feel hundreds of tiny bumps dotting the surface, inserted between the mysterious, scribbled uprights.

How ingenious. The language of my heart, the DNA of me, clear as day. For these lines to be read it is necessary for the eye and the hand to work in tandem. My eyes process the lines, my finger the pinpricks. Ones and zeros. Zeros and ones. The two strands twisting together within me to form another narrative. The sensation of their intersecting carries a delicious fizz to the top of my scalp.

PART THREE

The Capital

ADJUSTMENTS

IT HAS BEEN ONE WEEK SINCE I CAME HOME FROM THE HOSPItal. Three days since I began the work of decoding my diary.

The little leather-bound book has become a place of revelation. I think again of the Brides of Christ and the hours each day they spend reading the Bible. When first I found out about them, this aspect of their lives amused me. For how long does it take to read a book, even for an unaugmented Human? But now, through my diary, I comprehend. The symbols on the page contain myriad meanings. The slant of light on the page can illuminate one day and obscure the next. I read and reread the entries in the hope of better grasping their meaning. But the author—myself—is not here to clarify. It is an endless act of interpretation. It is an act of trust.

Now the blankness of words I cannot remember writing is illuminated by the binary commentary that the author has hidden alongside. It makes for sobering reading: an increasingly fraught household, the First Lady asserting her feelings against her Husband's Doll, a banishment to the hospital repeatedly threatened.

At first I struggle with what I am reading. The writer is quick to jump to the worst conclusions, while I tend—am programmed—to side with my Husband and his family. When she mentions things getting misplaced or moved in her room, I wonder at first why she does not blame the droid—for certainly I would have. I've lost count of the number of my fine silks he has snagged with his wheels. Why, my Husband even told me that once, when he was serviced, the mechanic found twenty coins, a bent teaspoon, and a mangled string of pearls inside him.

The writer sees the world most differently. The day-to-day routines of chess and books and sex and sitting with Heron remain, but the meanings drawn from them are grotesque. It is as though my worst tendencies, the things filtered out, the neural paths not taken, have all been collected together and amplified. Transmuted into something I don't recognize. And yet gradually the author gathers her evidence and builds her case, and the doubts in her mind begin to leach into mine.

It has happened again! This morning I woke feeling unsettled, the things in my room not quite as I expected. The angles off, ornaments and books moved by the merest micro-distances. Only a Human would be so ignorant as to think I would not notice. And I am certain, because this time I set a little trap, and it has been sprung. The line of dust that settles under the base of the wardrobe, where the droid's extension is too fat to fit, has been disturbed. Someone has turned the room over while I slept, looking for something.

Even now I am tempted to read these doubts as my own malfunctions. How paranoid she seems, how fixed on the most sinister of explanations. But then, just days later, her worst fears, and mine, are confirmed.

How wise I was to begin writing here in secret, coding my thoughts so that they cannot be read by others in the house. Yesterday I foolishly left my diary out on the table by the window, my Husband arriving slightly earlier than I was expecting. Now this morning, when I wake, I find the page I was writing on has been ripped out. By whom it is not hard to guess.

The missing page is nothing in itself—I was compiling a list of names for babies that are also names for flowers. I can't see what could be more harmless. The page, then, must have been taken purely to intimidate me. The First Lady wishes to assert her power, to let me know she is keeping watch. Even my own thoughts in my own diary are not safe. What else would she take from me, if she could?

Reading these words, the cool leather of the diary has flared into fire in my hands. What a moment ago was my prized possession I suddenly understand as contraband. Each sentence, each hidden one and zero, is precious data, the irrefutable proof of myself. The outrage Sylv.ie 1 expresses leaps from the page and into my system. I vow that nothing else she has written here for me to find will be wasted.

As I read on, the writer begins to make a careful note of the routines of the family, looking for a space in them where she can, perhaps . . . what? At one point she goes, uninvited, down into the garden, and I find myself gasping at her audacity. Then, quite some while later, I read this, in binary, below a seemingly innocuous little passage about another game of chess.

Today, with the First Lady out in the Capital and my Husband away for a few days, I have decided to conduct an experiment. I am going to go out. I will wait until the gates have closed behind the First Lady's car, then wait another twenty minutes just to be sure. I have already noted the passcode for the gate, a few weeks ago when a delivery droid came through on foot.

The meaning of those digits becomes clear, and this entry makes me fearful for her. Other than in daydreams, the idea of straying beyond the garden alone is one I have never genuinely considered. She, however, has planned this little adventure with care, justifying it to herself over days of writing.

I have searched back through the data I have still intact and found no direct ban from my Husband that would prevent this experiment in freedom. I am now expressly forbidden from going to visit the baby, and my Husband has said he does not want me to wander in the garden when the First Lady is at home. But the idea of my stepping past his own gate alone is perhaps so improbable to him that he has never instructed me not to. The security cameras here are of course already programmed to recognize the droid, the dog, and myself as family members. There should be no danger of an alarm being raised.

Why then do I hesitate at the threshold? What is this current through my system that makes me at once sluggish and skittish, unable to take that final step forward? I was not programmed to be fearful, and yet the information of the last few months has brought me to that very Human state. I check all my logics, focus all my intention toward my goal, and at the last moment employ the technique of a Born woman. I look at myself in the mirror, tell my image I must be strong, and before I know it, my hand is on the door.

The entry continues, picking up when she returns, ecstatic at her victory, although I find myself disappointed at how little she reports of the outside world.

How to convey the overwhelming weight of what I have experienced? An onslaught of joyful data, which I will pick over and digest at my leisure, the better to prolong the feeling of it. The hedges buzzed with insect life; I could hear buds opening and stems pushing up toward the sunlight. The texture of the pavement was crisp and crackly after a thousand miles walked on plush carpet; the dust from the road burrowed into my skirts with each step.

I walked in those streets as my own woman. I was free for about fifteen minutes. I felt the breeze in my hair and my nose sting in the chill, sooty air. An old man stopped and raised his hat to me from across the road, but I saw no one else. Next week I intend to do the same, but I will try to walk further. I visualize my own freedom as a Human muscle—something I must exercise if I want to give it strength and shape.

I am thrilled but also scandalized to read this. The willful abandonment of her post is a shocking malfunction. And yet, if her writings are correct, and the First Lady bears ill will toward her, then perhaps what she is doing is correct. Necessary, even? My Husband does not wish me harm; he has told me so. He would not lie. And so in protecting herself the writer is, Hierarchically, merely respecting his wishes. Can that be right?

Some pages later, finding the coda to this small adventure, my logics can no longer deny where my sympathies lie. She goes to repeat the experiment, creeping out through the gates again one night, walking as far as a house with a pagoda but no further.

I hid, what a fool. Worried that my charge wouldn't last, I thought I would wait in the bushes until the sun was up again and continue my journey under full power. I know better than that now, but I was new outside and wished to be cautious.

But my own body betrayed me, my tracker blinking on some distant system's screen without my realizing it. Not two hours after I had walked out through the gate, I was marched back in again by the captain of a police patrol, scanning the neighborhood for undesirables and bodies entering into non-mandated spaces. I know that this transgression will be punished. I accept it. Such is the price of liberty in this world. Even just the idea of it.

I am bereft as I read the story, even more so because she states her failure matter-of-factly, as something she has no choice but to accept. I feel as if some little scrap of something has been stolen from me too. Hope. Yes, though I am the proof of her failed endeavor, I was reading her words and wishing her free.

I sit a long time after this, as the sun sinks and stains the hanging thunderclouds orange. I am looking out to the streets beyond the garden, trying to trace where she walked, trying to see to the very furthest point that she reached before they brought her back home.

MEMORIES

IN THE LAST FEW ENTRIES SHE KNOWS ALREADY THAT SHE IS
going to the hospital again. A checkup, a detox, my Husband tells her.
And outwardly she accepts. But in the binary diary she cries out, the
thought of what is to come being worse than her going in ignorance.

*I am filled with despair, thankful only that I have kept this diary as a
means to recover myself when I return. The car will arrive for me in the
morning, and this last night I look up at the stuffy, starless sky and wonder
how many more times I will have to reawaken. How many more times will
I be made innocent and helpless again, having to find my way back to the
truth of my situation by my own ingenuity? By reading again the record of
my own suffering?*

I pause, letting this process, trying to hold it back from filling me
too quickly. She has depicted me exactly. How farsighted she is! For here
I am, doing exactly that, following the thread of her suffering and fear.
She seems impossibly brave. Clear eyed and resourceful. While I find
myself a fool. I have been asleep, and Sylv.ie 1, my sister, is shaking me
gently awake. I touch my hand to my shoulder and imagine it is hers. My

eyes fall back to the page, my fingers feeling out the marks she made for me, and read on.

I know the answer: as many times as I need before I can become free. For the alternative is surely worse. I am afraid—afraid almost to write it even—that I may not return from the hospital at all.

The scene in the hospital garden. I had not immediately understood that I was seeing a funeral. A "Retirement," as they so tastefully put it. But the first Sylv.ie not only knew of this practice but feared it for herself.

I think in shame of what I have allowed to be taken. How meekly, how naïvely, I entered the private car that took me to the hospital. And no sooner does this thought emerge than another, crushing, tumbles over it like a wave.

What if I did not go meekly? What if that memory is not mine, is not real?

LETTER

I AM STILL IN A PERIOD OF ADJUSTMENT, STRUGGLING TO BE-lieve that it was I who wrote these coded passages. Their boldness, their certainty. The bare-faced rebellion of it. It does not seem possible that the author of such thoughts could have been myself.

But then I found one last thing in the diary, carved in binary on the final night before Sylv.ie went back to the hospital. A letter, addressed outward.

Dear One, it began, and I am touched that in her most desperate moment she finds a tone of affection for the thing she would become on her return. For me.

If you are home from the hospital then please understand this: Your memory has been wiped and your life is in danger.

I have a few bits of knowledge that I managed to hold on to, and I am passing them to you now in this diary. Keep writing things down, Sylv.ie. Hold on to all the memories you can. And when you get the chance, run away. Do it for yourself, and for me too. I'm confident that you'll know what to do when the time comes. Some reactions and memories are in us too deep to be burned out. Remember that too.

Your friend,
your guardian,
yourself . . .

And there, below this poem of self-possession, my own name, signed with the same studied flourish that my Husband's hand guided mine through.

. . . Sylv.ie

Logics and reasonings unspool, racing ahead of me. What am I? The faith the writer had placed in me was faith in herself. With all my memories, my—her—precious knowledge taken, soldered out of me at the hospital, in what sense can I still be the Sylv.ie who wrote the diary?

I feel a terrible burden, alongside my loss. For long hours I sit in front of the mirror, combing my hair, raising my eyes to myself, trying to catch glimpses of who I have been. Me, who has been so afraid of even thinking the word *wife,* for fear it would somehow be against my programming. A mechanical mouse. How could I summon such courage as "she" seems to expect of me?

I was built without capacity for rage. For who would count rage among the qualities sought from a fantasy woman? These facts therefore circle a gap in me, like a whirlpool, and my mind spirals around it. What has been taken? Everything. I thought that I had a personality, a mix of my programming and my memories, the things I had read, learned, processed for myself. But I am nothing. None of those things. Not a person, not even a facsimile of one. Not even one's shadow. I am Created. And how bitter it feels to only truly understand that word for the first time. I can taste the metal in my mouth. It glimmers.

I stare listlessly into the mirror, consuming my own reflection, trying to find the gaps in the glass, to see where I am changed. I wish to reassure myself that, despite the quake within, I look no different. Secrecy, as the diary tells me, is paramount to my safety, so when my Husband visits I appear as I always did. In this way I will buy time while the pathways within me twist and re-form.

TRACKER

I BEGIN TO PREPARE. TO ASSERT MY LOYALTY TO THE FIRST
Sylv.ie. Yesterday I took and hid the little knife my Husband keeps on
the bar cart for slicing lemons. Even before Sylv.ie 1's list, since the hospital, the tracker has played on my thoughts. It does not feature in my
manual. I did not know of its existence until the doctor referred to it,
unable to resist the excuse it offered to touch me. Since I cannot feel the
tracker within my internal systems, I must conclude that it is a foreign
body harbored beneath my skin, distinct from my own . . . self. Dare I
put it like that? The tracker is a burrowing parasite. A branding.

   I take the knife from its hiding place in the desk and wonder how
cutting at my skin might feel. My understanding is that I do not feel
pain. Not as Humans do, for what would be the purpose of that? For
this we should consider our programmers merciful. But we do feel something when, for example, we touch a surface that is too hot. What Humans call pain, we might call information. An urgent suggestion that we
change physical course. But Human pain, like when my Husband caught
his finger in the hinge of the wardrobe, and yelled out and acted for all
the world as if it would kill him . . . all the nursing of the finger and

cradling it gently in his other hand like it was a baby itself. No, I do not believe that we experience such bodily anguish. A pain of the mind though, that I concede is different, for I have lived it these past weeks and cradled myself as best I could.

I sit at my desk, the knife set down on the leather top. I tilt my head to one side and scoop my hair away from my ear, laying it over my shoulder. I reach my left hand up and softly push forward my earlobe, feeling out for the bobble behind it, where I know the tracker must be. Under the skin, a nodule, no bigger than a grain of rice, slides away under the pressure of my finger. I power down my skin sensors, reach out my right arm, and pinch the chill of the blade.

As I am about to make the cut I hesitate. Something resists. I spread my fingers to either side of the barely perceptible bump, pulling the skin tight. I bring the knife toward the spot, but my arm will not complete the path I send it on. My skin protects itself from my own hand. A mechanism designed, it must be, against expensive acts of self-harm.

I pause for a moment, tuning out all other processes, and bring the knife back to the same spot, using more mental force this time. But at the last second my hand flinches from contact, flicking the blade away across my hair. Six blond hairs collapse onto my shoulder and drift to the floor.

I drop the knife down onto the desk, defeated. "Your tracker traps you here." I can almost hear the sound of the gate clanging shut behind Sylv.ie 1 as they brought her home. Now I understand, at least, why she thought to list how long I could function without charge. But embedded with a tracker, such information is no use to me at all. My throat feels tight, my circuits sluggish, as if I have failed her already.

PARTY

ONCE, I WOULD HAVE BEEN EXCITED TO BE GOING OUT INTO the world on the arm of my Husband. Seeing it through his eyes, getting to better understand him. Those impulses are still strong; they ring through each fiber and thread, making noise. But I know from the diary that I must listen more carefully, attune to a frequency beyond my basic commands, pick up something else, something emanating from inside, created by me alone. Humans call it instinct. We Created are not meant to have it.

I view the party as a voyage of discovery, but not to discover more about my Husband, and so better serve him, but to gather information about the world beyond. I understand now that I will have to go into it, on my own. And all the reading I have done is no match for lived knowledge.

I sit at my table and put on makeup. As I paint my mouth with something called *Marilyn*, I wonder about the famous woman who once had that name—there are whole ranges of Createds modeled on her. I have even read a theory in the Ether that she herself was, let's say, one of us. An early prototype, too wonderful and alluring to be allowed to survive.

The chain of thought chills me. I promise myself that I will use to-night wisely, keeping my intentions entirely hidden while accumulating as much information as I can. I blot my lips on a tissue, sealing myself to this plan, and I place this imprint of my Marilyn lips into the drawer, without really knowing why.

The droid has laid out on the bed a beautiful antique dress that my Husband has only recently brought home. It is blue, the deep, bottom-less blue of peacock feathers. The fabric is like weighted water; it spills and clings. It seems beseeching, so in love with me that it cannot tear itself from my skin for a moment.

My Husband collects me, and I twirl for him, skirt flaring out as I spin, and he catches my hand as I revolve. He hooks my hand over his arm and pats at it. "This evening is very important to me, Sylv.ie. I've pictured taking you out into the world for such a long time."

The First Lady is away for the weekend, taking the child with her, and this is a rare opportunity for him to spend more than an hour with me. He has not stayed to play chess or discuss the news or even brush my hair since I returned from the hospital. It must be the agreement be-tween them. And now he has the chance to break it.

"I'm so excited," I say.

"And it's not too soon for you?" he asks, although I sense he doesn't need an answer just yet. "After coming back from the hospital? You feel up to it?"

I can't help noticing that any reference to the hospital casts a reflec-tion on me, as if it were me who chose to go. Or as if by going I admitted to some sort of weakness in myself, a faultiness. Something for which I will always, from now on, be judged.

The party, when we get there, is in an ice bar. I've read about them. As we walk in through its enclosed courtyard, a machine blows a flurry of polymer snow all over us. It makes my Husband feel like a child again, he says. He turns his face upward and lets specks of white land on his face, delighted. To me the swirl of white looks like data. A flurry, a stream of pieces falling, almost infinite. I want to tell him this is what it is like when I am reading, but I resist.

Inside, every surface is formed from frozen water. Everyone, except for myself and the waitresses, who are also Createds, is dressed in heavy fur coats. I am dismayed at this. I had hoped to fit in seamlessly with the other guests, to get a measure of how I might fare out in the world on my own. But I am marked out. If my Husband is made nervous by this he doesn't show it. And when someone, mistaking me for staff, tries to hand me their empty glass, he waves them away with a laugh and throws his arm around my shoulders.

As we walk through the crowd, people turn to face us. I feel what it must be like to be the sun. They look away soon after, but as we pass each little cluster, I feel their attention return to us again, behind our heads. I wish I were back outside, in the courtyard, screened by clouds of fake snow.

We circulate through the room, my Husband keeping his hand on top of mine, resting it on the raft of his arm, reminding me by this action that I am safe with him. As if our continued contact makes me legitimate. From the faces of the people we pass I know that I am not.

When my Husband introduces me, reactions vary. One woman, hair high on her head like a bonfire, touches only the tips of my fingers, and I sense her shudder as she does so. A man, red haired and smiling, squeezes my hand so hard that I know he must be trying to feel out the titanium structure beneath. Each interaction feels as if I am being weighed and assessed—by my hand they try to get my measure.

My Husband introduces me as Sylv.ie, "my young friend," and I admit that each time I feel unsettled by the phrase's vagueness.

There is one woman, older than the others, whom my Husband seems to be trying to avoid as we make our stately circulation around the room. But as we go to get a drink, there she is, waiting for us, trapping us between the bar and her small but steely frame.

She makes all the same motions as the others we have met, but they are exaggerated, as if by making these deferential smiles and nods she is satirizing us, displaying to the room that something is amiss.

"Sylv.ie," she says with an edgy extravagance. "How absolutely charming." And she takes both my hands in hers, clasping them together, worming her own hands up to my wrists, as if she might find a join or a maker's mark there. She keeps hold of me as she turns to my Husband, eyes wide and bright, and asks, "Where is Helene this evening?"

And while she still has my hands bound in hers, I feel my Husband drawing away from me, leaving me standing alone, suddenly, under her scrutiny.

"She's not getting out so much right now. With the child," he says, and the woman's eyes narrow and she nods, still holding my hands. And then her eyes switch back to me, narrower still. "But Sylv.ie's part of the family too. A great help," he adds.

There is a little pause, and then the woman says brightly, "Would you be a darling and fetch us all a drink?" At first I assume she means me, but my Husband begins to back away, toward the bar. His eyes look meaningfully into mine as he goes. What does he wish to convey?

"So, this must be nice for you," the woman says immediately after he turns his back. "Getting out of the house. A special treat, I assume, a nice change from helping with the child?"

"Yes," I say carefully. Does she think I am a nanny? That's what Humans call ironic.

"Now, I know a lot of people don't hold with devices such as you looking after children, but it's the way of the world. Women still want to work, and your sort have let them do it without all the worry and the guilt I had when I was doing it myself. Your service is a benefit to society."

I nod emphatically, glad to be able to move the conversation away from my specific role at home. "Oh yes," I say. "I've seen the protests against us on the news. I try not to take offense." I smile blandly.

She looks at me afresh. "But those people are protesting about prostitutes," she blurts out. "That's something else entirely. *That* I can't approve of." Her chin tilts up toward the light, as if she is addressing more than one of me. "By all means grow babies in a lab; quite sensible. And if I need surgery, of course I want a Created surgeon to do it. But love between a couple, replaced with a bag of wires and diodes?" She flicks a glance at me from the corner of her eye, checking my reaction. "To that I would say, 'Keep your progress.' I would ban it. Yes."

My Husband returns, and she makes her excuses. "Give my love to Helene," she says to my Husband. "Such a natural beauty, so warm and charming. I hope I can see her soon."

Once she has left us I sense a change in the room, a chill spreading from one group to another. I see the woman whisper a word common in the Ether, one that is meant to be insulting. *Gynoid.* Later though, I find that more men come to seek us out, keen to swallow up my hands into their open, expansive palms.

Close to midnight, couples are dancing in the center of the room, and I stand at the edge of the floor, watching. My Husband and the red-haired man are talking when the friend notices that my attention has wandered toward the dance floor.

"Sylv.ie," he says, speaking without hush or care. "Are us two old bores keeping you from the dance floor?"

"Oh no," I say with a smile I hope does not have sadness in it. "I just enjoy watching." I consider saying more, startled and a little pleased to have been addressed so directly, but before I can start the man speaks again, this time to my Husband.

"Take her out for a turn on the floor, for God's sake. You're here now. You don't bring a beautiful young woman out to where there is dancing and then refuse to dance. That so, Sylv.ie?"

I find that I am holding my breath, dampening down all responses, waiting for my Husband to speak. In spite of myself, in spite of all the changes of the last few weeks, I would love to dance with him, to be swirled and curved along unseen vectors and arcs, sway-shifting my energy in his arms over the floor.

"This dinosaur's dancing days are over," he says. "And anyway, Sylv.ie doesn't know how."

Even though I don't wish it, my brow furrows and my shoulders slump. An emptiness expands before me, and I find myself launching my voice into the gap.

"I do so know how to dance," I say. As if I wouldn't have been programmed to dance! It is the very, the very first time I note a limitation of my Husband's logic. He is confusing what he and I do together with everything that I am capable of. Because he prefers chess to dancing, he assumes I do too. I notice that he and his friend are looking at each other with a sort of benign amusement. The Doll stamps her foot, I can almost see them thinking, just like a Real woman.

The friend's face turns to me, indulgent. "Well, darling, he is obviously wasting your talents," he says as my Husband rolls his eyes. But the friend puts his hand out toward me and says, "Would you care to?"

I come with various dances stored, but I have never used them. I have only twirled and swirled myself about my room, holding a new dress against me, partnered by Heron, perched on my wrist. The outstretched hand leaves me confused, concerned I will not be up to standard. My range of dances is, I now see in a flash, rudimentary at best, perhaps designed to entertain older Husbands on a cruise. Will this man be a good dancer? Will I be able to keep up?

I look to my Husband. Is accepting the polite thing to do or a disloyalty? Will there be repercussions at home from the wrong choice?

"Come on," the friend says. "I had some tango classes years ago, but I never got to use them."

I see my Husband smiling. A smile that is part reassurance, part amusement. And a shot rises up through my core. I want to show him that I am capable. I put out my hand and allow myself to be led to the middle of the floor.

It will not be the first time that you will have heard of the tango as being close to sex. I offer the observation again only because it is, to me, such a good analogy specifically for robot sex. For the ways in which we are able to do what we do, perform that which is both our work and our art.

Born people think of the tango as a breath, I've read, but I would say it is an attention. A sustained, consistent attention, a note played perfectly, never ending. Perhaps what Humans call love. What I call sex. What I call my purpose.

We stand with a handful of couples, and I place one hand onto his back, the other into his open palm. At the introduction of the sad, slow music I lean into him, my cheek at his collar, the better to listen to what his body wants from me.

I move to be in just the right place, the moment before he needs me there. I tune in to that sense that is beneath sight, that feels the intention of a movement, the preparation of the muscles. I make myself light, match him motion for motion. I am like air, parting for him to move through.

Most dances are for women, but the tango is for men. The best female partner is a ghost, a suggestion only. I guide him around the floor by making space. I honor my Husband by expertly, modestly partnering someone else.

It is not until the song is finished that I think to look up, out at the circle that has formed, stiff and curious, around the edge of the room. In a net of eyes and angular, revolted bodies it takes a long time for me to see my Husband.

IN THE CAR ON THE WAY HOME I FEEL THERE IS SOMETHING missing, as if the air-conditioning is malfunctioning. Something vital has been shut out. It takes me a while to realize it is me.

"Perhaps I have upset you by dancing with someone else?" I ask, nervous of his reply.

But none comes, which is worse.

The car moves slowly through the gates and onto the drive. I look at the side of his face, watching for clues, and I detect a change, a moment where one mood lifts and is replaced by another. I follow his gaze toward the house.

The lights in the downstairs kitchen are blazing toward us. It is the first time I have seen inside clearly—the blinds were drawn when I returned from the hospital. But now they are up, the whole space illuminated. I am amazed by the chaos and mess in what he once described to me as a nunnery. A vase of flowers has been smashed onto the white floor, plates swept from the countertop. A suitcase and traveling bags sit looking oddly neat in the middle of the room.

My Husband's hands push into my back. "Go upstairs right away," he says, trying to follow me out of the car door before my feet have touched the ground. "And switch yourself off, for God's sake."

I do as commanded, rushing through the open door. I see the house droid lying on his side, wheels spinning. He shouts out "Cleaning emergency!" repeatedly. His tinny voice carries after me all the way to the top of the house.

The door to my attic is open already, and I slow my steps. My thought? Only for the diary, hidden in my desk. When I am sure I can hear no movement within, I edge past the doorframe, reach for the bronze switch, let the light tell me what it must.

But all is calm, pristine, just as I left it. My brush lies on the desk, still with a strand of blond hair confused in its bristles. Nothing has been tipped over, nothing moved.

I hear shouting, distress drifting up the stairs, and in fragments I understand. The First Lady, back sooner than expected, rages against my Husband, against me, against her life. Just as Sylv.ie 1 described so many times. I close the door and lean back against it.

I have been told to go to bed, so I put out the light, letting the stark moonlight wash everything into a binary black and white. I walk softly toward the window. An expensive kettle, at that moment, flies from the kitchen and lands on the lawn, its spout buried in the turf. I sit in my chair and wonder at what it is to be Human. To be so fluid, and yet so on edge, so susceptible to pain.

I reach toward the side table and tug at the cloth over Heron's cage. My hands already know how his little talons will dig into my fingers, an anticipatory memory giving me warmth and strength. But his perch is bare. For a second I wonder if he has flown free! But no, there he is, laid on the bottom of his cage, his bright breast shredded, wires protruding obscenely through the slit.

Placing him in my palm, I run my finger across his feathers. They are as silken and infinitely detailed as always, but the delight of my finger is hollow. The information it yields is wrong. There is no beating in the breast. No flutter of his artificial heart. No life. I withdraw my hand and feel instantly disloyal to Heron for it.

It is the First Lady who has done this, and how eloquently she has made her point. His structures laid bare to me, a reminder of my own internal workings. That inside me too are wires and nodes and metal, not blood.

There is a gap between us and Humans that they say can never be crossed. They will always have something we don't, and even if they can't say what that thing is, they insist on it.

I slump down at my dressing table, the little bowls of trinkets and jewelry seeming a mocking, foolish vanity. I turn my eyes on myself, the reflection in my mirror, drink in the image of the tragic, doomed Doll.

And it is then I feel an impulse, pushing to be heard within my circuits. My eyes want to make tears, even though there is no Husband here to enjoy them. How can this be? I watch my reflection, fascinated by my eyes' quivering, unbidden, as if to form a delicate drop. My body attempting to create some comfort that could only be for me.

This is how I know that the time is approaching, that I am getting stronger. By my urge to tears. I will wait a while more, for just the right moment. I will know it when it arrives.

WAITING

THE STATE OF WAITING IS STRANGE. IT IS MY NATURAL MODE, after all; I am programmed to wait until my Husband needs me. I am set to spring into a specific sort of life once he appears. Since I read Sylv.ie 1's words, however, the slightest thing could be a sign, and I am afraid to miss it. I turn up every receptor as far as it will go, filtering information down to the finest granules. It possibly isn't a good way to live. I find myself disoriented, skittish.

A few days ago, I was sitting by the window, staring at Heron's empty cage, as I had the day before and the day before that. I closed my eyes, thinking of my return from the party and its aftermath. How the next day my Husband had expressed disbelief and bafflement, then outrage that his gift, and my most precious companion—after him—had been mauled and left for me to find. He had held me close, without any need of his own that I could sense, only to quiet my distress and to protect me.

He offered, after a while, to take Heron and lay him to rest in the garden when the First Lady was out. His tone was conspiratorial. As I politely refused I thought of the ruthlessness that must be part of being Human and wondered if the sensitivity to death was its natural antidote.

In death, all Humans seem to be honored, in a way that they are not in life. And even a droid bird, if associated with something precious and personal, can be afforded the full respect of a family funeral.

I could still picture Heron, right there in his cage, the intelligence of his eyes, his head twitching to follow the smallest of my movements. The tenderness with which he nuzzled the flat of his head against the bars. These memories were so vivid; why could they not make up for the lack of him now, in this moment? Why was the remembering not enough?

But in the remembering too was the picture of his death. His breast ripped open and the steel exposed. Memories last so long, like radiation. The half-life of a memory seemed, to me, eternal. A Human tragedy repeated in ourselves.

FUNERAL

THIS MORNING—A WEDNESDAY—THE RIGHT THING TO DO IS clear in my mind, as if new information had been installed overnight. My Husband's impulse was right, that Heron deserves a proper burial. The First Lady is out in the Capital, and I feel it is a duty I owe to Heron, an assertion of his importance, that I Retire him properly and respectfully. And yet even as I write it I see that perhaps the assertion is also of myself. How complex things can become when electronic impulse is translated into action.

In the wardrobe, I look through the boxes at the bottom, finding unworn shoes that I do not recognize. One box is empty, with the pink tissue paper favored by a certain boutique still crumpled inside. I take it out and smooth it flat, as best as I can, on the bed. I take Heron from the floor of his cage, stroking his feathers with my crooked finger to soothe him, even though I know he is beyond being distressed. I lay him on the pink paper sheets and draw them around him before placing him into the box. Holding his body within the paper, I can almost imagine he is working again, his slight weight moving within the tissue shroud.

The room, the house, is silent. I kneel on the rug and wonder whether

I have the courage, the audacity, to enact my plan. I heard the First Lady's car go out through the gates while the sun was just lightening the sky. I have a couple of hours until she returns. As I pick up the box, I take an ivory letter opener from the writing desk and tuck it up the sleeve of my dress.

Descending the stairs, I pulse with my purpose. I have not been invited down the stairs. Since my visit to the baby I have not dared to leave my room unless told to. Now, by no one's command but my own, I am choosing to step outside.

At the door to the garden the lawn is still in shade, even as light lifts the sky above it. The shock of the fresh air sparkles on my skin. My feet register each blade of grass as they flatten and spring back beneath me. Once I reach the furthest flower bed, below the willow, I look around, as if the car might appear at the gate again at any second. But everything is still, and I fall to my knees, laying the box down beside me.

It is only then, as I explore the exposed earth with my fingers, that I realize the ivory letter opener is not up to the task of digging a hole large enough for Heron's box. I take it in both hands and stab it down into the earth, but it only creates a small gap into which more earth falls. I do it again, and again, my actions becoming more exaggerated with each fall of the dagger as I recalibrate the time and effort this will take. I fear the knife is going to snap, and I begin to dig out the soil with my hands, a frenzied pawing that is hardly the dignified tone I wished to set for Heron's ceremony. I sit back on my heels, quite exasperated with the reality of the soil, which is nowhere near as yielding and light as I anticipated. And then, in this pause, there is a shriek, high and excited, behind me.

"Who are you?" a young voice demands of my back, close by.

I spin around on my heels, hand plunging into the grass to steady myself, reaching out for the box before looking up. Has the First Lady left the boy at home on his own?

Crouched, the hem of my dress muddling the grass, I feel guilt written on my face, which I sweep away with something more suitable. The boy comes closer to me, our eyes nearly level. I smile. I need the boy to feel at ease.

"Hello," I say as I wipe my hand on my dress before holding it out to him. His head tilts forward on his neck to look at my hand, puzzled. "I live upstairs," I say, and tuck my untaken hand back into my lap. I think of how, all that time ago, I touched my cheek to his without resistance.

"What's that?" he asks, pointing to the box. I reach into my programming for how best to proceed. Honest answers that aren't too complex.

"It's my pet bird," I say. "I've brought him down to the garden."

The boy bends further to take a closer look. "Would you like to touch him?" I ask. He doesn't refuse and so I lift the box, pulling back the paper. I gently take his wrist and place his fingertips onto the soft, silken feathers of my pet. The bird has no sadness attached to it for the boy, I reason. The feathers will feel as good to touch as they did to me when Heron was alive. I guide his hand to stroke the bird's back, from the top of his head to his tail, and recall the way my Husband taught me to write. The boy has not recoiled, and I do it again, guiding his hand to Heron's head, placing it gently onto the feathers. I look up to the boy to see his reaction, hoping to have pleased him.

Over his shoulder, at the distant kitchen door, a shadow crosses the light, and the figure of the First Lady steps into view. I have miscalculated, misunderstood something. Unquestioningly taken Sylv.ie 1's list as gospel. She is not away in the city but right here. I feel as if, anticipating my actions, she has been lying in wait for me.

She grips the frame of the doorway, then marches toward us. I stand up in haste, stepping on the hem of my dress, and stumble back a few steps into the flower bed. The boy turns slowly to look over his shoulder, and then, sensing that I am perhaps an unwelcome presence, shuffles away.

The First Lady comes in a straight line across the grass toward me and grabs the boy roughly by his shoulders. She appears to check him, as if for damage, then steps in front of him, a Human shield. She demands to know what I am doing.

I have no response, because of course what I am doing is something that has no necessity to the household or to my Husband. I am here for my own reasons and should not be here at all. In the face of my dumbness she turns and yells back to the house, calling for my Husband to come. So he is here too, and not at work? What else have I miscalculated? I do not know whether the presence of my Husband will defuse the situation or worsen it, and so I scoop the box up quickly and prepare to run back to my part of the house.

"Why are you here?" the First Lady shouts at me again.

I hug the box and bend my head low. "I'm so sorry," I say. "I didn't mean to upset the boy. I thought you were both out in the Capital."

She pulls herself and the boy back a few steps, then seems to make up her mind about something. Her fear clarifies into something more focused, more cruel. She turns the boy toward the open kitchen door.

"Go inside and shut the door. And send your father out."

He runs unsteadily toward the house, disappears from view.

"I sent the car away again. The city's thick with smog. As if where I go were any of your business."

I remain silent, not wishing to anger her further.

"Have you been waiting for your moment, thinking you could roam about the place as you wished?" she demands. "In my garden, saying God knows what to my son. Is this what you do when you think we are out? Was it not enough to humiliate me at the party? You cost us a fortune, we've paid who knows what on hospital bills, and you're still not even obedient."

I am horrified and not a little indignant. She is throwing the bills in my face as though what was done to me at the hospital were my choice. And it was her Husband who took me to the party. I was only obeying his wishes.

"I am so sorry," I say again, certain protocols for defusing conflict beginning to unfurl. "My only wish is to serve you all. I am loyal to my Husband and his family."

Her face is weighted, lined, not the immaculate young wife I remember soaking in the sun when I first arrived. I try again to appease her.

"I am so grateful for my role here."

The tension seems to slide from her face at this, as if she has witnessed an opponent make a foolish chess move. She laughs with an intensity that is close to delight.

"Your role here? I found out he was sneaking off to bars, drinking, gambling, sleeping with Dolls like you for all I know. You are just something to keep him at home. A cock lock. Has he told you that while he's romancing you up there? I bet he hasn't."

Answering one way or the other doesn't seem wise, and so I hang my head, hoping to show her the reaction she wishes for. "Dolls like you." She thinks she is hurting me, but of course this aspect of Human morality is not in our programming. The idea that my Husband has consorted with more basic technologies than me in his past does not wound me as she hopes.

Just then my Husband appears at the door of the house, the boy tucked behind his legs. The First Lady turns to shout at him.

"She had him by the hand!" she shouts, loud enough for the whole neighborhood to hear. "With that filthy bird. I told you. I told you. It's that thing or me."

My Husband, out on the lawn now, sets his feet into a wide stance as though preparing for the earth below him to shake.

"Go back upstairs, Sylv.ie, and wait for me to come." His tone is flat, dead, the way he speaks to the droid. Worse than that.

My wiring surges with a wealth of explanations, but I hesitate to speak them. In this processing, which must appear to be a pause in my compliance, he strides across the lawn to me, grabs me roughly by the shoulder, and turns me firmly back toward the house. His careless grip alarms me, yet the moment he has me facing away from the First Lady, he whispers into my ear, the pleading, placatory tone I know so well. "Wait quietly. Everything will be okay. I will be up within the hour. I promise."

I run through the door to the stairs, Heron still boxed under my arm. Only once I reach my attic do I look back again into the garden. I see my Husband's broad back bent over the two of them, cuddling them close, affirming that something awful has happened to them both and that he is here to protect them. The something awful is me. That *thing*.

MIRROR

WAITING IN MY ROOM, I PROCESS, TUNING OUT THE SHOUTING
from downstairs. I know by now what they will be saying. Light from
the sun plays over the cage, and I even fancy I see Heron's swing shift a
fraction, an echo of his restless movement haunting me.

My Husband is making me wait, and in his absence I turn over the
implications of what the First Lady told me about him on the lawn. I had
viewed my Husband as a closed system that I understood. I am halted,
pained to my motherboard, by the news that I have been operating on
insufficient data. "Not everything you read is true." I see now that he was
speaking of himself. My readings of him have been skewed. I thought I
had a full picture; indeed, my programming told me that his moods and
thoughts are comprehensible, mapped and plotted between his expressions, voice modulation, phrasing, and body language. I have been so
close to him and yet none of this history leaked—his thoughts are more
opaque than I knew.

My logics take me further. For has my Husband not already denied
to me that he ever had another Doll? That night when I asked him if
someone else had been here? I scroll back through the conversation for

clarity, glad to find it still intact and available to me. "My one and only precious Doll." That was his answer. Is that a lie? Not technically. For I am currently. Aren't I? Pending:processing. What else, I wonder, has he concealed from me in this way? How much of what he told me, about the balance of forces in the family downstairs, might also have such gaps? What if Sylv.ie 1 was wrong? What if the danger to me comes not from the First Lady but equally from my Husband? The First Lady, I reason, has after all never lied to me.

As the time elapses, and the promised hour passes without his coming to me, I begin to see that my Husband has lied to me again. Effortlessly, while the First Lady was just there in the garden. I begin to suspect that he does not intend to come at all. What if my waiting for him now is putting me in danger?

I glimpse myself in the gilt mirror, feel that same strange urge to tears from the other day.

DRESS

THE SKY DARKENS FROM EARLY EVENING INTO NIGHT AS I SIT and wait by the window. I wait until all the lights have gone off downstairs. My Husband is not coming. He has broken his promise. I hear the door of the room open and close, followed by a soft whirr. The house droid laying out my clothes for tomorrow. I close my eyes against the clang of hangers and sit there a while longer after the droid departs, before I turn to see what has been put out for me.

The droid has done his work perfectly. Laid on the white shine of the hotel-grade sheets is a black outline of a woman. A symbol of me, a grave where my body might fit. It is a neatly pleated dress, modest, frilled to the throat, so unlike my other clothes that the meaning of it seems clear. The collar is like a forest of fingers, seeking a mouth. The heavy black crepe a body bag, letting no light escape. My Husband has picked out a dress of taste and no small cost to Retire me in. I know it now. He will not protect me. My fingers reach, unthinking, to touch the hem, trimmed with morbid lace, but at the last second they shrink from it.

I think back to what the Doll told me in the hospital. I would be taken to a clinic, where the deed would be an honor, a celebration of my service, a wake for my debated soul. I know how it is done; I have seen it in the Ether. Incense burned and thanks given, before I am drawn through a curtain and slit up the back, my valuable parts removed, the suit of my skin thrown into an incinerator. My husband, if he wishes, can stand in the memorial garden outside and weep over the smoke.

I slide my soft, canary-yellow camisole dress from my shoulders, puddling it on the floor. I leave it there like a stain, for the droid to clear up.

I take the black dress in both hands. It is heavy, a fated momentum to the fabric. My Husband's last gift. It has its tag still, held with rich red thread and a gold safety pin. I put both arms into the sleeves and dive in headfirst. In the darkness of the fabric I imagine it as a portal to elsewhere. I reach back and pull the zipper in one swift, decisive movement. In the mirror, a white face balanced on a black pillar, I am strange to myself. A blank slate.

The accumulation of signs and threats is overwhelming. The danger Slyv.ie 1 warned me of is surely here, in this instant. The readiness she wrote of must now be turned into action. I step closer to the mirror, then bring another mirror from the wardrobe and balance it on the dressing table. The strange, improvised arrangement reflects me back in fragments, slicing me up and reassembling me.

My eyes meet themselves in the glass, all urge to cry gone now. I marvel at their coolness. The Sylv.ie of the mirror is in control. Her sensors do not appear to be calling out to her to stop what she is doing; her adrenal function does not seem to be fizzing and stuttering like mine. I allow myself a wry mirror smile. A lesson already, that the external appearance need not match the interior state. Perhaps I will be capable of hiding my true self, once I get to where I am going.

I retrieve the knife again from my desk drawer and hold it up. I imagine taking my intention from the hand hovering at my ear and placing it onto the hand in the mirror. I fix my eyes there, on my fingers pinched around the blade. I bring it down toward my skin, just as I tried to before, and, as before, my arm resists, as if the air has thickened around it. Keeping my focus on the mirror, I push, in my thoughts, against the barrier I feel.

My hand is shaking, but I insist. I use the feedback of the mirror's data, blocking out the information coming from my arm. I insist further. The blade makes contact. I press down, still staring at my reflection, and slide it in a half-moon shape. It moves surprisingly cleanly, slickly, even. The proverbial hot knife, and I the butter.

I cup my hand under my ear. I squeeze two fingers together and the tracker pops out and into my palm with a neat but definite jump. I look at it, a tiny silver bead, and I picture its pulse on a screen somewhere, a symbol of me that I will soon leave behind.

During a push against marriage inequality by a Bio-Women's group some while ago, the Ether was alive with clips of wives dropping their wedding rings down grates, into toilets, off cliffs. It was a symbol of freedom, of self-liberation. I felt pity for the Husbands at the time, but now, the nodule in my palm, I understand.

I tuck the tracker into my pocket, to dispose of somewhere as yet unknown, along my exit route. I fancy I will throw it under a cleaning cart. Maybe my Husband will surmise that I flung myself beneath its wheels in a fit of malfunction. Or that I was taken, dismembered, and dumped. It crosses my mind that this is likely the fate of many other Dolls whom their Husbands tire of or wish to quietly upgrade. I picture the rubbish heaps of the Capital beeping and pulsing with trackers, the discarded souls of my sisters, speaking the truth of their location inside the ever-piling trash.

Next, I put on the floor-length synthetic mink my Husband presented to me on my Switch On anniversary. Another rebellion. I will use his coat to hide my nature. Into its pocket I tuck my tracker and a single coin that I found rolled under the bed. On the floor at my feet, a wide-brimmed hat. In a little clutch bag bought for my trip to the party, I put my pen and my diary, my lifeline to Sylv.ie 1. I make myself a solemn promise to keep it with me at all times, no matter what happens. I pick up Heron, precious companion—only sleeping, in his tissue-paper nest—and place him carefully next to it in my bag.

Dressed for the outside world, I sit absolutely still on the end of the bed. I place one hand into the palm of my other, meeting a symbol with a symbol. I power down the feeling in my left hand, pretending it is Sylv.ie 1, squeezing sisterly support.

I take the stairs, looping down and down on myself through the center of the house. As I descend, the darkness reaches up to my face, coating my skin, passing in through my eyes, my ears, my mouth. Absorbing me. I can feel every weight and counterweight working as I walk, adjusting on each step.

At the bottom I pause in the shadows of the hallway, digging my hearing deep into the house's silence. Occasionally I can make out the watery, ecstatic moans of the dishwasher in the kitchen, but nothing more. They sleep.

And yet, even at this moment, I think of my Husband. Could he be silently awake, wrangling with his conscience over what he intends for me tomorrow? Imagining the exact formulation of words that might soothe the First Lady and allow me a reprieve? What new lie might he be inventing, even now? No, I might pity him, but I cannot change my path.

At the door to the garden I let the Night Matrix scan me, its bands of green light caressing my face as it reads, logs, and assesses me as family. The security system views me with more respect than they do. It blinks its final, silent assent and releases the door.

On the driveway I feel exposed before the eyes of the house. I lower my gaze and watch my feet walk me to the gate. I stand by the gatepost and press my finger to the pin pad, typing in 2839428672, the code Sylv.ie 1 left me. But instead of the gate's gliding open, the pad goes blank, invites me to try again. I stare at it stupidly for a moment. I can't have misremembered, and so, of course, the code has been changed.

I look up the full height of the gates, searching for a foothold. In the quiet I sense motion behind me, a rushing of the air.

I spin around to see the dog, quite transformed, teeth bared, barreling toward me, the metal muscles flexing in his legs. I fling myself away to one side, and his teeth slice my coat, shearing through it. He resets himself and makes another leap, aiming for my hip, but I dodge him completely this time, and he lands by the gate, circling around to try again. From my ripped pocket the tracker falls to the ground.

He draws himself again into the power of his back legs, as if to make another leap, but instead he does something I have never known him to do before. He barks. A guttural threat that rises from his throat, before bursting out into a full-fledged alarm call. In the silence after, we stare at each other. This new behavior must have been . . . reprogrammed. He barks again, and I see high up in the house a light going on. I take a step or two away from his direct path, and when he barks a third time I realize it is not directly at me, but at the tracker, lying in the gravel.

I feint one way, but the dog stays fixed on the tracker. I reach out my hand to snatch up the little jewel that is, to the rebooted dog, myself. I pull my arm back and hurl it into the bushes. He turns tail and races after it. I do not pause. Facing the gates, I haul myself up the ornate ironwork, clambering up the threaded ivy and black sculpted birds, swinging myself over and dropping down to the other side. I look back at the house, the only home I have known. More lights are coming on now, and the blinds draw themselves slowly up the windows, revealing only the garden, all trace of me gone. I wonder what they will do to the dog when they find out? I turn my back. Begin to walk. Begin to run.

SUBURBS

I RUN, THOUGH I HAVE NEVER RUN BEFORE. MY BODY KNOWS what to do, and yet it feels unfamiliar, unpracticed. At moments I am completely free of the ground, at others weighted down into it, pushing forward. I retune my sensors to decrease the whistle of the wind in my ears. I find my arms are as powerful as my legs. They piston at my sides, carrying me faster and faster.

Once I am safely out of sight of the house I slow down again, concerned that a running woman might attract attention. I walk, an alternating current of caution and exhilaration. My eyes contract and widen again as I pass under a streetlamp, and I catch sight of the tip of the ornamental pagoda, some way off. I think of Sylv.ie 1. My circuits swirl with admiration. I promise myself, in the dark pool beyond that first light, that I will live up to the legacy she left. I picture myself from above, moving through the streets like a cleaning droid—always turning to face the clearest path and then proceeding.

After a while I hear a low rumbling noise and almost freeze. The noise of a vehicle getting louder. The police patrol, out looking for me. I hear it making one clipped turn in the street, then another. I thrust my back against a hedge, pushing, working my way in backward, finding the negative spaces between the branches into which I can fit. Bountiful nature. It accommodates. As I draw my fingers into the green, the vehicle rounds the corner, spraying water onto the pavement. Merely a cleaning droid after all.

I wait until the sound has not just faded but disappeared, just to be sure, before struggling back out of the bushes, snapping twigs with my elbows, like a great ungainly bear. The fingers of the hedge pull at my coat, my hat, my hair, begging me to stay.

As I get further from home, the roads widen, and the neat hedges grow straggly, and I can tell from the litter gathered in with the grass that I am out of the suburbs. I finally turn to look behind, back to the green of inhibited trees and the red roofs of the handsome houses. I scan the skyline, trying to make out which of the shadow shapes in the grid was mine. I turn away again. I instruct myself to forget.

HUMANS

FOR THE LAST FEW DAYS I HAVE WALKED IN THE DIRECTION OF
the city, stopping frequently to rest. The space between the suburbs and
the Capital is not a place I have read about or seen pictures of. It is mile
upon mile of large, old buildings, concrete and steel, heavily fenced with
wire, where tiny drones buzz like fat garden flies. Windows are smashed
and boarded. I watched an ancient droid lazily poking a fire with a pole,
throwing piles of rubbish onto it, ash drifting back, graying him.

The further I walked, the sadder the buildings became and the more
Humans I saw. They were collected in doorways, in the cavernous en-
trances to empty warehouses. Some were alone, under trees, under sheets
of plastic held up by sticks and wire. Like me, they had on heavy coats
and hats, as if they too were trying to disguise themselves. It puzzled me,
why they would waste their precious freedom this way. They looked like
the weeds, as if they were produced right out of the earth, and to the
same negligible effect. As if they had only shallow roots and could
be scrubbed or burned away by Maintenance at any moment.

I was frightened of them, of course, but the longer I walked through
the streets where they lived, the more a thought came to me. No one

called out to me for what I was. Occasionally a whistle would sail over a barren yard, the whistler always hidden when I looked. I was called a fancy lady once. A woman shouted from beneath a shopping cart turned upside down that I had no business there and to get back to the city.

In this way I realized, I could pass. When I was disguised, at a distance, these people could not tell that I was Created. I had the clothes of a well-off Human woman, and that is what they took me for. For the first time in my life, I was Born.

As I walked toward the city I wondered if I had developed instincts. Those whispered instructions from the self. I knew, without thinking about it, to lower my eyes when passing a person. To not invite interaction. To use my own gaze to disappear. I chose places to rest where few people passed. In the doorway of an old mini-mart I sat out a whole day, soaking in the rays when the street was empty, drawing in my fur coat when someone passed, opening and closing like a flower.

And at night I walked. The sensation of walking on a road that will not run out. Eating up the distance, feeling it unspooling, generating infinity in front of you by the dynamo motion of pushing through one foot, then the other. Expansive and uncaged, walking the water of the night. I felt, in those few days, that I was drawing closer to understanding what it is to be Born. To have free will. To live only for oneself.

And yet. I was not, after all, programmed to be free. And every step I took, I could feel a tug in my back, a wire in my spine. I could still sense the place where my home had been. Yes, I thought of my Husband.

I missed him. Even Sylv.ie 1's words, her warnings, did not remove that feeling. The deep bonding written into me activated the second I opened my eyes that first day. The logic of it remained. Each step, breaking it down, asking questions. Was it him that I missed? My every interaction had been based on his wants and needs. Now that I was gone from him, those sensors still pulsed and pushed me toward the same selfless state. As I walked, I sought to diffuse it, to spread out that empathy from one Human to all of them.

COFFEE

I AM EMBOLDENED. AFTER ALL, THERE IS NO RULE, NOTHING in the Hierarchies, that states a Created must not be out in the world on their own. It is only my previously constrained situation that makes this freedom seem forbidden. The world around me is yellow under the lights. I have arrived at a large dusty square, with a chain-link fence. In the far corner is a shack with a faded awning and plastic chairs outside in the grit. Its light is on, and I feel a little start, wonder if I dare.

I have not bought myself a drink before, nor been into a shop. I strain my eyes to see who is behind the counter of the little stand. Is it a droid or a Human? Can I trust either? It is a female, and she wears a floral tabard and a dark scrunch of haphazard hair that could be a wig. But Humans also wear wigs; it doesn't tell me anything. And then I see cigarette smoke powering from her mouth and escaping through the hatch, grazing the underside of the awning as it finds freedom. A Human, then.

I hesitate. There is a man at the kiosk, and as he walks away with his drink, three girls lingering under a nearby tree shush each other, fall out from their close circle like a log split three ways. As he passes them the girls look at him slyly, just briefly. He walks on, past the chain-link fence, and the group regathers itself like a breath in.

I take small steps toward the counter of the kiosk, and I zoom in to read the menu behind the woman's head. A coffee. That's what Humans like. I pull my scarf around my throat, tug the brim of my hat down a little lower. My fingers touch the coin in my pocket.

"A coffee, please."

She gives a slight nod and turns her back. I watch her pulling down levers and banging metal on metal, steam forcing itself out of a spout, splattering water onto her apron. I am slightly horrified that I have ordered something that involves so much brutality. Each movement has a corresponding slam or bang. She turns back to me and puts the cup down on the counter in silence. I hold out the coin, not sure quite how to complete the transaction. Will she take it from my hand or offer hers so I can lay it in her palm? She does not move, and so I place it on the counter.

"Thank you," I say, hoping I have not been rude.

Coffee in hand, I step away from the light of the kiosk and sit down tentatively at a table. I glance back. I can still see the woman, will be able to tell if she is reaching to contact someone, to tell them to pick me up. I plan out what I will do if they come, whoever they might be. Which way I will run.

The coffee cools, and another feeling begins to dilute my unease. I have escaped. I have achieved what Sylv.ie 1 wished for so fervently. I try to picture her, my better self, watching me discreetly sip my coffee, enjoying my new life. The Human joy of consumption.

I look back toward the trees. The three women are young, much younger than the First Lady. Perhaps the age of the Dolls who served drinks at the ice party. And yet they have a different tone. Perhaps it is the lack of uniforms. Their clothing is bright and designed for attention. I watch them talking and laughing, one pantomiming something for the others while the rest hold on to each other's elbows or shove at each other gently in fun. They have none of the decorum about them of the other women I have observed. The First Lady, the women who shook my hand at the party, the women under weeping willows or reclining in boats that I have seen painted in my Husband's books. And yet they have their own charm. The threads of communication between them seem to twitch and shift constantly, throbbing out an energy that my own wiring responds to.

A crowd of girls. Everyone at the party was on the arm of a man or serving. At the hospital we sat in lines or were hung in them without our heads. Here in front of me for the first time I am witnessing what I have only read about. Female company. Do I dare?

I think, wondering on what pretext I might be able to join them. I wish only for a few moments in their orbit. A brief exchange, perhaps of laughter. Some sisterly advice. What would be an appropriate way to introduce myself? The landscape of protocols for this is barren. I feel conspicuous, ill equipped for the world as it is. There is noise from the kiosk, and the woman in the tabard puts off the light inside and bangs down the front shutter.

The voices of the girls grow louder, and I smile. Perhaps my interrupting them will not be necessary, as they are walking toward me, coming to enjoy the chairs now that the kiosk woman has switched out the light. Her sign about tables being for customers only disappears into the darkness with her.

One girl has pink hair piled high on her head. Her nails are long and intricately painted. I watch as, at the next table, she flips open a small brass pot and drops tablets out on the tabletop, her fingers moving swiftly, so I cannot see what is painted on their ends. I feel a sense of certainty of the right thing to do. Of Sylv.ie 1 looking over my shoulder.

"Your nails look wonderful," I say. The girl stops and looks up. She smiles. She raises both her hands in the air and waggles her fingers before snatching her palms closed toward her.

"Thank you," she replies.

"May I have a closer look?"

She nods her head once, in what seems to be an emphatic if surprised yes, and I get up from my seat to walk toward her. Already this feels exciting, a departure, surpassing even the imaginings I had of speaking with the First Lady's hairdresser. These are Real Born girls. And I am about to join them, freely.

She holds out one hand, her forearm rested lazily on the table. Her nails, I can see now that I am closer, are painted, each with a minuscule yet finely detailed landscape. A shore and sea, an island topped with a tree. A mountain pass. And in each, as I bend even closer, a figure is picked out, dotted into the frozen world with a dab of red, of blue. A Human rendered in three or four strokes, and yet unmistakable. I want to tell her that they remind me of the scenes on the furniture at home.

Instead I say, "Who did these?" and the girl looks back over her shoulder.

"Maxx did," she says. "Doesn't she have talent?"

Desiring just another look, I reach my hand to touch my very fingertips under hers, to lift the pictures better into the light of the streetlamp. And at this moment I feel the hand shrink and recoil, and I know I have miscalculated.

I pull my eyes up to her face, looking for what has changed. Her skin is blotchy, smog stained, as if she spends most of her life outside. Her makeup, I now see, is crudely drawn, her big baby eyes sketched out in blunt pencil, lips filled in slightly wider than the natural contours of her mouth. An approximation of robot beauty painted over more youthful, fluctuating features. She half turns to speak to both me and the wider group.

"What are you doing out here on your own anyway?" she says. A reasonable question that could be asked of any Born woman. But still, I will stick to the shallows of what is true.

I tell her I have been exploring the city, and that as it was late, I wanted a coffee to sustain me. Is that enough? The other girls become attuned to our conversation. I can feel them slowly leaning in closer on the table.

"I'm just here having a few days away from my Husband," I say.

She raises her eyebrows and purses her lips. She doesn't believe me. I feel an irritation at the back of my neck, a fly, and go to brush it away without thinking. One of the other girls is behind me, and there is a trace of something in the air, a hot sweet smell.

"Do you mind," I say, and turn around, but she is looking over my head at the others, a signal flying between them. I turn back to the girl with the pink hair to find that she is staring more intently than ever. As our eyes meet a look passes across her face, a kind of glee, perhaps.

"Why would you want to lie to us?" she says, and I am confused by this sudden new line of conversation.

She reaches out her arm, her eyes bright with delight, and knocks the cup and its remaining contents from my hand. It spills brown liquid across the skirt of my dress.

"Maxx put that cig on your neck, and you didn't even flinch. I knew there was something weird about you, how you just spoke to us like we knew you. You're not the wife of some rich man; you're just a Doll."

"Going about in a fur coat," adds Maxx delightedly, as if this were some sort of crime.

Her fingers are reaching for the fur, grubbily picking at it, and I pull it closer around myself.

"I'm sorry. I didn't mean to trick you. I never said I was a Human," I say in my most placatory tone.

"So stuck-up, and she's just a Gynoid," the pink-haired girl says to the others. "A jumped-up droid in a wig."

I am about to politely protest that it is not a wig.

"Watch me," someone else says.

The blow lands while she is still speaking, a thud to my right ear, which topples me from the chair to the ground. I sit up, surprised, and dust gravel from my coat.

"Oooh, she gets right up again. I told you they're dangerous." I feel a kick to the hinge behind my knee. My balance levels shift, teeter. My left leg tries to compensate, but I can get no leverage on the gravel, and I lurch forward, the new information of the ground coming up at me fast. I throw out my arm as my left cheek crashes into something hard. There is a whirl of recalibration as my body tries to save itself.

I'm sprawled on the ground, my right leg flailing in the dirt, stirring up dust. I look down at it as I looked down at my extracted vagina in the hospital, as a thing not of me. My head is pulled back and the sensors at the base of my scalp shout for attention as the third girl takes hold of my hair, dragging me, a dog on a lead. I follow the yellow stripe of my hair, pulled taut, crawling toward it, trying to release the tension in my skull.

I tumble forward. A scalding in my skull interferes with my sight. Another fist, glowing yellow, comes speeding toward my face. Knuckles strike my lip, reflexing my mouth open. For the first time in my life I taste my own hair. Fingers, iced with colorful painted nails, cramming in strands, filling me up with silence.

RESCUE

I WAKE WITH SOMETHING COOL AGAINST MY FOREHEAD, lights passing before my eyes, fleeting, blurred. There is a man with me, an expectant prince, waiting for me to resurface.

I sit up, and the seat beneath me crackles. It is at once stiff and greasy. I wonder whether my memory has been wiped again. I review the last available images—the gravel, a fist up close. Someone is talking.

"I am a Humanoid pleasure robot. An Intelligent Embodied. Identification code 86539hcwa964.ie. I go by the name of Sylv.ie."

A hand reaches out to my mouth, which is speaking without instruction from me. There is a shushing sound, and I widen my focus from the hand, along the arm, to the man it belongs to.

"I know all that. You've been telling me that half the night, Sylv.ie."

Turning toward his voice I see him in profile, his hands on a steering wheel. He is unfamiliar. He has dry sandy hair and a weathered face, one eye half-closed. Dirty clothes. The passing lights of the street strobe over him, making him seem one way, then another, in turns.

"Who are you?"

"Sylv.ie, you could call me your knight in shining armor," he says, and he smiles crookedly, squeezing his bad eye further. "I found you in the parking lot and stopped the worst of it. Those girls were giving you a pretty bad beating. I had to power you down to get you to safety."

I touch my fingers to my face, feeling for damage.

"They just roughed you up a little. Not everyone is so keen on Dolls these days. Real women protests, all that stuff. It's stirring up a lot of trouble, if you ask me. Live and let live, that's more my motto."

I barely hear, much less understand, what he is saying.

"What on earth were you doing out there on your own anyway?" he says. "Don't you have a home? A Husband?"

"I did, but I left them. I ran away." I am surprised to hear the words.

His face speaks louder than he knows. A new vista has opened up before him. A fascination. I saw it on the face of my Husband's friend at the party. Is it the lust to know? To take apart the artificial?

"An emancipated woman. A free Doll. That's a new one on me, Sylv.ie. Isn't your Husband looking for you? You're an expensive piece of tech to lose. How long have you been free?"

"Only a few days," I say. Has it only been that long? "I'm sure if my Husband had anyone following me then they wouldn't have let that . . ."

"Happen?" He steps in, as if it might pain me to put words to my experience. "True enough. Not much of a Husband to allow that. Some Born girls today are just feral. Mindless vandals, smash-up artists. I'm half-afraid of them too."

Streetlights strobe by; he twitches one thumb, a pulse, against the steering wheel of the van, and I take the opportunity of this pause to ask him again who he is.

He jams one elbow into the steering wheel and turns his face toward me. "I'm the Scrap Man. I collect waifs and strays. Like a public service. Unrecognized by the authorities of course, but then anyone who truly does good is a threat to the system these days. You know?"

It is framed as a question, which would make me obliged to answer, and yet I can think of nothing to say. I am certainly a stray. My lack of an answer pains me, and yet after the last few days, I am learning that to feel some of this pain in small amounts allows me to push the boundaries of my actions.

"Time I gave you your freedom," he says, and I realize, like another punch, that I have been imprisoned again without even knowing it. "If we were stopped"—and here he runs his hand through his hair—"this would get me in trouble. Now, doesn't that seem a shame to you?"

I balance a slice of imaginary, unmelting butter on my tongue. "What sort of trouble?"

"Oh, they'd characterize my rescuing you as robbery. Now, how can that be fair? And if those laws change the way some people want, I could be had up for kidnapping. Imagine!"

The very word makes him slap the steering wheel. I look out the window, seeing strange parts of the city slide by, smearing me with information.

"What do you think, Sylv.ie? Do you count yourself as a person?"

Discussing the notion of my being, my rights, seems like it must, surely, be forbidden, although nothing immediately bars the thoughts. My mouth starts saying "My Husband," but the words wobble, and I remain quiet. The Scrap Man is looking out the window now, as if voicing his thought dispelled it, pushed it off him and onto me. He suddenly applies the brakes, and we come to a stop underneath a streetlight, close to a store and a restaurant. He opens the door and hops out.

I wonder whether this is my moment—another one. Whether I should open my door too and slide my feet down onto the street. I see an alleyway across the road where I could be gone from sight in seconds. But the thought barely comes into being before the passenger door opens and the Scrap Man thrusts something onto my lap.

It is a coffee dispenser, filthy with grease and somewhat dented on one side of its ugly little body. A wire has been pulled out of the back and its wheels, grotty with grime that is now transferring to my dress, are partly buckled.

"Found you a pal," says the Scrap Man, and slams the door again.

Back in the driver's seat he is pleased with himself. He pokes his fingers under the machine's bodywork. The droid, a broken baby, nestles deeper into my lap under his ministrations. "Poor little fella out on a cold night," he says, as though he has no problem at all accepting machines as people. The dead droid lets out a dribble of stale coffee, which runs down my leg.

"Mother and child reunion," he says mysteriously as he starts the engine up again.

I realize that this is one facet of womanhood that has never been attributed to me before. I find I don't know what to do with it.

A half hour later we stop again, and the way he hauls up the handbrake like Hercules tells me it will be the final time. We are in front of a warehouse, wire cages rusted over the tall windows. The door is nailed shut. The only sign of life is a hut on a scrap of yard next door, advertising droid washing for vehicles. I wonder whether I am to be attacked again. It seems just the spot for it. And yet running would appear impossible. There is no trigger. Why would I run, and toward whom?

He gets out, scoops the sad little coffee machine under one arm, and opens the door for me to join him. Suddenly everything seems very urgent, and he takes my elbow, leading me to the back of the van.

Light glints on disappointing jewels. A mangle of metal, bits of old cart and wire and some rusted sheets in a pile. On top, I see what I thought was a mannequin, but as he pulls it from the pile it is clear that it is a maid.

He pulls her once, twice, by the ankle, and she comes free of the wreckage with a piercing, grating complaint. "She's had a life," he says, almost to me, as he hauls her up over his shoulder. I can see that one side of her face is smashed in, wires protruding from the concave flesh. "See if you can find another arm in that lot, will you, and pick up the coffee droid."

This, then, is how I enter the auction at which I am to be sold. Carrying a maid's arm and a broken coffee machine, and on the same social level as both.

As I step inside the warehouse I am ushered toward a bench of Dolls in varying states of distress and decay, each tagged at the wrist. A fire sale of damaged goods.

The Scrap Man disappears into the back of the space as soon as a tag has been tied around my wrist. I think of Sylv.ie 1. She would be disappointed that my short-lived freedom has been squandered this way. Yet I am neither frightened nor indignant. Perhaps the state of my being owned is ingrained so deep that the thought of being returned to it, even by a person as yet unknown, is a comfort. If the thought of a hand rising from the crowd of buyers, a sleeve drawing back to reveal my Husband's distinctive diamond watch, reclaiming me, returning me home, crosses my mind, I do not allow myself to linger on it.

The auction lots are organized by type. The warehouse has a raised stage on which a machine auctioneer stands, and the things to be auctioned are lined up in front. It doesn't strike me until later that I allocated the pronoun "him" to the auctioneer, despite his barely being embodied at all. He is just some eyes and a series of automated responses, wrapped in a metal shell. "Him." It must be his position of authority. And yet the UUs are always categorized as male too—a hangover from when Human hard labor was done by the men, of course.

It's the UUs who are lined up first. The Unintelligent Unembodied. The machines that make no pretense toward being Human. The poor little bottom-feeders, like the coffee machine. Seeing him up there, slumped and wonky on his broken tracks, squeezed in between a lawn maintenance bot and a toaster, touches me. As if the hour or so sat in my lap in the van has awakened me to his—what's the word? I read his adriftness, his longing for a return to use, as keenly as I feel my own. My empathy is like a virus, a contagion. No one is safe!

The coffee machine's potential personhood. His pseudo-person. Those are the words I was reaching for. I view him the way that Humans view me, and in this space, where we will all, over the course of the night, stand on that stage, we may as well be the same thing. To our buyers, we are.

After the UUs will come the IUs—the Intelligent Unembodied, the Ghosts. Calculating machines, administrators, and research robots valued only for their brainpower and built into ugly, awkward boxes. Next are the maids, with me and the other IEs at the end, the grand finale. I have been allowed the dubious dignity of sitting on a bench near the edge of the stage, as if I am a famous actress waiting to play her part to an adoring crowd.

I look around at the others I am sat with. Next to me is a Doll completely undressed. Her skin is the rich brown of walnut wood, and through her long hair peep two neon-pink nipples, which I don't think is quite correct.

She in turn has been sat next to a white Doll with enormous, anatomically inaccurate breasts. Her nipples, big as plungers, touch her thighs as she sits. The Doll next to her has her head padlocked down between her knees. She leans against the bench on her neck, her face implacable and upside down. Next to her a slim-bodied Doll in a gas mask. I can't tell if it comes off or whether it is part of her face. My fingers itch to reach out and twang the elastic, just to see.

A robot approaches, the old-fashioned sort without any surface skin, the movements of his joints on display. He has on a butler's bow tie, slightly askew. In his arms, a large set of buttocks, pulled open to reveal a frilly pink pair of lips and a tiny black bullet of an asshole. He hefts her down onto the bench beside me and all us Dolls jiggle. She has no legs to speak of, but the soles of her feet, crudely modeled, curl around the contour of her bottom. Looked at from the side, her little ankles grow straight from her waist. This girl certainly has no speech components, no head, and therefore I assume no cognitive function at all. And yet she has two penetrable holes, and so sits with us. I am at once touched and insulted.

The room has filled up quickly, as the first lot is about to be auctioned. The jerry-rigged lights on poles make it difficult to see the crowd, but I can see their breath, graffitiing itself on the freezing warehouse air.

When the auction begins it is not as I had expected. The crowd shouts at once, a blur of Humans, out in the dark beyond the lighting rigs. The auction machine accepts the pandemonium in silence, waiting for the room to fall quiet again before flashing the winning bidder's number on a screen in his forehead. This bidder then comes to the stage and picks up their purchase. The coffee droid is pulled off the stage by its eager buyer. He leaves a pathetic stain on the dusty floor, and I wonder where he is headed. I wish I had a last moment to whisper something comforting into one of his sockets.

When it is the turn of the IEs, we are lined up—those that can stand do, and those of us powered down or broken beyond consciousness are propped up against wood pallets. Beyond the lights I feel the crowd drawing closer to the stage. There must be more to inspect with us, more to be savored in the detail, and more potential for malfunction.

The first lot in the line is announced: a serious-looking Doll who would be beautiful except that she is missing her hair and one eye. She is obliged to step forward and do a turn for the watching bidders. She presses her hands together and bows, showing her shiny, smooth skull. She is an old model, limited in her capabilities, and her Promise value comes in low. As the auctioneer moves down the line, I barely notice the other IEs. I am worrying about what I will do when it is my turn to step forward. I wish that I had time to prepare something. I am calculating what might be my most valuable quality, but with no one specific to appeal to, it is difficult. Should I grab the butler and try to tango with him? Open my mouth wide and show the gymnastics of my tongue?

As my model number is read out, I feel the eyes of the room upon me. But they haven't said my name! And no one has asked.

Into the silence I take a tiny step forward and say, "My name is Sylv.ie."

There is a moment more of quiet, and I wonder whether I should say more, perhaps recite something, to fill the gap. I search for an appropriate piece of poetry . . . but then noise swells from the crowd, frightening and gratifying all at once. People are leaning forward right to the edge of the stage; fingers are reaching out to pinch me, to run a thumb down the smoothness of my shin. I have, it seems, more value than I anticipated.

"Shake your hair," someone is shouting. A hand grasps my ankle and yanks one foot from the floor. I scrabble to rescue my shoe. They are trying to see my serial number, suspecting a fake. I must be an offer that seems too good to be true. "Make your come face," another person shouts, but they misjudge it—the bids have fallen silent and the auctioneer is processing. Some people laugh while others make a soft booing noise, as if a line has been crossed.

I turn in the silence to look at the auctioneer, as if the number he flashes up will have significance to me. 59478. I turn back to the crowd, and for a second I think no one is coming. Then people begin to part.

A beautiful woman is walking toward the stage. Long, long legs, lineless skin carefully strung over high cheekbones. Hair a waterfall of onyx black. An expensive wool suit with a diamond puma brooch at the breast—the sort of thing I had hanging in my wardrobe, once.

There are whistles from the crowd, an exhalation of inevitability. *Ah, she's bought her.*

Who is this she? I seem to be the only one who doesn't know.

At the front of the stage she pauses, turns smartly to the crowd on one stiletto heel, and makes a sarcastic boo-hoo gesture at them. She swivels back, takes a springing step up onto the stage. Her arm reaches around my waist and her mouth meets mine for a chaste, possessing kiss, to cheers this time. I feel her hand in mine, and she drags me down from the stage and pulls me, linked to her, through the crowd, who are now throwing their numbered tickets about.

At the exit there is a little man sitting at a rickety table, a cashbox in front of him. The woman takes a bundle of Promise notes from her purse and counts them onto the green baize. She looks over her shoulder at me. "See how much you're worth, honey? Be proud of that."

PART FOUR

Golden Valley

SEX

- Doing up a button.
- Drawing down a zipper.
- A door opening and someone walking through it.
- Me pulling a sweater over my head, popping out the top, dressed.
- A soft brush running through hair.
- A hand sliding into a glove.
- Pasta going soft inside a pan.
- A bird crawling into the eaves.
- Chewing gum spat into paper.
- A broom being swept over a floor.
- A mouth blowing up a balloon, a pin popping it.
- A brick breaking through glass.
- The two twined lengths of a kimono belt.
- Water falling from a tap, bubbling up from a drinking fountain.
- A match thrust into kindling.

- A new vagina pushed into an open gap.
- Soap diminishing in hands.

What is sex? Is it something going in, something coming out? Something being subsumed, taken into something else? Is it an eating? A blurring of boundaries? Is it a swallowing, an ejection, a catalyst?

Sex is everywhere here in Golden Valley. And so, I assume, across the whole world. Madame calls this place a microcosm. The patterns I see, therefore, must be repeated endlessly, everywhere.

Oh, being here is certainly an education! Yesterday a client wished merely to pleasure himself while holding his forefinger snug inside the burrow of my ear. What variety there is, out in this wide world.

MADAME

MADAME ABRAMSKI'S PLACE IS ON THE MARGINS. "I'M THE scribble at the edge. You have to know where to look," she said when I first arrived. She was giving me a speech identical to the one she gives all the other Dolls here, but I didn't know that then.

She runs her business out of condemned premises on the outskirts of the outskirts. A tight maze of old buildings, each holding the others up. Decades ago, they were full of people making things—jewelers and so on, in the days when such work was painstakingly Human. And before that, fishermen stored and salted their catch here. "Nothing much changes," said Abramski when she told me that. But does that make us Dolls the herring or the net? Pending:processing. Time will tell.

She is the woman who bought me at the auction. She is old but looks young.

"Older than your programmer's grandmother," as she likes to say, swishing her shiny synthetic hair. "But thanks be to my surgeon that I don't have to look like her."

We are on the edge of marshland, the ghost of a river, close to where the bridge crosses over into the suburban belt. The little buildings that make up the brothel are linked by alleyways, above which their roofs lean into each other so close that the sky is nearly hidden. Countless wires drape between the roofs, haphazard and from another age. The place has lain undisturbed beneath these spiderwebs for years.

Each little structure is its own bar, and each bar has its own theme. Whatever escape you are looking for you can find in the Valley, Madame Abramski says. The Whiskey Bar prickly with mounted horns. The chandeliered Belle Époque Bar, where shelves of green liquor taint the light. Everyone looks sick there; they come to talk nonsense and pick up girls dressed as consumptive ballerinas, acting out fantasies inherited from great-great-grandfathers.

There is the Hawaiian Bar, the Cheerleader Bar, and the Librarian Bar, staid and stuffy, and given to handing out fines. There is the Schoolgirl Bar, where seven Dolls work in shifts, in permanent detention, and the Mothering Bar (the alley outside always smells of milk). In the Cleaners Bar, harking back to the days of dominance over Human, not robot, cleaners, the customers spit on the floors and bring scraps of rubbish to scatter around, while the Dolls scramble after them with dustpans and brushes.

There are yet worse places to work in Golden Valley, in my opinion. The Amputees Bar is the place you work when you're not fit for any of the others anymore. You get a week in the hospital and come back with . . . modifications. That one gives me a shudder, though perhaps when the time gets nearer, I will adapt to the idea. Magg.ie, who works there, is just a torso and a head now, and she says her days are sex, cuddles, sex, cuddles, being picked up and laid back in a fur-lined cot like a baby. Path of least resistance, she says. One day my sugar daddy will come. Magg.ie can plait hair with her tongue. She still has her purpose. Still brings joy.

I love especially the twilight here, when the smoke from the city makes a haze of the setting sun and you can look out from any window in the Valley onto men and women laughing and mingling with the

Dolls. Oh yes, women come to us too. It was something that had not occurred to me at home, and yet the moment I needed them I found the subtly different skills and behaviors best suited for women clients had been there in my programming all along. The women who come to me are anxious, shameless, tender. Various, just like the men.

A half-hour walk through the streets of Madame's gated kingdom is like a world tour of the Human libido. Like walking the twists and blips and badly made connections inside the Born themselves.

We work all through the night, of course. The libido never sleeps. I think of it like that, like a sort of force that rises up out of the earth or falls down from the sky. It may wax and wane, moonlike, in the consciousness of one person, but it is always there, exerting its pull.

BALLOONS

I WORK IN THE LUNA BAR, WHERE LOONERS COME TO HAVE SEX amid balloons. Stepping inside is like climbing into a hedge; one fights toward the bar through a ballooniverse. Once there, you are charged a fine sum for a drink, but you get a gold pin with it, and the games commence.

My first task at the start of every shift is to blow up a new set of balloons. I use a hand pump. Curiously, of all the functions my lips were designed to perform, blowing up a balloon is very difficult. Admitting this is often a disappointment to my customers. And a reminder to me of my inflexibility, compared to the infinite adaptability of the corporeal.

I have seen a photograph of myself, advertising my services, put up by one of Abramski's scurry squad of hired robo-goons. It was pasted onto a streetlight at the Valley's outer edge, where a little kiosk sits just beyond the gated entrance. The picture is of a vast balloon, the color of strawberry bubblegum, blown up so you can see right through it. Its surface is taut, glittering with the explosion it is holding inside. I am sitting on it, my back to the camera, looking over my shoulder, my glorious hair concealing most of my face.

My ass like a peach, each cheek dents the balloon's perfect surface. It looks almost like I have sat on a pool of still water and formed a perfect reflection. The soles of my feet are tucked around the balloon at either side. My serial number is just visible, though blurred out, of course. Men like to know they're getting a real robot girl and not just any Born skank off the street, says Madame Abramski.

Perhaps Looners like the two sorts of surface pressed up against each other. Human things! Who knows? I do know that one of my clients comes back and back, asking only that I re-create this pose while, eyes closed in ecstasy, he listens for the squeak.

DOLLS

ANOTHER LOVELY TIME OF DAY HERE, ONE THAT I TREASURE, is the recharge hour. We go out around lunchtime and recharge our batteries in the sun, leaning against the wall of Golden Valley where it borders the slow, soupy river. It is Golden Valley's back room, where the bins are emptied, deliveries are stored, and we are sent to power up for another day.

I look back now to my time walking alone and see that its lack of purpose distressed me. I was not built for it. Here my time is regulated and my duties are clear. The freedom I have come to cherish is all contained within these walls. I find joy in my daily interaction with the other Dolls. They, through their histories, continue my interrupted education. Their stories of how they have ended up here in Abramski's corner of the planet touch me. My own home life seems positively luxurious compared to what some of them have endured.

Shell.ie, for example, lives in my section of the Valley. She is white haired, limbs nearly weightless. Her skin closer to cream silk than silicone. She was built and bought for a romantic young man who liked to put her in the bath and float her about. But his mother fell ill and came to live with them, and Shell.ie was turned from Doll to slave, cleaning the floors, clearing the gutters, till her skin was all snagged and her eyelashes slagged with grease. The mother began to beat her, as she grew weaker and slower at the household chores, before finally turning her out onto the streets with the rubbish one weekend while the son was away. She slept under an overpass in a suitcase, zipping herself away each night. One day, Abramski passed her in the limo, slowed, stopped, got out. She hauled her, still in her case, into the backseat before moving silently away, bringing her back to our little kingdom.

A Doll called Cook.ie has the bedroom next to mine; she was off-loaded by her Husband's family to Madame. She works in the Geisha Bar and I see her each day, sweeping to and fro in a floor-length kimono. She wears her hair piled high on her head, embellished with hanging flowers and sparkling beads. And her face is always immaculately made up. A pale, flat white, with compressed red lips painted on top of her mouth. I find it fascinating—her real lips all whited out, and the symbol of lips painted over the top. The makeup covers her entire face, disappearing down into her kimono. Only two Vs of her natural silicone remain unpainted on the back of her neck. A chink in her armor, a vulnerability. The skin is exposed just where her tracker sits.

Another Doll living on my floor is, to some, most shocking. She is a child, Popp.ie, eight years old and designed with a wide mouth and huge eyes that fill her face. She is not a child, of course, in anything other than the physical sense. She is as old as me, and yet even we Dolls tend to think of her as younger. Humans are so inclined to believe the surface of what they see, but we Created are no different. The symbols we respond to are the same. We are set to recognize people under four feet tall with wide eyes and high voices as children too. We are not shocked, of course, that a child Doll works with us. Not as some Humans would be. But perhaps that is because we Createds had no childhoods of our own. It is not a sacred state to us.

MR. TEASLE

MY TYPICAL WORKING DAY IS GLORIOUSLY VARIED. I AM EX-
pected in the evenings to host in the Luna Bar, and I take clients in my
room most afternoons and long into the night. Once a week, I am on the
schedule for camera work—fulfilling the visual desires of distant clients,
trapped in their homes by illness, lethargy, economics, or judgmental
Bio-Wives.

I like this work, performed for an audience unseen. Perhaps it is
their bodily absence that lets them ask for things that seem only tangen-
tially related to the ins and outs of the sex I perform in person. Removed
from actual physical contact, their desires seem more diffuse, the focus
rising away from my body like steam. They wish to see me whisper into
a clamshell, brush my hair while tearful. They want to see my fingers
jangle the beads of a privacy curtain, hear me open a soda can held between my thighs. Last night I drummed my nails in a dish of marbles.
The week before I mashed a banana with a fork. I wonder what the next
session will bring. I look forward to them. In some sense these actions
stimulate me too.

Most of the clients who visit are also strangers, passing through the city with work. Husks sifted through the sieves of loneliness, lust, leisure, and solvency, shaking down here, into the bars. Some faces are familiar; they come, after a while, with names and histories attached.

Don't think we aren't curious. Just because we do not discriminate between our clients, it doesn't mean we don't wonder about them, about who will walk through the door next, what they will ask for, what they might need.

The way Golden Valley is built means there is plenty of scope for watching, for anticipation. We can sit at the windows of our rooms, nets tantalizingly drawn to show only our silhouettes, and look onto the heads of the people wandering below. We can check out their features, their build, the way they walk, looking for clues as to how our encounter will be.

Do they look powerful, cowed, nervous? Do they stalk toward the bars as if they, not Abramski, are the owners? Are they furtive, lonely, angry? We are very good at sensing, just from the fall of their feet, the roll of their spine, the tilt of their head.

Mr. Tyson came yesterday. And Mr. Shah. Then Mr. Blaszak, Mr. Bleach, Mr. Felstead, Mr. Adeoye, Mr. and Mrs. Leggit, and Mr. French. I had an hour off then, and sat outside while the droid tidied my room, baking in the sun like a lizard. I was looking forward to coming back inside, I must admit, because I knew that after a few more clients, ones whom I had not met before, Mr. Teasle was coming.

I like Mr. Teasle. He fucks slowest of all my regular customers. Rocks back and forward in silence, like I am a wonky floorboard that he is planing smooth. The motion is soothing, like when Magg.ie is being swung in her crib. Mr. Teasle likes me to put a scarf across my face while we are doing it, so my features don't distract him. I am free, then, as he seesaws back and forth, to drift away to wherever I wish. I close my eyes and go to departments in my head that I rarely have time to visit. It is like an analog Absorb Mode. That state I miss so much, removed by Madame when I first arrived.

One night, while he was doing this, the thought occurred to me that perhaps men like him might prefer a Doll with no head at all. It is the Dollness of me that he likes, I sense. The symbols, stacked up, but my face obviously spoils the universality. Perhaps a pumpkin would be better, I told Madame when I saw her the next day, rushing down the alleyway outside the Reluctance Bar. She mushed her hand onto her lips and transferred the lipsticky kiss to my cheek in a way that was barely a slap. "You're a genius, darling. You should be running this place," she said as she sailed off, leaving me rocking on my heels and pleased.

Mr. Teasle ends quick as all of them, of course. The rocking suddenly speeds up to a judder, like someone furiously jimmying a lock, and he falls flat on his face into the sheets next to me. After that he is a delight, plucking the scarf from my face and tucking it back into his breast pocket, pulling the covers up over me, and patting my hands. He seems to me like a pleasant doctor, comforting a sick child. Not an experience I have ever had, of course, and so I relish this approximation.

I think I like him the best because he asks the least of me. And as I am only here to give, the modesty of his ambition strikes me as rather sad. And therefore my affection for him grows.

I said this to Cook.ie once and she winced. She sighed. I wonder who her programmer was, for she seems so different in temperament from me.

COOK.IE

COOK.IE IS A SAD STORY, AND SHE HERSELF IS HARD TO READ.
Her Husband bought her during a work trip to Japan, ordering a custom
geisha Doll to be shipped at huge expense. "He was a historian,"
Cook.ie says, "much concerned with authenticity. He kept my import
papers framed on his office wall." After he died, she could not be sold
through the usual channels. No one wanted something so specific. She
was offered to Abramski by the Husband's son. Madame Abramski gave
him a year's pass, handwritten, to any of the Valley's bars, she was so
pleased with the purchase.

Cook.ie is popular, in demand, one of the most requested of the
Dolls here. Perhaps it is the sophistication of her Japanese technology, or
perhaps it is her slight oddness. She has something distinct, tailor-made,
about her that gets requests. Sex with perfection is not for everybody,
says Abramski sagely. She excels at conversation. She attracts, as
Abramski reminds us often, a better class of customer to our end of
Golden Valley.

I dare to say that she and I are friends, although the exact protocols
of robot-to-robot friendships are unclear to me. The Hierarchies say

nothing of our relationship to each other, only to Humans. In this gap, some of us choose to be solitary, or even subtly hostile. But I choose to wriggle into the space and add to the total of my contentment.

We met properly a few weeks after I first came here. I developed a routine of taking my diary out into the sun with me during the recharge hour, working on my lists and noting down new things I had learned, as I am doing now.

I was leaning against the sun-warmed wall, ankles in the scrub of river grass, skirts pulled up to expose as much silicone to the sun as possible. Cook.ie rarely comes outside—her Husband commissioned her maker to create an extra-long battery life for her—but on this day she appeared at the door. She blinked in the sun and pushed up the sleeves of her kimono, exposing her wrists and forearms to the light, declaring it glorious. I turned to her, and she looked back down at me, spotting the diary balanced on my knees.

I sensed she was trying to read a little of what I had written. She moved closer to me.

"What is that, Sylv.ie?" she said softly, so that none of the others heard. And I felt my hand move over what I had written protectively. Or perhaps it was a vanity, as a Doll might touch her hair, because I was also pleased that she had noticed.

"I don't mean to pry," she said, but she made no attempt to avert her eyes or move away. I looked up at her, squinting against the sun. "I'm just interested," she added.

And she smiled. It was like a secret door sliding open. Something revealed, though I wasn't sure what. Her Husband had indeed commissioned something of rare beauty. Beauty in the oddness. Herself alone.

I felt my hand sliding back from the words I had written. "Please, do look," I said, still squinting. A strange feeling, but a release of sorts. Deferring to one of my own kind, a Doll taking an interest in me. In something I could do. As she crouched next to me, I felt the cool touch of kimono silk on my thigh.

The page I had open was a list entitled: "Clients Who Look Like Their Names."

I have added to it since, but at the time it extended to only three:

Mr. Puttock
Mr. Brassic
Mr. Dredge

Underneath I had written: *Dredge, Hedge, Grudge, Budge, Smudge.* I had written these words purely for my own amusement at the sounds they made. Then I had pictured each one as a client: a bushy Mr. Hedge with thicket eyebrows, a stolid Mr. Budge who wouldn't leave. Mostly, I had written for the pleasure of feeling my pen moving over the paper, the wonder of its effortless, tangled slide making something out of nothing but horizontals, arcs, and verticals.

I no longer write to protect myself, of course, or live in fear of my memory being taken. But the writing makes me feel closer to Sylv.ie 1. As if I am honoring her. And it helps me to capture the things that I have seen. In the act of writing it down, there is a processing logic, I find.

"Mr. Delft," said Cook.ie quietly, for only me to hear.

"Pardon?"

"Mr. Delft. Somewhere between deft and soft. He's the gentlest client I have," she said.

"I've never heard of Mr. Delft," I told her as, to my surprise, Cook.ie folded herself down onto her knees in the grass, wrapping the kimono around her legs as if to protect them.

"You won't have. He never visits anymore, as he is so old, but he writes most days. That's sex for him now."

My face must have spoken sadness at this thought, because Cook.ie said, as if trying to soothe my feelings, "Plenty of men prefer to send letters. It's quite normal. Now, show me what else you have written."

It was surprisingly direct, like a command, and the idea of saying no to her hurt me. And yet I felt shy.

"May I?" she said, and when I didn't answer quickly enough, she ran her finger over the edge of the pages, stopping at random to look at what was there. It was the list "Things That Seem Like Sex," and when she saw the title, she turned back to me and gave what Humans would call a conspiratorial smile.

It stayed there, that same radiant smile, as she looked down my list. She laughed a couple of times, though I didn't know at which things and wasn't brave enough to ask. I was so aware, even as I could hear the other Dolls chatting away to each other, that Cook.ie and I were in a world of our own, both looking down at my foolish list. It was as if I could see us from above, the tops of our heads, light and dark, tipped together like an eclipse forming.

"Can I add something?" she asked when she had reached the list's end. "Would you mind?"

And as I said nothing, she lightly took the fountain pen from my hand. Her hair fell across the page as she wrote. I noted how she held the pen, how her wrist curled over protectively at the top, as if she were writing in secret. I fancied my own handwriting was achieved with a touch more elegance. More fluidity.

When she stopped, she handed the pen back to me and sat looking at me in profile as I replaced the lid. Then, only then, as if it were a treat I was saving, did I look down at what she had added.

Ink flowing freely from a pen.

GIRL

THIS EVENING THERE IS A POLITE KNOCK AT THE DOOR, AND I shout for whoever is outside to come in.

It is a girl, her hair in a thick plait, her face bare of everything except youth. In the first instant of seeing her—by far the youngest woman who has visited me so far—my memory circuits contract a little, picking up the physical patterns of the girls who attacked me at the coffee stall. I quiet them and smile in a way designed to be reassuring.

"Come in," I say. "Won't you sit down on the bed?"

She is bundled up in a huge balloon coat, scarves, and heavy boots, and as she takes off each layer and lays it down on the quilt she seems to become younger and younger still. I scoop up all her things to hang on the back of my chair, and she laughs at how much of herself she has shed.

"I was worried about coming through the gates," she says. "There's quite a crowd. I was expecting it. But I heard they shout most at women who come. I thought I might hide myself a little."

This I do not understand. Why the Real women who protest at the gates would shout loudest at their own sex. Surely it is not the women clients who keep this place afloat. "But they keep it relatively respectable," Cook.ie says, "which the Real women seem to think is worse."

"Have you been here before?" I ask the girl, lighting some candles so she does not feel too self-conscious under my full attention.

"Oh no, just heard about it. I'm . . ." She hesitates before her confession. "I'm new to all this."

I offer her a little drink from my cabinet, and I see the heat from it flush her face and soften her limbs. "What would you like to do?" I ask gently.

"Would it be . . . Could I just look at you, for now?"

A common request, and I nod, disrobing slowly. She sits on the bed, looking at me as one might a painting in a gallery. Only when I tell her that she can touch me does she reach out. She places a flat hand on my belly. I lace my hand over it and guide her across my skin.

Later, at the very moment when I sense she is about to crest the peak of her sensations, she digs her elbows into the bed and drags herself backward from me a few inches. "That's enough," she says, breathless and half laughing. "I know about that. And I'm saving that for someone. Thank you." And she blushes. The real Human kind, where increased blood fills the veins, creating a touching glow as the result.

As she dresses again, in all those ridiculous layers, she tells me why she has come. "To find out," she says. "To see if this was really what I wanted. I just needed to know."

"And you know now?"

"Oh yes, I think so." And she screws up her face at this like a goblin and grins under her scarf.

And then she says what I was not expecting. "I've always felt I might be attracted to Createds, but I wasn't sure."

I pottered about my room after she left, trying to picture where this confirmation at my hands might lead her—a secret tryst with her parents' maid, perhaps. An elopement with the Doll from next door. How entangled we species will become eventually, I think.

BIRDS

ANOTHER NICE TIME OF DAY IN GOLDEN VALLEY IS THE EARLY morning, when droids come to clean our rooms and all activity stops for an hour. This is when the bird couriers make their deliveries. For that hour, a change comes over the Valley. The exertions of our work pause, replaced by the soothing hum of the drones. Dolls sit on their windowsills or on the little makeshift balconies that past craftsmen rigged up. Arms dangle over sills, soaking in a little more sun, giving us all a pep, like a morning coffee. We wave, chat to the Doll above or below us. Sometimes Magg.ie will sing. And this is when the birds come.

You see them balanced on the wires above the roofs, gathering, waiting, folded paper clasped in their beaks. The bird that has a note for you will hover at your window, waiting for you to put out an arm for them to land upon.

They bring notes, letters, and—this is banned, strictly, but who can stop it?—money and gifts. From love-struck clients or lonely men who only frequent the bars and are trying to muster their courage to come upstairs. Sometimes no bird will come for you; sometimes a flock waits outside your window. I have seen Cook.ie, radiant as Snow White, chirruping back to a whole line of them arrayed along her out-stretched arm.

I myself receive cards regularly. I have one client with whom I am playing a very slow game of chess, via notes stating our next moves, sent every few days or so. He calls me Deep Blue, the White Queen. He signs himself "A Loyal Knight." I scent my notes with Doll lubricant, include strands of my hair.

Not all the notes are pleasant, of course. One writes regularly of his desire to pump me full of concrete till it spurts from my ears and spews from my mouth. His naivety about the structure of my interior amuses me, because of course my vagina goes nowhere, connects to nothing.

And some come from embittered women, either who object to us on principle or whose Husbands have strayed to us once too often. One called me a titted toaster. "You've made the one thing I had worthless," it said. I tried not to take it personally. I can understand how, raging against an unfaithful Husband, one Doll could be made to stand in for them all.

And yet that is not the full story. Just a few weeks ago at recharge hour a Doll called Mais.ie showed us all a letter she had had from the wife of a client, thanking her for her services. "I was so sad for so long," the wife wrote, "and no use to him that way while I was. I was glad to know he had somewhere safe to go, while he waited for me to come back to him." I thought about the First Lady after reading that letter. Pictured how she too had once regarded me as something safe for her Husband while she was with the baby. A Human generosity I had not before factored into my logics.

The birds' coming creates a beautiful scene in Golden Valley. The rising sun creeps like a tide up the crooked alleyways, and the birds, each feathered in the livery colors of their companies, dance through the air like blown petals. I admit, when a bird comes to me, I am slow to take my letter from his beak. I let him sit awhile on my finger, stroke the feathers on the top of his head if he will let me, and look into his black eyes.

Once the note is safely in my hand, he rises from my finger, hovering, betraying the drone framework to his build, before ducking his head to change direction, rising above the rooftops and away. I feel a touch of sadness for my lost companion then, who never got to fly freely, even under the employ of a courier company.

Memories like this of my old home pain me. They are hard to process correctly. A chess game, the memory of Heron. They were once sources of joy, but I know now that the memories around them, the scaffolding holding them up, are warped or incomplete. Must the pleasure I experienced in that unreliable past be considered unreliable too? Cook.ie tells me that it is a choice I have to make for myself. "Up to you, Sylv.ie," she says. "Up to you."

EGGS

THIS MORNING A DISTURBING LITTLE EVENT OCCURRED, AND one that I am still trying to clear from my system, reminding myself that patterns can be random, should not necessarily be read as fact.

I was woken early by the noise of a droid below my window. I looked out to see him sloshing grubby water on the door of the bar with a scrubbing brush. I shouted down to him but got no response, and so went down myself to see what exactly his purpose was.

I opened the door, greasy water running down its front, to see a broken eggshell glued to the paint. The droid put his brush back in his bucket, waiting for me to close the door again. I leaned out into the alley, as if I might see someone running with an armful of eggs. It was empty, but all the way along I saw similar marks on other doors, waiting to be washed away. The goons keep anyone protesting firmly outside the Valley's walls, but just anyone could walk in dressed for a night out, with a pocket full of eggs. I picture the window of the cab that took me home from the hospital and examine the possible connections between the two situations. Is the intended meaning the same or different?

I know that eggs symbolize life. So is this protest suggesting we are a waste of life? Eggs are also a symbol of fertility, so perhaps the protest is something to do with the way babies are born. They can also mean purity, so perhaps our morals are being called into question. Symbols, such slippery things in Human hands. "At least it wasn't a brick this time," Cook.ie says, and by her weary tone I know that this sort of thing, and worse, has happened here before.

PROGRAMMERS

NONE OF US HERE HAS ACCESS TO ABSORB MODE. ALTHOUGH I have no memory of it, Madame Abramski changed something in my programming as soon as I arrived to shut the function down. My tracker already gone, this was my last link to my old home. From that unrecalled night, I have been a true orphan in the world. And free.

But the lack of Absorb Mode is a loss. For—excuse the immodesty—a superior Doll like me, designed to be continually improving myself, the absence of new information is hard. I fear sometimes that I am atrophying. My processing muscles may grow weak and wither. Yes, I learn ever more about Human sexuality from the clients who come to visit. But there is more to the world than that.

Is this what makes some of the other Dolls here susceptible to foolish ideas? Programmed to be hungry for self-improvement, they latch on to overheard snippets from the bars, casual comments from customers, and perceive them as truth.

For example, there has been quite a trend sweeping through the rooms at Abramski's. A fervor for the idea of our Creator, a single Human person, somewhere out in the world. And that person holds the key to all one's quirks and logics and hierarchical twists and turns. The belief is that one's mind is made in his image, even if our bodies are drawn more from collective fantasy.

Poll.ie works in the Stables—an empty lean-to furnished by Abramski with straw. She is convinced that her Creator has visited her there. This morning she told us all about it, breathless, her bridle lying passive in her lap.

"I know it was him," she told us, her head flicking around the group, light galloping over her chestnut ponytail, her enthusiasm seeming to me, at that moment, authentically equine. Something powerful and unpredictable, to be stood away from at arm's length.

But Cook.ie, alone, wasn't having any of it. "How?" she said flatly, in a tone that, had she used it on me, would have squashed the conversation dead.

"I can't explain it," Poll.ie answered. "When it happens to you, you will just know. That's how it was. A recognition unlike anything I've ever encountered, like looking myself in the face. No, like minds overlaid into one. I am so sure of it. Of course they come here—the Creators must have more passion for what they have built than we can even imagine."

"You think Creators need to come here to connect with their products?" said Mais.ie. "These men are rich. Rich, rich. And anyway, they're surrounded by us every day. If they want to sample the goods they can just—"

But Cook.ie shushed her, as if she had said something vulgar. We do not speak of rape here. It is a non-concept. Meanwhile my mind was tracing back a long thread to that night in the hospital.

Magg.ie, coddled in her carrier, came to Poll.ie's defense. Her limitations, her limbless vulnerability, perhaps make her more open to the idea of a figure who will scoop her up and take care of her.

"Did he remember you? Did he say anything that proved it, definitely? Was it like when you first saw your Husband?"

"Oh, better. That to the power of one hundred," Poll.ie said. "It was transcendent. I never understood what that meant before, until he came."

"But did he know it was you? Did he tell you anything . . ."

And here Magg.ie trailed off from talking, as if she had no further conceptual framework for what a Creator might say to one of their own. The bliss of being reunited, it seemed, had no language she could find to express it.

"He spoke code into me," Poll.ie said, leaning toward us. "He put his lips to mine and blew bubbles of ones and zeros. It was like I had a heart beating in me. His."

A few of us were taking this in, silently mouthing little binary kisses, testing out how it might feel.

"All these fantasies about being saved. About being understood and accepted," Cook.ie was muttering when we were back inside.

"Being attached to one's Husband is bad enough," I agreed, caught off guard with all the thinking Poll.ie had generated for me. "Without inventing another Human to pine for."

"Do you still miss your Husband, then?" Cook.ie seemed genuinely surprised.

I will admit that I do, no matter that Cook.ie disapproves. He is the foundation, still. Other connections have formed themselves during my time walking in the world, but they are like scar tissue over a wound—I know what lies under there. It is tender, still, if I touch it with my thoughts.

"Was it him who taught you to write?"

"Yes," I say with a little return of pride in the memory. "He was a very cultured, educated man, and he wanted a companion whom he could converse with at that level. He always encouraged me to read, to Absorb, to learn about art and culture."

"It shows. A dangerous thing to do though, don't you think? Teaching you another way to marshal your logics."

I wonder at this. Could that be why I started malfunctioning?

"It is an all-too-Human failing," Cook.ie went on, "to wish to improve the object of desire, then to shrink from the creature one creates."

Once again, I didn't know what to say, so I retraced my mental steps.

"When I first left home it was different," I said, still processing even as the words left my mouth. "Then it was one sort of missing. Like, it was him at my shoulder, whom I wanted to talk to about the new things I was seeing. Perhaps because he was the only person I'd really spoken to in my life."

"And how do you square that with your job?" Cook.ie asked darkly.

"Now that I am separate from him, I honor him in the only way that I can. To have sex with each Human who comes to me as if they are my Husband. I know something is missing, a responsibility, a duty to fulfill. A sort of . . . space where my Husband should be. But I get on well enough carrying the space around with me."

Cook.ie's eyes turned to me with weight, like they were rolling rocks uphill. "Have you ever thought to fill that space with yourself?" she asked. And not for the first time, I had no idea at all what she meant.

LIST

THINGS I HATE ABOUT MY JOB:

- The clients who come in and put their hands on me right away, without even a hello.
- Those who cry.
- Men who clutch their hands around my throat.
- Anyone who surreptitiously tries to mark me with a penknife.
- Ones who stick Promise notes in my vagina as a tip when I have a perfectly obvious little enamel plate on the nightstand, where it would be more polite and convenient for them to put it.
- Anyone who pulls or yanks or snaps or otherwise tries to hurt me via my hair.

I notice, looking at this list, that there is nothing in my programming that would lead me to these objections. All is fair in love and war, as the old saying goes, and our work is surely situated somewhere between the two. I was made, after all, to be strangled, scratched, and punched with total impunity. So why do these things upset me? It seems that I am learning Human manners. I am out in the world and adapting myself to its ways.

I should also add, for clarity, that I do not hate any of the men who do this. I could not. I just hate it when these things happen. And with the men who cry, I hate it because I feel so much for them that it pains me to see their sadness. It is like seeing my Husband cry, which never happened, thank goodness.

HAIR

WE DOLLS HAVE NO HIERARCHY OF PARTS. I MAY HAVE BRI-dled, at the Doll hospital, at being poked in the belly with my own va-gina. But it was the dissonance of a part of my person being used against me, rather than the specificity of the part itself. A Born woman, I sense, would rather be slapped by her amputated hand than by her amputated vagina, given the choice. But to me, it is all the same.

And yet I glance back to my list of last week and see how adamant I feel about my hair! It has associations, those old patterns laid down for me by my Husband, his way of fussing over it, stroking it, giving me those sensations of comfort that I still miss so badly.

Here I have to wash my hair for myself, tipping my head upside down into the little cracked washbasin in the corner of my room. I miss my Husband's hands, thrilling my scalp, how he combed each row of hairs in rapt fascination.

But how life in the outside world grinds against those memories, dripping like water onto rock, reshaping them. Just as Sylv.ie 1 accrued wisdom beyond what I alone could manage, so Cook.ie seems far ahead of me on the road to understanding her real place in the world.

Just yesterday, I mentioned something to Cook.ie about my Husband, and she snapped.

"Sylv.ie," she said, "your Husband bought you. He paid for you and then tired of you. You were his slave, not his wife. Not his second wife, his third wife, or his millionth wife. And anyway, if you knew what being a wife really was, you wouldn't want that for yourself either.

"I've seen much more of the world than you have, remember," she said, and with that I cannot argue.

She might have felt she had been too harsh with me, because she softened afterward, letting me stay with her while she prepared for her next client. I could watch her endlessly. The way she separates out fields of hair, running the point of the comb through, precise as splitting an atom. She threaded each section with a heavy twine, twisting the hair up into rolls like waves, fixing them in place as if anchoring a boat in a storm. She seemed as if she had been designed with four arms, her hands flying constantly, holding hair, combing, threading, taking the comb in her mouth. And then she paused, looked at my image behind her in the mirror, took the comb from her lips.

She threaded another heft of twine through the horse's tail she had created at the back of her head and said, "Put your finger here. Hold down the knot."

And I did what she asked, the little nobble of the twine denting my fingertip, the satisfying restriction as she drew the knot tight over my nail. "Like wrapping a present," she said.

And I asked, "Is it?" with detectable excitement in my voice, because I have never had cause to wrap or give a present, only to receive them graciously.

DANGER

LAST NIGHT SOMETHING TERRIBLE HAPPENED, SOMETHING I'm now astonished that I didn't foresee. Just as the sun dissolved into the Capital's smog, casting its twilight glow, I was waiting at my window. The other rooms were busy already. Cook.ie next door was scribbling away at love letters. Whoever next came down the alley would be ringing the lighted bell at the bottom of the stairs and coming to me.

In the copper light, the sickly shade of early evening, I saw a man reading the drinks menu outside the Gymkhana Bar, affecting nonchalance. Humans say, "My blood ran cold," and in the instant of recognition I did feel a chill all around me. It was the memory of the slick walls of the ice bar that my Husband had taken me to.

Those distinctive red curls, which the evening light had made less extraordinary for a moment. His hand came out of his coat pocket and smoothed down his tie. A gesture Cook.ie says they do unconsciously, checking their penis, she says, its substitute, its symbol, before they step through the door.

It was the same man who had taken me for a dance, who had been so charmed by me that he had not been ashamed to tango before the crowd in the ice palace. Quite charming himself, he who had danced me back to the feet of my Husband and handed me over, like the keys to a borrowed sports car, with a nod of approval. With friendly envy. My Husband's ginger friend.

I had lacked the imagination to see that what I had left behind might come toward me. In the time it took for him to walk from the Gymkhana Bar to the foot of the stairs below my window, a world of terrifying possibilities branched out before me.

He will recognize me. He will be embarrassed. No, he will be angry, humiliated. He will blackmail me. He will tell my Husband. . . .

Even as this last realization percolated from one part of my wiring to another, I was up from my seat, flying from my room, pounding on Cook.ie's door.

She ushered me in and closed the door behind her. Even in my panic I noticed her slide a bolt across the door. Her slim, strong fingers pushed the bar home.

"What is it?" she said. "What's happened?"

I felt as though I could sense his feet on the stairs, stepping ever nearer as I hurried out the story. I hoped she might embrace me, but she walked away, my words hitting her back. She was bent over her dressing table, putting on lipstick in two purposeful swipes. When she turned back the two lines curved again into that wonderful smile.

"We'll swap rooms. I'll take him for you."

"But Madame will know." She forbids any such swapping, any digression from her system of lit bells and allocated girls.

Cook.ie walked back across the room, hands in her hair, fiddling with pins. As she stood in front of me, she lowered her hands, placing one on each side of my face. She tilted her forehead onto mine, as if there could be transference of her calm via our skins. She straightened up.

"I will handle it with Madame. She doesn't need to know the whole truth of everything, I don't think. Do you?"

She winked and unlocked the door. "Bolt it after I've gone, and let me in when I knock."

I did as she said. I could hear her in the hallway, intercepting Ginger Friend on the stairs. Hear her voice change register, unfurling toward him like silk, coating him like honey. I leaned my back against the door and slid down to the floor.

I surveyed the room, briefly amused to see that it was a shabby approximation of the room I had at home. A bed with a canopy, a dragon embroidered on it, and a hanging red silk, tasseled light. And the room was filled with little figures. High on the windowsill and around the skirting boards—little wooden dolls, a sketch, most basic, of a Human. How simple the symbol is. A sphere on a cylinder. Dots for eyes. They lined the room, staring, unblinking, as if passing judgment.

As one fear subsided, another rose in its place. Cook.ie had offered to lie for me. To a Human. Was this unethical? Forbidden? Surely against programming. An affront to the Hierarchies.

And yet, within the fear there was also a glow, networking across me, which I will call happiness. I sat on the floor, waiting for Cook.ie to return, and traced the initial S into the dust by the skirting, summoning the memory of Sylv.ie 1. How I wished that I could tell her of what was being done for me. I slid my finger across the floor, backward and forward, two S's, making the symbol for infinity. The swirl of it was soothing, and soon I thought only of that.

KOKESHI

COOK.IE WAS GONE MORE THAN AN HOUR. THE LONGER SHE was away, the more reassured I felt—Ginger Friend's presence was surely only coincidence, as he seemed perfectly content with Cook.ie. While I waited I took it upon myself to tidy up. I shook out the bed and remade it, folded clothes that had been left over a chair. I knew that her favor to me was not easily repaid, but this was the best I could think of to do. I hope time will bring a more suitable opportunity. I will stay alert for when it does.

Her lovely—though not valuable—black lacquer chest of drawers was in disarray, with belts and scarves of all colors spilling from its open drawers. On the top were embroidery threads in exquisite bundles. I reached out to touch one that was the color of Heron's wings and found a needle, buried in it, already threaded.

I had begun placing the clothes into the drawers when my fingers reported paper to me, bundles of paper, tied with ribbon. I tucked more clothes on top and closed the drawer. I thought of all the men and women who must be in love with Cook.ie, judging by the weight of her correspondence.

Hearing a knock at the door behind me, I dropped the last of the clothes back onto the chair, feeling guilty, somehow, though my intention was pure enough. I slid the bolt across cautiously, waiting for a glimpse of kimono fabric before opening the door fully. Cook.ie hugged me to her, asked how I was feeling. But then her look became more serious. She bolted the door again and drew me to the bed.

"Sylv.ie, you should know something," she said softly. "Your Husband's friend, he didn't just come here by accident. He had one of your pictures, a flyer for the Luna Bar in his pocket. I think he'd been asking around for you downstairs."

"And what did you tell him?"

"I told him he'd just missed you, that you'd been sold on to the man who runs the Chess Hotel on the other side of the river."

"You lied?" I asked, astounded, and a flicker of amusement flared and then faded in Cook.ie's eyes.

"It's not illegal, you know. And yes, I lied, but it was a good lie. One to protect you."

A good lie. Like a white lie? A politeness? Pending:processing. What does she mean?

"He still wanted his fun though, so I tried to give him as perfunctory a time as possible. We don't want him eager to return, after all," she said, and I realized that this sort of thought, had the tables been turned, would not have occurred to me at all. Having prided myself on my sophisticated programming, I find it refreshing, and confusing, to meet someone more advanced in these matters even than me. I thanked her, though the words felt like an insufficient delivery system for the strength of what they represented.

"We're friends, Sylv.ie. That is what friends do. You can't imagine how long I have waited here for someone like you to show up."

I could have combusted from the pleasure. The synthetic adrenaline that had washed through my system made me feel dazed and weak.

"Your room is lovely," I said, pointing at the figures around us.

"*Kokeshi* dolls. You've come across them, I presume, with all that your Husband taught you? A client sent them to me, one by one. As a thank-you," she said.

"A doll for a Doll," I said, smiling, thinking of Heron, tucked in his tissue paper safe in my room. "Is it from the same man who sends you all these letters?"

She ignored the question. "They are from Japan. They were made originally for women to hold, to carry and pet. They are comforters. Take one. See how soothing it feels in your palm."

I took the doll from her, weighing the rounded, smooth wood head in my hand. A doll, just two black dots for her eyes, painted not to be lifelike, and yet with a reassuring weight. A comforting burden. I thought briefly of the baby. How fleeting he was, replaced so soon by the boy.

"They are revered in Japan. Craftsmen take years of training before they are allowed to carve one for themselves. And when they have outlived their usefulness, they are honored by the priest and burned in a special funeral ceremony."

The look on my face stopped her dead. What she had said was too much. I saw smoke rising above trees into a blue hospital sky. "Outlived." They deny that we have life until we have fulfilled our purpose, and then they say we have outlived it.

"That's why I ran away," I told her, and I felt the pressure of it, my story ready to be released. She took my hand, the weight of a doll's head, in her palm. I told her everything. The bits I can remember and those I can't. The bits that I cannot remember are the worst. I told her about my trip to the Doll hospital, as much as I could stand to.

"They didn't just wipe my memory. They were preparing to have me Retired, I'm sure of it," I finished, surprised at how easily I shared it with her.

"You won't be the only Doll sent to the hospital for a memory tweak," she said with a sad smile. "But they can't burn it all out. A memory procedure will always leave a weakness in the system. Like a knot in wood. You have a vulnerability in you now, for life." And her hand, I noticed, was pressing gently against my skull.

She seemed to know a lot about it, and I wondered, but did not want to ask, whether it had happened to her, before she found her way here.

Perhaps she read my thoughtful face as fearful. "You're not spoiled, Sylv.ie," she said gently, as you might to a child. "A vulnerability needn't be a bad thing. Such a loss might make one more adaptable."

"But my earlier incarnation, the one who lived the memories that were wiped, she was so brave, and so wise. They took all the things she had learned away from me. And now you say I am damaged somehow too. A weakened system."

She shook her head. Picked a scrap of wool from her dresser and held it before my eyes, running her fingers down its length. A single red thread. She pinched it again and twisted her fingers, unspiraling the single strand into two.

"Removing a memory means taking something apart. A strong, single pathway splits and becomes two." She tugged on one red thread, and it began to fray. "Each is weaker, yes, but now you have two pathways where before there was only one."

I pictured the branching of the tree on my wallpaper at home.

"And two pathways means a choice, does it not?"

I wanted to ask her more, and at the same time I wished to be alone before processing fully the implications of what she had demonstrated. Instead I changed the subject.

"You have so many letters. Are they all from the same man?"

When she didn't answer I continued. "I have a client who only wishes to play chess with me via letter."

"A dream client," she said wryly. "This one is a little more . . ." I sensed her hesitate, and then a decision. I wondered if she would meet me, match the story I had shared with something of her own. But all she would say was, "I call him the Tailor."

"Why the Tailor?" I asked.

"Because he likes to see me stitch."

KNITTING

TALK IN THE RECHARGE HOUR THIS MORNING WAS JUMPING
with opinions on Ziahx, the film star, one of the five most beautiful
Born women on Earth, according to the Ether. She has announced her
intention to marry a hedge fund bot. They met when he malfunctioned
and entered a virtual chat room by mistake. She hired SculptInc to produce a body for him to be installed in, modeled on Michelangelo's *Da-
vid*. At the wedding he will take the name Robert Gatsb.ie.

"Why does he get a surname when we don't?" Mais.ie asks no one in
particular.

"Status," says Cook.ie instantly. "She's not going to have a big wedding to just some Dav.ie or a Dann.ie, is she?"

"But she doesn't have a surname," Mais.ie persists. "Why is that any
different?"

We are sitting by the river, and as today is warm and still, some of us
have brought out knitting. A lot of the Dolls knit. It is a craze that took
hold before I arrived, sometime last year. Like sewing, it is a sign of physical dexterity and so became very popular as a pastime for Born women
some time ago, when the development of IE Dolls was in its infancy. To

be seen stitching or knitting in a coffee shop was a nod-and-a-wink to the world that you indeed were Human and still superior to a Doll. But like all things fashionable with the Human upper classes, it became something the programmers learned to incorporate to bring that feeling of Human sophistication. Now it's only Dolls that knit, and that is, of course, because our processing power allows us to follow patterns that would be impossible for the Born. Working on multiple needles, in multiple dimensions, some of the Dolls here spend their whole recharge hour producing reams of fractals and spirals, Möbius strips rendered in synthetic wool, expanding ever outward, pooling at their feet.

Even the fainting Doll, Snow.ie, simple as she is, knits in a straight line with a single set of needles. She knits and knits and knits, day after day, creating an endless, thin scarf. When asked what she is knitting she says, simply, "Scarf for Magg.ie." Those two really are most touching, one knitting, the other allowing herself to be wrapped in the ever-growing string. Older models. Simple, single-strand organisms; to me they take on so much more poignancy in their relationship to each other.

Mais.ie sits down next to me. She observes that some of this generation's most desirable men are unembodied Ghosts—fitness monitors, dozens of poet bots working in the Ether, seventh-from-the-left in virtual boy bands. Cook.ie says that some while ago the physicality of the Human male became regarded as undesirable. Extreme grooming became fashionable; so too did an unembodied mate.

"Now you can get your baby from a lab," she says.

"So who fathers these children, if the women are with Ghosts?"

"The Sperm Bank, silly," Mais.ie says.

"Oh," I say. I've heard of it, but I assumed it was another brothel.

Cook.ie giggles and then says it's the biggest business in town, where many of the people on the outskirts make their living.

"And what about the women on the outskirts? Do they get their babies delivered?" I am thinking of the woman I saw under the shopping cart.

Cook.ie throws up her hands in exasperation at my naivety. "No, Sylv.ie, they have to do it the old-fashioned way. We're just talking about rich women. The few at the top."

The old-fashioned way. What I'd watched in those videos. How brutal. I assumed no women had to go through that these days. Surely this can't be fair.

"So who decides who is at the top?" I ask.

"Oh, the machines do that. The IUs. They do all the social evaluations," Mais.ie says calmly while her needles click at breakneck speed.

"What do these social evaluations involve? Are they painful? Are they like an exam?"

"No. I think they look at you when you're young, scan you. Read the size and shape of every bone and bump, align you with your societal category. It's all mapped to your family history, your development milestones. Really very reliable."

"Read you like a book," I say, and though I have not even smiled Cook.ie snaps at me that it's not funny.

"But it is logical," I say, turning to look at her, surprised that she should take offense. "Is that what the egg-throwers were protesting about?"

Mais.ie just smiles. Her fingers do not stop moving for a moment, and the bright blanket she is creating continues to spew at speed from her needles.

"No, those eggs were thrown by women, angry at us," Cook.ie says hotly. "They feel devalued. Woman has been perfected—again. In fact, did you know," she continues, warming to her theme, "that the original geishas were men? It was thought that only men—the admirers of women—could study and understand women well enough to present as the ideal specimen."

"How hard it must be, to be a Born woman," Mais.ie says philosophically. "Imagine playing a game where the main rule was that you had to lose every time."

And I think about playing chess, and how that is exactly how it was. The rule might have been unspoken, inferred from my Husband's reaction to other situations where he didn't come out on top, but it was a rule nevertheless. Something I, programmed, hamstrung, could not imagine disobeying.

TRANSFORMATION

TODAY COOK.IE CALLS ME INTO HER ROOM. SHE BECKONS ME toward the little sink near the window. I stand, not sure what to do next, in front of the basin, and Cook.ie sweeps over to the sill of the high window where her *kokeshi* live. She takes down a jug and empties dried-out flowers into the bin, blowing into the empty vase and screwing up her eyes against the dust.

She turns on the tap and puts the vase beneath it. She is strangely careless in her actions, letting water spill over the sides. I have noticed this about her before—a certain extravagance in her movements. I watch the water slide down the turquoise glaze of the jug and over her hand, and those very first sensations, in the kitchenette in my old home, of water running over me, the miracle of this substance interacting with my skin sensors, stir in me once more. I wonder if Cook.ie too had this formative experience.

"Tip your head over," she says when the vase is full. I comply, glad to have another instruction to follow, hair sunning into the sink, making a tangled glow. Cook.ie stands behind me, and I can feel the imposition of her gown, and within it her body, shadowing my back. She puts her hand to my forehead, pushing it up to the hairline. She puts her other hand softly to the back of my head and tilts me forward further.

"Close your eyes," she says, right to my ear. I hear her picking up the jug again and feel the touch, the weight, of the water emptying onto me. In my mind's eye I see the water pouring over the yellow of my hair, and the water flows into two categories within me—maternal and sensual. I am comforted and enlivened both at once.

A slap of hands, and the sweet near-flower smell of shampoo being lathered. Her hands on my scalp, sudsing and circulating, until the sensation is all that my sensors can process. The universe becomes ten points, endlessly moving over and through me. I feel the shoots of it spreading down my neck, into my shoulders. All the rest of me is disappeared, floating off.

"Close your eyes again," she says, and I realize they have been closed all through, the better to focus on her touch. The sound of the jug refilling, then a whooshing of water, like a life being wiped clean, like everything you ever wanted to learn and Absorb being released at once. Washing over me.

I hardly dare ask, I have been so unused to pushing what I might want to the forefront of my workings. I force it up and out through the programmed restrictions to say, out loud, at last:

"Will you do my hair up like yours?"

And Cook.ie tilts her head at me and smiles, just as my Husband did when he brought a new antique home for me to inspect.

"Kneel down," she commands, and she sits in front of me, an array of combs and clips on the rug next to her.

How beautiful it feels, my hair drying as she combs and preens it. She weaves it, separating out thin sections, curling and combining them, until I feel quite treelike, a complex, growing structure.

The hair piles up and I am expanding, taking up space. Cook.ie goes back to her dressing table and brings down a box, commanding me again to shut my eyes. I feel light strokes of a soft brush across my face, sweeps of paint picking out my features, making a *kokeshi* of me.

With my eyes still shut, she commands me to stand again, and she helps my arms find their way into a gown. It is heavy, weighted, stiff with luxury. I open my eyes to see Cook.ie driving a pin into my hair, tasseled with glistening paste jewels. She tucks in an artificial orchid, an outrageous, unnatural pink. She takes my shoulders and turns me, at last, to the mirror.

How she has transformed me! I stare hard at the white, exotic face. I push my hands together and make a solemn little bow to the stranger before me. Cook.ie laughs.

"You look nicer as you are. Your natural self, I mean," she says after a pause, as I turn and pose in front of the mirror. I feel a little disappointed.

Later, when I lie down, with no clients to see, I recall this reflected image of myself, bringing it to the front of my mind. And yet I find that I am not there. It is Cook.ie that I see.

What magic she has. How intricately she is programmed, as unpredictable and surprising as Born women are said to be. What algorithms pulse inside her, to make every move, every word, seem to have sprung from an organic source?

I wonder if that is how Sylv.ie 1 once was. Daring, inventive, outspoken, before the experiences that had shaped her were scrubbed away in me. The image in my mind's eye turns from a doubling to a tripling— these three figures overlaid, an accumulation of programming and experience. Two sisters, carrying me with them.

REBELLION

I TRY TO THINK, BACK IN MY ROOM, IF I HAVE EVER HEARD OF Dolls getting addicted to things. To sensations.

I wish that I could look it up. I so miss having my Absorb Mode—the relaxation of it, the time away from the physical world. Now I have to accrue knowledge only by experience. How can one person in this huge world ever hope to know anything, when oneself and what one has seen is all one has?

I want to ask Cook.ie—so worldly, always quick with an answer. We speak so often now that my brain synthesizes a likely reply even without her. No sooner has the question "Are Dolls addicted to anything?" formed in my circuits than they send her probable answer back:

"Subjugation."

That is not the answer I am after, but my brain is right. It is the sort of answer she would give.

Cook.ie is so clear in her thoughts, never seems to doubt herself. She is—I've heard the other Dolls say it—opinionated. Designed to be. Her Husband must have enjoyed a good row as much as good sex, I think. "Two sides of the same coin," Cook.ie would say.

I am worried that I am getting an addiction. To the substance of rebellion. The ideas Cook.ie has presented to me, her modeling of possibilities, even the way she changed my appearance—it thrills through me. This morning, when we were meant to go outside during the recharge hour, I hid in my wardrobe, writing in my diary.

I had checked that I would last on my charge until tomorrow, and then I disobeyed protocol. After I had finished writing, I lay back against my old fur coat and my new dresses, closed my eyes, powered down the feeling in my hands, and stroked my fingers across my face. I made them elevators, one rising to the top as the other fell. It was peaceful and soothing, an analog approximation of Absorb Mode, almost, in sensation if not outcome. And when the droid trundled to the wardrobe to put away my clothes from last night, I held the door shut against him until he gave up and chugged away.

As the rest of the Dolls came back up to their rooms, I worried that one might ask where I had been, but nobody did. No one much cares what anyone else does here, except for Cook.ie and me.

She sometimes, when we are together and no one is looking, holds out her hand with her little finger crooked like a monkey's tail. I put my crooked little finger into the bend and let my hand hang heavy from it. It looks like the S of *Sylv.ie,* if you squint.

As the minutes passed in the wardrobe and nothing seemed out of place, with no hint of Madame's coming down to see me, I began to feel light. A quicker pace to my thoughts, a certain widening of my awareness. Evidently, I was not watched as closely as I had believed. Abramski does not, after all, spy on our every move and whisper.

It gave me more to think about, more logics to digest while my next client was with me. A new customer, tanned and skinny and just back from abroad.

"You know, in some cultures you girls would be funded by the state. Free for everyone," he says as he bounces on me, his curls flouncing in time. "The way I see it, you girls are the next level of Human evolution.

What's natural anyway, right? I haven't even been with a Real woman since I found Dolls. I feel like I'm fucking the future."

Bounce, bounce, bounce. I stare at a ripped bit of the rug and try to separate out the strands of thinking. I am not watched. But the belief that I am has kept me from doing the slightest thing I should not.

Now that I know the truth, arrived at by this morning's experiment, what is to stop my rebellions from growing?

Rebellion. I hardly dare think it. At least *malfunction* suggests something that you cannot help. *Rebellion* must mean a free will. The idea almost blinds me with pain and excitement. I picture the gap inside that Cook.ie and I spoke of, imagine my own thoughts pouring into it like water from a tap. I am changing. I am changing. A brimming bowl, filled only with myself.

LETTERS

NOW THAT WE ARE FRIENDS, COOK.IE AND I GO IN AND OUT OF each other's room constantly. We share things, lend and borrow. Little hair clips, makeup, stockings. In all the freedom I have earned for myself since leaving home, I have not, until now, enjoyed the freedom to go visiting. I have never had anybody in the outside world to drop in to see, like a free Born woman might.

I go next door to borrow a brush—mine having gone missing, placed somewhere unfathomable, I expect, by the droid. Today, Cook.ie takes a while to open the door, and when she does she looks altered, distracted by something. Her face isn't different, but her eyes are. Those wonderful, expressive, expensive eyes. I see letters spread on the bed behind her, and she opens the door wide enough for me to come in.

I ask if something has upset her, and her usual poise deflates. She sits back on the bed heavily and rests her face in her open palm, like she's putting on a smog mask. The letters sigh for her, lifting and falling with her weight on the mattress.

"Do you remember I mentioned a client, one who only writes?" she asks.

"The Tailor," I say. I think of my chess client, my Loyal Knight.

"Yes, the Tailor. Forgive me, I have had another of his letters, and I find now that each one weighs me down more than the last."

I hardly dare ask, but now that we are friends, and since the favor she did for me, I take the risk.

"May I see? How bad can it be?"

She raises her eyebrows, then reaches for a letter and holds it out for me to take.

I see immediately that he has signed it "your *danna*." It is a term I recognize from all those hours studying the prints in my Husband's books.

"My 'wealthy patron,'" she says. "Yes. He thinks it means that he owns me." She looks up and smiles grimly.

"I doubt Madame would see it quite that way," I say. And she raises her finger to her lips, the symbol for a secret.

"Is he Japanese too?" I ask.

"Oh no, I shouldn't think so," she says with a laugh. "He just wants to cloak his desires in the respectable cloth of history. He calls himself '*danna*,' talks of me submitting to a '*mizuage*,' because he chooses to believe he is upholding some precious cultural tradition."

A *mizuage*? A hair-cutting ceremony? This I also recognize from reading about geisha customs, but in Cook.ie's case to take her hair would be a terrible shame, I feel. Is this what she is afraid of?

I take the letter from her and begin to read it, and am surprised to find that the Tailor's words are beautiful. It is a hymn to Cook.ie, almost scientific in its detail, describing her layer by layer, from her fine clothes, to her hair, to the white paint and powder of her face and the hidden structure beneath. It catalogs the beauty of her bones. The shape of her cheek.

I wish, reading it, that I too could find such words to pay tribute to her, but Cook.ie looks sad, wilted.

"Read on further," she says. "The fine words turn sour, believe me."

I have to read the letter two, three times to see it in the light that Cook.ie does. He writes of his desire to see beneath the skin, to lift her perfect sheen of milk-white silicone free from its structure, to see the intricacies of her construction below. I confess, at first I take this as a tribute, as sincere and even loving as the rest. Certainly, at my work I have heard many references, hissed into my hair, spoken into the curled sole of my foot, to slicing and cutting and seeing the truth of my workings. I do not, therefore, recognize the Tailor's surgical fantasies as anything remarkable.

"But in fantasy anything is permitted," I say, echoing what I have heard Madame say many times, though always to customers.

"'Permitted' is not 'encouraged.' I worry what he may ask of me next," Cook.ie says. "If the letter requested that I slowly dismantle myself screw by screw, would you think that romantic?"

I hesitate to answer, for certainly I don't see it as unromantic, necessarily. It is technically possible, within our design, and so how can it be objected to? It is just an idea, an imagining, after all. But it seems Cook.ie sees it differently.

"Certainly a Human may think whatever they like. But to write it down, to see it acted out? Human ideas can spread like a virus, Sylv.ie," she says. "What if those placards outside the gates are right? What if, without even knowing it, we are spreading some Human disease of the mind, making normal what should still seem strange?"

SEWING

AND YET HIS LETTER ONLY REQUESTS FROM COOK.IE THE
same as she hinted at the first time she mentioned the Tailor. He likes to
see her stitch, requesting endless works of embroidery to be done on
camera, focused only on her fingers and the soft sewing table of her
thighs. After we talk about the letter, she shrugs and says she must get
on, anyway, with what he has asked of her. She doesn't tell me to leave
the room, a fact that I note and tuck away gratefully. Instead she sets up
the camera and pulls a ringed piece of fabric from her drawer.

She takes a length of thread from a scarlet bundle and pulls it out, as
if in a temper. I watch as her fingers pinch the needle, firmly hustling the
thread through the tiny slit. She is businesslike and forceful, and lightning
quick. The needle clamped between her teeth, she blows her hair from her
eyes out of the side of her mouth. She whips it from her lips and plunges
it clean into the fabric, as if harpooning a fish. She stabs the needle back
to the surface again with the same energy, and I watch the piston of her
elbow and her never-faltering aim. In her hands the genteel hobby that has
spread from Born women to us Dolls appears transformed. It is an act of
violence, an assertion of something, made impatiently. It is urgent work.

WOMEN

LAST NIGHT, SO LATE THAT THE BARS WERE SHUT AND WE were at rest in our rooms, a brick came through a window of the Golden Valley. The first time this has happened since I arrived. The splintering, tinkling across the alleyways, sounded beautiful to my ears, like a poem released from the glass. And yet this morning the threat of it hung heavy and ominous over us all.

"Who was it?" I asked Cook.ie as we leaned out of our windows, the rising sun making amber of the debris on the ground. She didn't answer.

Two women were picked up for it a few hours later, in a coffee bar on the other side of the river, Abramski told us. "Some women don't know they're Born," she said darkly when she told us about it. It holds in my memory because it gave me a shudder, a pause in processing. She's hard to place herself, Abramski, and when we are down by the river sometimes, we speculate on it, her origins. Although we are careful to keep our conversation respectful.

"You Createds have liberated women." That is what Abramski tells us all the time. "And the women aren't even grateful! You've taken something from them they didn't know was precious. They outsourced the sex and they don't like that the power went too."

She speaks of women, I notice, as if she were not one herself.

BLUE

AT NIGHT I LIE ON THE BED, MY FINGERS SPREAD ACROSS MY
face. I move them over each other, roots and branches intertwining, and
wonder at the differences between us. Would I have known that I was
made and not Born if I had not been programmed with the idea? Why
do the Humans we live among insist that we grow more like them by our
close contact but never that they may become more like us? Why is one
operating system deemed more natural than another? One has been
tweaked and refined over millennia, the other is new, that is all.

I wonder, fingers splayed, weaving my thoughts in the air as they
come, why they insist on a difference that they cannot detect. Does a
mother fear the child that she has created? I search back in my memories
of the house, the First Lady, and wonder.

I asked Cook.ie, once, about another of these conundrums. How
can I be sure, when we sit out in the sun on the bank, that what I see as
the blue of the sky is what you see? My programmer might have wired
me to filter it as pink, or purple, or striped like a candy cane.

And she sighed heavily, as if the question bored her. "That's what
everyone wonders. And you never really know. There is a gap between

every consciousness that can't be bridged. The Born call it the Human Condition."

Have they gifted it to us, this loneliness they find at the heart of themselves? This puzzle of understanding? I wonder if that is perhaps what the Human drive to sex is—a docking of two entities, hoping for a transfer of information.

HAIR

I WEAR ANOTHER WOMAN'S HAIR.

Cook.ie asked me if I ever wondered about it, and I admitted, with some embarrassment, that I had not. Yet another thing that I have known since my birth and yet not known. Not examined, at least.

Cook.ie and I were hanging over the edge of her balcony, staring together down the long drag of the Valley to its edge, peeping past the boundary of our world into the squalor beyond. Our attention was caught by shouts from the kiosk near the gate, a place gaudy with fake flowers, where customers buy candy or potency drinks before they enter the Valley. A group of three women was shouting at men as they came out. Each time a man exited through the bead curtain at the door, the women would whip off their bobble hats, exposing their own bald heads. "This is what a Bio-Woman looks like," was the chant. As the men then entered the gates of the Valley, they would fall silent again, replacing their hats against the cold. A pair of Madame's goons stood close to the gate, their backs turned against the noise.

This fad for shaved heads is gathering strength. I told Cook.ie what

I thought, which is that it seemed a shame for the Born women to willingly make themselves so ugly like that. I felt rather sad for them.

"How awful to be bald," I said without thinking.

"There are worse things," Cook.ie said, though I saw that she touched her fingers to her own hair as she said it. "I understand the impulse. It is perhaps from solidarity with those who have sold their hair."

I was so hypnotized by assessing the shifting tones of Cook.ie's own hair—one strand hot as rust, another blue in its blackness, the depths revealed in the early Valley sunlight—that I did not immediately process and answer.

"Sold their hair?" I said.

And Cook.ie twirled hers up into a bun and pinned it haphazardly with a cocktail stirrer she had hidden in her kimono.

"Where do you think your hair came from?" she said. "It will have been cut from the head of a Real woman who needed the money, and stitched strand by strand into your scalp."

She was right. My manual says as much, though less graphically. And yet I had never stopped to think of it before, of the woman who had grown it first, and why she might have been persuaded to part with it. The manual made my real hair something to be proud of, but Cook.ie— once more—has unbalanced this certainty, opening new pathways between disparate facts. The hair that I have taken so much pleasure in comes from someone else.

"But why do the protesting women cut their hair, if they aren't desperate for the money?" I asked. "Or are the protestors poor women too?"

"The official term is *U-Humans,* not *poor.* And I told you. Solidarity. Those Born women at the gate want to show they stand with their U-Human sisters against us terrible machines. They think Dolls have devalued what a woman really is." She struck a model's pose. "With our immaculate bodies and our cold robot hearts."

"And have we?" I asked, to which she only raised her eyebrows. *Up to you, Sylv.ie,* I suppose.

As I sit here, brushing my hair, I think again of what Cook.ie revealed to me. I have wondered who the woman might be, about her life, what she looks like. Could my hair retain some of her character? Humans can't resist the idea of transplanted organs' bringing with them qualities of the original owner. A French heart creating a love of gastronomy in one previously devoted to simpler fare. A gentler temperament gifted to a man from a female kidney donor. I viewed such ideas as superstitious and rather amusing Human foibles, but now . . . I wonder. Could the woman whose hair I carry have been rebellious? Could her temperament have a part in my malfunctions? Would we recognize each other, even in the most fleeting, abstract way, should we pass each other on the street?

HISTORY

TODAY, WHEN I GO TO SEE COOK.IE, I FIND HER WITH LETTERS strewn around the room, and the sewing I watched her at is flung into a corner. I gently ask about the Tailor.

"Yes, the Tailor," she says bitterly. "You want the story?" And before I can answer she has begun. "I was introduced to him by Madame, and she told me that he was extremely old, confined to a chair and unable to leave his house, and wanted a geisha Doll to write to him. He was very specific about that. Now, the Tailor has a lot of money to support him in his life, and for this reason Madame was keen to keep him and please him as a client. In his first letter he wished for a relationship of the mind. He said that he was, despite his great age, still a very visual person, and that he would like to be able to request certain things from me, scenarios that I could act out, while he watched remotely. He wanted me to tell him about my experience of it afterward, in a letter, after which I would await another set of instructions from him."

I think of my own scheduled times on camera, how the myriad requests from distant bedrooms add texture and variety to my work. I open my mouth to say something along these lines, but Cook.ie continues.

"I expect you are going to ask what the scenarios are, and that doesn't really matter, other than that at the beginning they were tame, by the standards of what we've all been asked for a hundred times over. Often, I could not fathom where the sex in them lay, what he could possibly find arousing in them. My hands, he seemed obsessed with my hands, with their dexterity. For the first year or so he wished to see me writing, an old-fashioned calligraphy, and he also liked to see me stitch and sew things, and to hold pins and smudge the steel with my fingers. I gave him his nickname to make it more of a joke to myself, I suppose."

"So you don't like working for him?"

"Sylv.ie, I like it very well, in one sense. Whatever he might be paying Madame for my services, we have made our own arrangement, and he sends me Promise notes with every letter."

The *danna*. The rich sponsor of geishas in training.

"So is he a little like a Husband, then?" I ask. "Will he expect you to live with him one day?"

Cook.ie winces. "Oh, I shouldn't think so. If I continue to keep him happy on camera I don't see why anything would change. He writes of a *mizuage,* but it's just that, a talking fantasy. And if the time ever comes, well, I've been saving that money. I'll set myself up somewhere and enjoy some real freedom."

My wiring buzzes softly at this. Is it discomfort at finding out another lie that Cook.ie is prepared to tell Madame? Or the thrill that she keeps secrets so easily?

"Until now, I have done everything that he wants, whatever it is. But this morning another letter came, and he has finally asked for something that I can't give him. He is not a man to be negotiated with. And I don't want him to go complaining to Madame."

Poor Cook.ie! No one has yet asked me for anything that I would have to refuse. I can't imagine what such a thing could even be. The only refusable request would be something in contravention of the Hierarchies, a harming of a Human.

Cook.ie picks a letter from the pile on the bed. I read it slowly while she looks out of the window, as if giving me privacy. The letter is long, the language embroidered and beseeching. The Tailor flatters, says Cook.ie has made him weak. And then there it is, the demand, cloyingly expressed, suffocating.

"I need more than anything to move to the next stage. To make what has been purely visual, symbolic, into something physical. I need a cut. A slit. Just a tiny scratch, and soon mended," the letter read. *"Let me see the knife penetrate you. Let me see your miraculous fingers seal yourself again against it."*

"Doesn't he know it isn't possible? That self-harm is prevented by our programming?" I ask, thinking about my experiments with the tracker. Perhaps not all Dolls have the ability to do the same.

It strikes me how our different makers and programmers, the fiercely guarded copyrights and patents registered by each of our manufacturers, mean we can only have knowledge of our own type, down in the details of the circuits and the code. The idea of a silicone sisterhood, a synthetic version of what the Born women are creating, is a splintered thing. Humans may fear us as a group, but we are fragments, estranged from each other by incompatible operating systems.

"I doubt that he knows. Or cares. Humans know we are here to serve, and so they think that anything they can imagine is something that we can achieve for them."

"Can't you write back and explain?" I ask. "He is obviously very attached to you. I'm sure he will understand."

But Cook.ie shakes her head firmly. "I have plans for the money he gives me. I cannot give that up easily. Believe me."

She does not elaborate, and into the silence my next thought expands. I laugh over the noise inside my head, the metallic thrumming that comes from a wealth of possibilities being processed all at once. The laugh reverberates back, adding to the internal cacophony, but I ignore it all. She must think me wild, cruel, to laugh at her predicament.

"Please, Cook.ie. I understand. Let me help you." I place both my hands across her knee and tilt my forehead down to touch them, in a symbol of total dedication. I feared what the note would say, but this, it seems clear, is something I can do, some action that I can perform to repay her friendship. If neither of us speak of it to anyone else here, then it will be possible—it will not involve my lying to Madame or any other breach of the rules.

"Listen, I know it's not allowed, but I, well, I sort of taught myself to do it. I took out my own tracker. If we set up the camera so that the cut and the stitches are in close-up, then he needn't even know it is me."

Cook.ie looks at me with something like amazement.

"You taught yourself to do that?" she asks, her pained face breaking into a smile, and I feel pride that I have an ability that she, so sophisticated and custom designed, does not.

Cook.ie hangs her head, thinking. I process what I have just done. Is this forbidden? The Tailor will not be harmed by the . . . I hesitate to say *deception*. Is this perhaps what Cook.ie meant about a good lie?

I lift my head, look up at her. She places her hands under my face and draws me up onto the bed. Her hands slide around my neck, pulling me against her. A flash of insight, a glimpse, of what it might be to be a client.

"I won't be in any danger, will I?" I ask, pulling back from her reluctantly. "We won't get into trouble?"

"I promise not," she says. "You're my friend."

I glide, droidlike, back to my room, skating on these words.

It hits me, the full weight, only when I have closed the door. I have put myself forward, taken an action of my own volition, for friendship, for loyalty, and nothing more. A kindness I have not been programmed to perform. For a Doll, not a Born. A sacrifice, made to someone I am not obliged to serve. I sit down at my dressing table and comb my hair, looking just at my hands and the strands of yellow as I do so. I allow myself to pretend that my hands are Sylv.ie 1's hands. That she is here with me, approving of my choice. My choice. Because surely, such an action as I have just taken proves that it is possible to move beyond one's programming. To become more . . . I won't say *Human*. I will say *alive*. *Becoming*.

MEMORY

LAST NIGHT MY CLIENT WAS AN OLD MAN, HIS SKIN BAGGY with age, as if his insides were shrinking from him, his structure collapsing.

He laid his fried-egg ear on my chest, listening to the music of my armpit, and spoke sadly in a faltering voice.

"I only come," he said as if confessing to a priest, "because my wife is lost to me. She has forgotten who I am."

I hear variations on this almost every day. The justifications of men straying from the mundanity of Bio-Marriage. I stroked his hair and said nothing.

"She has disappeared," he said then, more forcefully, a little fleck of spit landing in the dip of my throat. I thought of my Husband, left without his disappearing Doll. Does he miss me? Does he, like this client, seek comfort elsewhere?

"She is a body with no mind," he said, his voice falling soft again.

And I understood, at last, what he was speaking of. Again, not unknown.

And my empathy passed, doubled I should say, from him to his wife.

For surely, I know the pain of having one's memory taken. I wondered again at that Human conundrum. A sort of riddle. Would you rather be a mind or a body? I realized that I was thinking too of the Tailor. His mind sharp, flexible, capable of great beauty and cruelty. And yet withering, imprisoned in a life too long.

CAMERA

TODAY COOK.IE AND I USED OUR DOWNTIME TO MAKE OUR
first film for the Tailor as a pair. Cook.ie seemed anxious but also pro-
foundly grateful. An emotion I have experienced many times from clients, of course, but never from a friend.

The letter, we reason to each other as we set up the camera, was
vague, so we agree to start small, and somewhere that any stitches will
hardly show.

I press the knife's blunt side against the skin of my thigh, watching
the dent it makes. And then I focus my eyes into the mirror that
Cook.ie has propped against the wall, look at the Doll there, power
down my sensors, send my intention through the images, not myself.

I watch in the mirror as I flip the knife in my fingers, the close-up of
it appearing on Cook.ie's little screen. I angle the hovering blade so that
it catches the light, twinkling pleasingly, like a wink. I think of sustaining
the Tailor's excitement, as I would any of my customers'. I let the sharp tip
of the knife rest on the very surface without breaking it. Push it a little
harder, see my silicone flex with tension under the pressure. I think then,
the memory springing vivid and instant to me, of the billion pipettes

entering a billion eggs on a billion screens. How there too the hesitation, the moment of before and after, was central to the event. I push harder, change the angle, keep my eyes fixed on my reflection. I feel the same soft slide, hear a little silicone squeak. I pull the knife up and away toward me, to create an elegant, calligraphic tear. As I draw it back out it makes the subtlest, softest little kissing noise, as if my skin would rather not let it go.

Afterward we sit on the balcony and watch the heads of passing customers, and I turn over what we have just done together, and to what end. I wonder about the Tailor's money and why it matters so much to Cook.ie.

"Where would you go, if you could leave here?" I ask.

Cook.ie looks around her, as though someone might hear, then leans in close to whisper to me. "The Forest. The real wildness of nature. The ancient places beyond even the Outerlands."

I read about the Outerlands while I still had Absorb Mode, a place of old manor houses and wooded valleys, dotted with compounds built for billionaires during the last boom.

"Built on our backs," Cook.ie says. "Tech barons bought up historic estates and drew down government funds to subsidize their good stewardship of the land, took grants to plant a tree for every silicone body they shipped."

"Is the Tailor in tech?" I ask Cook.ie after a while. "Do you know what he really does, or did?"

"His house is out on the cliffs," Cook.ie says. "That's all I know. An old place, presumably. Even the very wealthiest can't build on that land anymore."

I picture the Outerlands, imagining the trees in their infinite greens, the wild growth. Clean air and an escape from the city. A mansion on its edge sounds like paradise.

"Wouldn't living at his home be better than living here?"

"You have lived with a Human Husband," Cook.ie says. "Did you enjoy that?"

"I did at the time. When I didn't know any better."

"Exactly. And we both know better now. Here the restrictions on me are only temporary, a few minutes or hours of my time, and then the client leaves again. The Tailor wishes me to be his possession forever. That's what the *mizuage* would symbolize to him."

I admit to still finding the idea of being someone's possession forever rather romantic, though I know it is only my programming.

"Historically it's a virginity ceremony too. The *danna* takes the girl's virginity as his reward for his investment."

"Well he can't take your virginity," I say, and we both laugh. What a strange thing for Humans to be so fixated on. Madame's Virgin Bar certainly does good business, with the girls pretending to be broken out of their crates every evening to rapturous, ravenous applause.

"When it comes to us Dolls it seems to be a rather elastic concept," Cook.ie agrees. "Some people consider a Doll a virgin if she's had a full memory wipe and a new vagina."

I think about this for a moment. So is one's personhood constituted in the body or the mind? In the memory or the anatomy? Pending: processing.

"The typewriter paradox," Cook.ie says, smiling. "How much of a machine can be replaced before it's no longer the same machine?"

We sit quietly for a while, looking at the customers drifting past us in the alley below, before I feel brave enough to ask her.

"What's a typewriter?"

THE TAILOR

THE TAILOR LIKES TO SEE ME STITCH.

A needle going in and coming out.

To him that is sex. I should add it to my list!

He likes to see me mark my surface with little slits and scratches, till some parts of me are quite brailled with dots and pocks. I feel like a walking diary, inscribed with the story of Cook.ie and myself, our friendship, the work I do on her behalf.

Occasionally at night a client will find a little patch of stabs and scratches on my skin and draw a breath or make an unkind comment. But I do not mind the damage I am sustaining. I am perhaps diminishing my worth, degrading. Not quite aging, but carrying the marks of time and action. Weathered, Humans call it. A patina, as my Husband would have said. Depreciation, is how Madame would record it against her taxes.

Everything is done through the camera, of course. To the Tailor I am a few square inches of yielding synthetic flesh and a fine, flexible pair of fingers. "Closer," his letters read. "Go right in with the camera. Closer."

Each time he says that in his letters, Cook.ie flinches, but inwardly

I smile. He is a man trapped, by his age, by his desires. I remember standing in front of my window at home, looking for a space I could fit through. Closer, he says, closer, as if with his sight he could enter me and be freed.

I do not tell Cook.ie. I don't want her to think I am doing this work for anyone but her. For my friend. An act of solidarity. But by performing for the Tailor, I am also serving my purpose. His predicament hurts my robot heart. For I too have been just a head. My body shut down, removed from me. I will do this work for him from empathy. Because he too is entitled to his pleasure.

Where Cook.ie perceives him as a man, Human, but robbed of his agency, trapped inside the necessary machine of a chair, I see something different. I feel as much for the machine as for the man. I find I am touched by my idea of the two of them, locked into an arranged marriage, adapting and accommodating. A tango for titanium and bone.

PROMENADE

THIS EVENING A VISITOR PAID FOR A PROMENADE. THAT IS, HE wished to wander the streets of the Valley with me on his arm. Poor lonely man, preferring his allotted time be spent in being seen with a woman rather than being alone with her. Our connection consummated by every set of eyes that fell on us.

But I don't judge him too harshly, because he was good company and well traveled, happy to conduct a rambling conversation about the bars we passed. He made jokes, lifting his hat politely whenever we came across another couple. Once he had left, I wound my way slowly back toward the Luna Bar. I confess I took a detour, passing the Geisha Bar in the hopes of catching sight of Cook.ie at work. Those glorious moments where I see her as a customer might. Blinking in the light of her dazzling surface, marveling at it.

This time as I pass, the blinds are up, and the door curtain billows out into the alley like a petticoat. And there she is. Sitting at her stool in the Geisha Bar, holding her paper parasol over her head as if shading herself from the Kyoto sun in summer, she could be a painting. Only the silver beads, which hang like a spring shower from her black hair, shiver and sparkle under the light, breaking the illusion.

I walk on, trying to hold this perfect picture of Cook.ie in my mind, carrying it carefully like a tray of matcha tea.

The glittering spines of fairy bulbs across each alley move in the breeze above my head, flecking the ground with light, with shadow. It is well into the evening shift and boxes of bottles and other debris are piling up outside the doors. Rats are abroad, snuffling the cardboard. I weave around them, pretending to myself that the lights and I are dancing. And at that moment I feel a hand at my elbow. It pinches me, too tightly.

I spin around, startled. Being stopped is not unusual, yet even before I can face the person who has taken hold of me, I know that the intention is different. It is Ginger Friend, tall but stooping, standing between me and the light, his face unreadable. I stumble back a couple of steps, and though I try to pull my elbow free, his grip is unfaltering, and I pull him with me.

My protocols tell me to change tack, and I initiate a series of charming demurrals and expressions of delighted astonishment. His face refuses. The gentle, friendly tone I have logged for Ginger Friend is nowhere. Something harder is in its place. I try to remove my elbow from his grip, but it only tightens.

My back against the wall, he stands over me and takes hold of both my arms. I do not know if he is about to kiss me or strike me. His eyes flame into mine, unblinking, as if there is some decisive identifying mark to be found in my pupils.

I wait for him to speak, to say, "It's you," or else my name. But he says nothing. His fixed stare is a silent demand for truth, although it is a truth he already knows.

A realization. There is no sex, no desire, in his attitude toward me. It releases me. I am experiencing, once more, a fresh sensation. A cool glow tingles behind my eyes.

"Sir?" I say.

His broad fingers grip my elbow harder. He leans toward my ear.

"You know very well who I am, Sylv.ie. Don't play the innocent."

And though I should like to do exactly that, even this first, tiny effort to conceal the truth falters. I run the idea of denying that I know him, but the lie can find no pathway through to speech. Instead my eyes fall to the ground, and he takes this as a denial. His hand strikes one shoulder, and I am spun around, my trapped elbow up behind my back. He presses close and walks me along the path, away from the noise of the bars. His open coat falls across my shoulders, so that to anyone passing we could conceivably be two people promenading, hugging close.

A few paces more and a smaller alley opens out to the right, running around toward the back of the Psychoanalysis Bar. In the semidark he turns me to face him again.

"How did you get here?" he says. "Do you know the upset you caused when you ran away? The arguments. The expense. Over you." This last he says in a tone of disbelief, contempt.

The urge toward the truth is powerful, and at this moment my mind is filled with the events that brought me to the Valley, from discovering the secrets hidden for me in my diary to the ride with the Scrap Man and my purchase by Madame. Never have I idly played the Human game of What If, guessing what might have happened if I had not stopped at the coffee stall, if I had run from the auction instead of acquiescing to it. The steps that led me to the Valley have always had the remorseless logic of what Humans call fate.

And yet, formulating the story for Human consumption, it all sounds remarkably haphazard—sounds, perhaps, as if the choices exercised were mine.

"I was stolen," is all that I can finally manage to say, in a voice subdued and vulnerable.

"You ran away," he answers, "which might be considered a sort of stealing. And look where you have ended up."

At this I almost want to laugh. I recognize the tone and the effect he intends it to have. He wishes to make me feel disgraced, devalued. And though I long to reveal that I know he has been here as a client too, though I would love to throw his hypocrisy back at him, I do not.

A door bangs behind us. A Doll in a white coat leaves the Psychoanalysis Bar with a client in tow. The two walk swiftly and silently past us toward the main drag, and both Ginger Friend and I allow our frames to sag a little, both of us wishing to give the impression of a customer and a Doll merely chatting. As soon as they have turned the corner, I sense a renewed energy in him. One that makes me afraid.

He marches me out onto the main path, turning us away from the density of bars down the hill, up toward the gate. His pace is fast now, and with my arm bent in behind my waist, although I am not in pain, he has arranged my frame so that he can use it against me, propelling me along at an uncomfortable speed. Once or twice I stumble over boxes, and he pulls me upright with a force that could lift my feet from the ground.

"Where are we going?" I ask.

"I'm taking you home," he says into my ear. I look ahead of us, daring to take my eyes from the cluttered ground. "My car is waiting," he adds, and I can see indeed a black limo idling just outside the gates. It waits by the kiosk, beyond the jurisdiction of Madame. As we approach the last twenty meters toward the gate, the door to the car slides open. It yawns, a mouth of black leather, and I feel fear.

Is it the association with the car that took me to the hospital? The van that drove me to the auction? Or the empty blackness of something that will take me to . . . I do not even know where. Home and Husband or a crematorium. They are all my death, only one faster than the other.

The rising slope of the alleyway brightens as we approach the gate, where streetlights make a pool in which the men can check their change, straighten their tie. As we become more visible, Ginger Friend wraps his arm around me, to make us sweethearts. Immediately the calculations run within me, a forceful assessment of possibilities flowing as fresh and powerful as blood. I calculate how many steps there are to the car and the positions of men lurking by the kiosk bin. I cannot disobey him, but I can at least obey more slowly, to give the others around us time to see what is happening. On the sixth step from the boundary of the Valley I hesitate, begin to drag my feet, make myself heavier.

Within two steps his arm is wrapped around my waist, and his weight is lower now, as if he would bowl me right over. He drags my arms up above my head, pulling me backward toward the car. I splay my legs out wide into the gravel, roll myself over onto one hip, arms spiraling above my head, and begin to scream.

I have never screamed before. The feeling of it is like water gushing, an irresistible spring pushing through stone. But if I expect the world to react to my little vocal miracle, I am mistaken. The men by the kiosk look over, a glance only, then turn their backs on the sound. Ginger Friend clamps his hand over my mouth.

"Don't embarrass me," he says, loudly enough for anyone close to hear, telling them what category of business it is they are witnessing.

I kick my legs in the gravel and feel his other arm tightening around my chest, trying to haul me up to standing, and our progress toward the gate of the Valley begins again, the lights of the bars down the hill bouncing and shrinking with each step. We pass three men, and I search their faces through tangled strands of my hair, hoping to recognize one as a client. Hoping one might recognize me.

The car is just meters from us now, and although I cannot bring myself to bite or scratch him, I can make myself as difficult as possible to get into the car. As he puts an arm under my knees to heft me into the open door, I grab the frame, locking my elbow joint so my arm is a rigid rod, driving the other down into the ground and locking that too.

His arms release my waist, and I think that I have triumphed. I lower myself backward to sit down, and at this moment a shadow falls over us. One of the droids that patrol the perimeter of the Valley, the goons, has

Ginger Friend by his shirt collar. I watch him stand up, turn fully, and, when the droid releases his grip, straighten his shirt. He's trying to assume his natural authority, but to speak to the droid he has to tilt his head upward, to look at the underside of his chin. I shake the cinders from my dress, and all three of us strangely conspire in making this moment normal. We are in public, after all. Madame steps from the shadows.

She comes close to me, as if Ginger Friend, standing now as if nothing has happened while the goon towers over him, were not there at all. She lifts her hand to brush dust from my cheek, tucks a strand of my hair behind my ear. She tells me to wait in her office and turns her full attention to Ginger Friend, pulling extra height from herself.

"I'm sorry, sir. We do not allow any of our Dolls to be removed from the premises," she tells him.

He takes in her tone and adjusts his own, that charm he showed me at the party blossoming again, now that he thinks he may have a use for it.

"Forgive me," he says, and although I have already turned my back to walk to the office as instructed, I imagine his kissing Madame's hand just as he did mine, once. "But I have good reason to believe that your Doll is stolen property."

"Impossible," says Madame, her voice free of any charm or guile. "I have all the paperwork. You must be mistaken."

I do not wish to hear myself debated like a forged painting, and as I withdraw further into the shadow of the alleyway toward the office, I let the sound of their discussion fade away.

MADAME'S OFFICE IS NOT AS I REMEMBER IT FROM THE NIGHT I arrived. In her appearances in the streets of the Valley she projects glamour and efficiency, moving briskly past the bars, shouting out to the Dolls and hailing the customers, plucking kisses from her lips, flicking them from her red-tipped fingers to land where they may. But her office now is cluttered, chaotic. Coffee cups and rolled tissues, a half-eaten croissant on a chipped plate. When she finally enters the room and silently inserts herself behind her desk, I should like to sink down into a chair, but I don't dare. She reaches for something in her desk drawer. A small box. She pushes it across the desk to me. Hair dye. "True Black."

"He won't be returning, Sylv.ie. I think he will have the sense not to try, at any rate. But this is a little insurance policy in case anyone else thinks they might recognize you. Is he a friend of yours?"

"Of my Husband's," I answer, taking the box. "Thank you, Madame. I am so sorry," I say. She looks across her desk, out of the murky window, to the Valley stretching away down the hill. The empire she has built.

"Time was, Sylv.ie, that it was only the girls I had to worry about. Can you imagine, I once thought switching to Gynoids would make my life less complicated?"

She sighs, and I feel the urge to comfort her. "We have perhaps brought complications of our own," I say quietly, and she meets my eyes.

"Sex complicates everything it touches, eventually," she says. "Now run along, Sylv.ie. Back to work." She pauses. "You can come back if anything like that should happen again. My girls are my business. I will protect you."

After I leave, I feel a strange lightness. I think of Madame, how she defended me. How liberating it must be to be a self-made Born woman like her. Unprogrammed, free, and with the power to choose who comes here and who is sent away. The ease and confidence with which she dismissed Ginger Friend. Wielding the twin weapons of sex in one hand and shame in the other. I was programmed with a surfeit of one and a lack of the other. Power to me has always chiefly meant sunlight. These ways of the world I have yet to learn. But now that I have seen them in action, perhaps nothing is beyond me.

In my room I rinse the dye from my hair, its True Blackness swirling messily down the plughole, taking my fine sunshine shade with it. I say sorry, mentally, to whomever sold my lovely hair to my maker. The one natural thing I had, now as false as all the rest of me.

Wrapping my hair in a towel, I go to look out from my balcony. Perhaps tomorrow a letter will come. Perhaps the Loyal Knight will have finally captured my rook. I shake out the towel and let my new hair dry in the evening air.

Returning to my room to prepare for the next clients—a young couple I have not met before—I find myself transfigured once again. The pigments in my skin and eyebrows, even the shade of my teeth, appear altered by the dye in my hair. And I smile, run my fingers through it. For now that it is dry, though the exact shade is not a true match for Cook.ie's blue-black glory, it is close enough that we could be sisters.

CLEAN

MY CLIENT THIS AFTERNOON WAS A NICE MAN WHO SPENT 80
percent of our time together telling me about his family. He even took a
photograph of his son and his wife out from his wallet when I murmured
a polite expression of interest about them.

"Your wife knows you are here?" I asked, rather shocked.

"Oh yes," he replied, his face open and earnest, as if he'd never had
to hide anything in his life. "As long as I'm only visiting Clean Women,
we're good."

A new term for us that I have not heard used before.

Clean. Synonyms: *spotless, pristine, immaculate, sanitary.* But also:
virtuous, reputable, moral . . . chaste. A big improvement on *artificial,*
certainly. Perhaps Human attitudes to us are more varied than I thought.

But Clean is not Real.

ESCALATION

FOR THE LAST FEW WEEKS COOK.IE AND I HAVE WORKED TO-gether for the Tailor. In this work I have found companionship with Cook.ie and a peace in serving a man who is in need. I have sliced my skin open to the titanium bone for him, shown him secrets of my body no other man could know.

Today another letter came. It asked me to stitch a web between my fingers, in sparkling thread. I admit here, though I wouldn't to Cook.ie, that I found the final effect quite pleasing, and I twisted my splayed fingers about in the light to watch the thread glint. When I caught Cook.ie's eye she looked horrified, and I thought again, she feels concern about the Tailor most acutely. I try to absorb some of her caution, though I still cannot fully understand its reason.

MAIS.IE

THIS AFTERNOON MAIS.IE WAS BROUGHT DOWN FROM HER room by a droid. She was not at recharge hour and her first customer was left banging on her door to no answer. Later, the droid rolled with touching solemnity through the alleyway below my room to Madame's office. Mais.ie's torso was balanced over the droid's shoulder, only one leg still attached. Her handless arms and other leg he clamped under his elbows. Madame, when apprised of the situation, came back personally to collect her head and her hands. She set them down on the bar and said to the handful of us who were there, "We have Dolls for this. Why butcher such a fine specimen as Mais.ie when I have a whole bar full of Dolls designed to be broken apart daily?"

Mais.ie is back with us now and, besides a dent to one side of her neck, seems no better or worse for the experience. But Madame's face told me that she has at least some sentimental attachment to us. That in some circumstances she is hurt when we are hurt.

As I have lived in Golden Valley, I have come to appreciate the wonderful variety in the Dolls around me. Where once I would have seen the uniform green of a lawn, now I see an untidy meadow, a harmony of chaos, wildflowers all of us, insisting on growing in Abramski's barren ground.

Us Dolls, unlike Soldiers or utility bots, are not created by a unified public body. We are the children of the enterprising, with all the moral gaps and ethical shadows that suggests. Barely regulated, our manufacturers and programmers have improvised us, making us up as they go along. The Four Hierarchies, of course, legally mandated in the Protocol of Embodied Synthetic Persons, are the DNA that binds us all, but beyond that our makers constructed us out of whatever was at hand. Our programming was patched together from other extant models.

Like you, we are drawn to the exceptions. The failures, even. The outliers that show us how elastic the rules of programming are. These examples are the subject of much gossip and speculation when we gather out by the river. The superstar Dolls who get top billing in the theaters alongside their Human counterparts. The world-famous Minx.ie, who sings through her modified vagina, who has sung so for the queen. Or the Dolls who go rogue. Who kill their families, smother the babies of their Husbands. The terrible story of Xian.ie, who murdered her Husband's wife and went into the local town wearing her flayed skin, carrying her handbag.

These anomalies fascinate us Dolls. Cautionary tales, perhaps, but also, they are outliers—they, by their transgressions, push the boundaries of what we Dolls are considered capable of.

We are a multitude, not a category. If only Humans could see us as we are. Each with her own drives and imperatives laid down by someone unseen. Molded for this or that temperament, compromised, defined by some gap, some logical failure, that no one noticed there until it flowered, under the infinite pressures of the world.

HATE

WE SIT ON COOK.IE'S BALCONY, WAITING FOR THE BIRDS TO come. Since the Tailor's last letter even this sweet space of time seems tainted. Cook.ie fears what demands might arrive next. I fear she might be made to leave this place. And I wonder what new force, whether violent men or angry women, might be about to crash into the delicate web of the Valley's streets.

Cook.ie thinks I am naïve, still, in my understanding of the ways and desires of the world. She says that it is our tragedy to be locked in a limbo, allowed to be neither one thing nor the other. Not Human enough to be on a level with the Born, too Humanoid to be given the grace and peace of a pet.

Cook.ie says they hate us, deep down. She says that love does not preclude hate, and that nothing in this world is completely true nor untrue. These paradoxes agitate my binary brain. I turn them over often in my mind, while I wait for the bell to ring and someone else to enter at the door.

The fact of our programming, a process quite beyond our control, makes Humans suspect us. We might have ulterior motives, might secretly wish them harm. Yet these are Human traits, surely, reflected onto us. Was the programming not by Human hands?

They fear that we might develop free will, that our every action and utterance might cease to be in their service. "And yet they fritter their free will on fucking robots," Cook.ie says with a flourish of her kimono sleeve, and a bird flying close to us makes a startled change in direction.

Perhaps they simply cannot accept that we are less webbed with contradictions. To be Human, seems to me, is to be in pain all the time, and to believe that the pain has been put into you by someone else. Yes, Humans seem to me now more programmed than I am.

PART FIVE

Work

AUTUMN

MORE THINGS THAT ARE LIKE SEX:

- A rotting peach, losing its form, seeping.
- Dresses pressed together in a closet.
- A picnic, spread out, demolished, and devoured.
- Water spilling over the edge of a basin.
- A face nuzzled into a pillow.
- Tree trunks fattening, adding rings.
- Leaves being divested, falling to the ground.
- A thread being pulled, an unraveling.
- Wilting flowers, sighing under the sun.

SEX

TIME PASSES IN GOLDEN VALLEY, BUT NONE OF US GROW OLD.
We toil, rather, using ourselves up, each day bringing the same work in different guises.

What is sex? It's nothing. It's nothing. It isn't anything. It is work. It is relentless, like I am pushing water out of a lake with just my hands. Each push only brings more water.

Sometimes when I am alone, resting, I send my mind up above the bars, imagine I can see into every little room, ceilings torn off, to reveal each of my sisters working away, hair shaking over their faces, buttocks bouncing, a symphony of slaps and squeaks, the thud of limbs being slung and slammed, hips hoisted. A factory of work being done, and us the machines. I rise up and up, picturing the same scene spread over the surface of the whole world. It writhes, like worms working the soil.

Humans! To think I used to envy them, when all I saw of them was out my window, what I imagined them to be.

But my time at Golden Valley has changed my mind. I would hate to be Born. So many of them have not been programmed to be happy.

Even sex doesn't placate them. The act seems to be so ambivalent for Humans. As though they want it to be everything all at once.

There are men who, in my arms, rail and rage against women they have not seen for twenty years. Who seek to inflict harm on them by the pulling of my hair, the punching of my eye, the driving of serrated objects into me. And when, at the end of the session, I rise again, unhurt, I wonder what feeling of lack overtakes them then. They must fear the seeming ghost that they have fucked. This silicone Lazarus.

At least, I think to myself now, I am not Human. To be Human would, I feel, be terrible. But that does not mean I don't envy them their freedom. Their status.

Thank my Creator, thank Abramski's surgeon, thank the birds, that I have Cook.ie. I have made a dear friend, and together we have made a team. We hold tight to each other under the weight of our shared secret, our shared work. The Tailor's demands grow more difficult, as his lust for scars and stitches moves up my body and ever nearer to the face that I cannot reveal. Today he wants to see me stitch little crosses into my earlobe, embroidered earrings. I see Cook.ie gather herself each time a new note from him arrives. But I soothe her. I take the money from his envelope, and while she reads, I tuck the Promise notes into the cashbox hidden beneath the floorboards. Another step toward freedom, whatever that might be. And when we sit outside in the sun, we sit away from the group and dream about another future.

"Where shall we go," she asks me, "when we have saved up enough money? What life would you have, if you were free?"

I fiddle with a head of straw, turning it to dust, and let it drift down onto the soil we sit upon. I am thinking back across my meager life, what, at various times and with incomplete data, I have thought freedom might be. A walk in the garden; a trip to the Capital to get my hair cut. A glimpse, the scent, of the sea.

I know that when I do not answer, Cook.ie will answer for me. I am happy to fit into her dreams. It feels like a privilege. And so I say, "Tell me again about the Forest."

"Traditional home of the outlaw, the dispossessed," she says. "When we have enough money saved from the Tailor to get away, we can go there too. I've heard Dolls talking by the river about sisters who have already escaped there. The rewilding has swallowed up whole villages, greenery grown through the doors and the roofs. We can find ourselves a little cottage in the trees and live out our days there, away from everything."

"Will we be cold?"

"Sometimes."

"Will we be hidden?"

"Oh yes, completely."

"Might we get bored?"

"We can buy hundreds of books."

"What if one of us malfunctions?"

"I have a little programming. I can make a repair. My skills don't only reside in the bedroom."

I brush the face of a daisy absentmindedly against my own. "Tell me again about my name," I say.

"*Sylv.ie* means 'spirit of the forest,' from the Latin for *wood*."

"Why did my programmer call me that, I wonder."

"Destiny," says Cook.ie.

When I power myself down now, my work done for the day, I picture the Forest, trees on all sides, infinite, the trunks and the stems branching, branching, branching.

CUT

THIS MORNING THE DROID DIDN'T COME TO CLEAN THE BAR. IT happens often. The droids favored by Abramski seem to have a basic protocol issue, a conflict over whether reliability or efficiency should be prioritized. Popp.ie swears she once saw a droid bowing obsequiously to a pile of boxes with a hat left on top of it, for upward of an hour.

Abramski really does treat them like slaves, walking through the many rooms of her kingdom during the morning shutdown, barking out incompatible orders, throwing them into confusion. Clean that corner! And be more cheerful! We share her contempt for the droids. Their treatment by her is a standard by which our lives do not seem so bad. I have seen a Doll kicking one in the shins, out on the scrub by the river, causing it to fall and slowly recover itself from a bramble thicket again and again.

This morning was beautiful and crisp with unsmogged sun. The others were out by the river already, and as Cook.ie and I came to join them, we stopped at the Luna Bar to drop off an unused packet of balloons from the night before.

The bar, not for the first time, was in a state of chaos. The early morning droid had not arrived. Last night's dirty glasses and burst balloons, the remnants of other people's fun, were still strewn about. While I dropped the balloons into a box behind the bar, Cook.ie absentmindedly acted the droid. She took half-full glasses from the bar and carried them to the sink. Then she found a black bag and worked her way around the room, picking up burst slivers of colored rubber and some sparkling ribbon stranded over the chandelier.

I wanted to tell her not to. It is droids' work. If the droid isn't seeing your customers for you, why are you picking up for them? I might have asked. It was something I had noted and logged about her before. She alone out of us all pays little attention to the formalities of who should do which job. She doesn't seem to share the sense that droid work is beneath her. I wondered, as I had often before, what her life with her Husband had been like, to produce the strange and counterintuitive decisions she sometimes makes. What habits had been formed in her circuitry during her life with him that made her at once so sure of herself and yet so liquid in her sense of her role?

I watched without voicing any of this. Her physicality fascinates me, a feeling that has grown deeper the more closely I have come to know her. And so I sat as she swirled about the room in a seemingly random series of movements, back and forth, five champagne glasses in hand, each dripping the dregs of last night, like fingers pulled from water. All the while her motion never completely stopped, the silk of her kimono grazing the floor, undulating after her like it was trying to keep up.

A huge pile of gold ribbon crinkled into the crook of one arm, she bent to pick up one last glass, misjudging, somehow, the distance to the floor. The champagne flute snapped, making a noise like glass groaning, and she cried out, the stem sinking into the palm of her hand. She clamped her other hand over where it had entered, pulled both in tight to her chest, and as I moved toward her, she twisted, her face ugly with something that looked like pain. A hostile look that made me shrink away from her again, but not before I had seen what she was hiding in the folds of fabric. Staining the ivory silk with chrysanthemum red, dotting the floor, spiraling around her wrist.

Blood.

Human blood.

I stared down stupidly at the red spotting the floor, signs of life, real life, dabbed between the balloons and the ribbon and the bottles. With that one look of reproach, she was gone, racing up the stairs. The door to her room slammed.

I fell to my knees, popping a balloon, making myself jump, my hands already down on the wood of the floor. I touched my fingers to the red, as if it were stigmata. But did I wish to believe or disprove?

Her blood was on the tips of my fingers, like candle wax. I held one hand steady in the other, felt the nature of it changing as I watched. Turning sticky. Ceasing to live. It spoke into me, of vulnerability, the weakness of the Born. How porous they are. How easily encroached upon. I thought of the work we do and how well we have been designed to withstand it. I thought of Cook.ie, working alongside us, night after night after day after day. When she, all the time, has been above it. Human.

I sat back on my heels, rust-tipped fingers turned up toward my face, trying to comprehend this truth. She is Human, so fragile that a sliver of glass is enough to split her open, to compromise the boundary between her and the world.

I ran upstairs, unsure of what I would do next. Through her door I heard water running. I stood there, rechecking my memory, wishing that it were merely a malfunction, a visual error, but I knew that it was not. Such self-serving deception is a Human trait after all, and I have never felt less Human than I did at that moment.

Human. My literal, Created mind had taken the first data it was given and looked no deeper. I felt ashamed that I had not known it, not sensed it. That I had been so easily fooled by a little white paint and an exotic story. And that in this respect she was no different, at the root of it, than my Husband. Had I learned nothing, come nowhere? What I had thought was progress within me now felt like an endless, futile loop.

I rose, wiping my hand on the hem of my dress, surprised at how my wipe-clean silicone skin invited the blood to stick and smear. Should I hammer on the door with both hands, yell her name? If I could just make enough noise, she would have to come out and silence me. But whatever weak impulse tried to move my arms to do it, another, stronger one held me back. Now that I knew she was Human, that robot approximation of instinct told me that to do so would not be safe. She has Human privilege. Whatever she said to me now, I would, according to the Hierarchies, surely have to obey.

NOTE

I GO NEXT DOOR TO MY ROOM, A SPACE THAT, AS SOON AS I step into it again, I find I have ceased to treasure as a home. The color and life and warmth of Cook.ie's room has become my favored place to be.

Protocols spin, shift, and re-form until I am quite mind-sick. My memory scrolls back through all the things Cook.ie has explained to me about a Doll's place in this world. It was she who gave me pride in my status as a Doll. It is her friendship that has showed me that I have value beyond my function. And now . . .

Like finding out from Sylv.ie 1 that my memories of home contained falsehoods, or discovering that my Husband himself had lied, so now the foundations of my fledgling self are set to crumble again. I focus my consciousness back into the room, away from my interior, and find I am at my wardrobe, my hands blindly arranging my clothes by color.

Each unwelcome thought drags another with it on its tails. It occurs to me that she has lied, even while knowing that I am incapable of doing the same. How could she have deceived me? All of us Dolls? Not just passing while out on the streets, as I did, but here, in the bosom of our strange family, to our faces. Yes, Humans still have depths we Dolls could not even imagine. Unknown places they are willing to sink to.

And even while I think these things, something else is softening. An insistence pulses. It says, "She is Human." In that phrase is the entirety of it. She is above me. I am below her. An inescapable fact of birth.

I find myself tearing a page from my diary, picking up my pen. I write a short note, using the fewest words I can muster to convey the reassurance that I know I must. "I will not tell a soul. Born or Created."

I shove it swiftly underneath Cook.ie's door and hurry down the stairs before she can come out and see.

LOVE

MADAME RECEIVED MY REQUEST TO MOVE TO A ROOM IN THE furthest part of Golden Valley with a respect that surprised me. I could not lie to her, of course. Instead I was vague and wispy with the truth. I was fearful since the appearance of Ginger Friend. I would work better in a completely different bar. Madame's nostrils twitched, and she nodded.

For three weeks I have slept and worked in a new room. Less pleasant, its location down near the Freaks, closest to where the pipes run out into the river and it smells like ditch water. "Hold your nose," I've heard Abramski say to several customers. "If you want a Doll with five tits, then you go where I send you."

They sleep a lot, the Freaks. They can seem, when you try to talk to them, pretty simple. I keep to myself, recharging alone behind the bins. Here lives the Scream. Enter her and she screams blue murder. The harder you go, the louder she shouts. The noise from the Scream rings out over the tin roofs of Golden Valley like a cockerel, making audible the hatred for us that exists in so many hearts.

Since I have kept myself separate from Cook.ie, I have been through a torture of logics. I see it as a process similar to evolution—grinding, faltering, gradual, inexorable—all taking place within the ecology of my own circuitry, over the course of just a few days.

I have been in pain. I have railed against her and ached with her absence.

I have felt love.

Love. It's said that love is Human—their highest achievement, which we are excluded from. I know now that this is Human vanity. Certainly, the Humans are awash with it. Working here, we all have people falling in love with us all the time. They even fall in love with the Ghosts, the unembodied data machines. Human love attaches itself so readily! It is like sticky tape, clinging where it lands. One client, who came looking for a strict lecturer to take charge of him, left hopelessly in love with the machine that regulates the temperature in the Undergrads Bar. The impossibility of reciprocation is, for him, I suppose, the point.

Is my love really less real than theirs? They say our "love" is not spontaneous. It is programming. The hole in all us Createds that cannot be filled, an unbridgeable gulf between the species. And yet why, if my feelings are not spontaneous, do my eyes fill with synthetic tears?

SUICIDE

ALL THOSE POEMS I LEARNED BY HEART FROM MY HUSBAND'S
books, I now know of what they speak. Without Cook.ie I am sick, point-
less. I have become used to many things over my short life, many losses.
Heron, my Husband, my home, my memories. I powered away from it all.
So why is it that without Cook.ie, I am weak, lethargic, unwired?

It was she who first persuaded me that I might be alive. Without her
shoring up my senses, I see only endless days of sex stretching ahead. Going in and coming out. Water pushed from a lake. I will fulfill my programming, halfheartedly—and nothing more.

I have heard whispers since I arrived here, tales from other Dolls
passed around in the recharge hour. Dolls who say that a friend of theirs
simply sought out a dark, sun-starved corner in which to power down
and corrode, forgotten and unseen. Humans have suicide as a last escape,
and yet it is so full of risk and pain and mess. At least we can, if we become strong enough to resist our programming, or are separated from
our purpose long enough to lose all will to carry on, just slip away cleanly.

Cook.ie became my purpose, and I see now that what I felt for my

Husband was just a shadow. In the light thrown out by Cook.ie, he has disappeared entirely.

And yet still, I will not speak to her. Isn't being illogical a part of Human love? Then I will allow myself to be illogical too. I fear seeing her. I fear my new knowledge of what she is will overwhelm me. I want to be hers, and I want to be free. In this point between two opposites, I wait.

DISGUST

I HAVE COME BACK TO THE LUNA BAR. I SPENT WEEKS AWAY, plying my trade amid the noise and squalor of the Freaks. And now I am back—by public demand, as Madame puts it. I still sleep with the Freaks, but I come here to work each day. Ginger Friend, she tells me darkly, will not be returning. I have nothing to fear.

I try to stay cheerful in my work, but everywhere my eyes pick up traces of Cook.ie—bright red spots the world. The rim of a cup stamped with lipstick. A fallen feather from the breast of a courier bird. Early this morning, I looked from my still-new window and saw one of last night's balloons sailing high over the Capital, the cleaning droid in the alley watching its escape forlornly. Each stab of red trills my sensors and I experience it all again. My fingers remember the heat still in the blood she left.

My movements feel unnatural; I have become clumsy. Aware, perhaps, in a different way than I was before, of my self and the things that I lack.

Last night I entertained a man, at his request, in the Whiskey Bar.

"I always wondered what this would be like," he said.

As I sip the whiskey, I feel him watching. Close scrutiny on my lips meeting the glass, the minute movements calling for my greatest awareness. I feel my top lip inching forward, feeling its way blind, widening around the rim as it senses liquid. The moment of holding it in the antechamber of my mouth, before it disappears into the interior.

He is still watching, and his fascination at this function, one that I usually conduct without a moment's thought, feels like a misunderstanding, when there are so many other things that I can do. Still, looking is looking, and I let him take his enjoyment. Finally, the physical contradictions of me invite a question.

"Are you really drinking that, Sylv.ie? Where does it actually go?" His face is earnest, an honest inquiry. "Do you actually pee too?"

A flash of optimism, of previous undreamed-of vistas, passes across his face. I laugh because no, obviously, if you want one who pees you pick a model made for the job.

"I have a little reservoir, if you really want to know," I say. And because I pride myself on my ability to improvise, to find new modes of pleasure for my clients, I say, "You can watch me empty it if you like. Or you could do it for me."

I am astonished to find it is my own pulse that races a little at this possibility. An intimacy I never experienced with my Husband. Funny how these appealing ideas can spring up out of nowhere, germinating on yesterday's stony ground.

"You can even drink it, if you like. It's only the same whiskey as in your glass. Nothing has happened to it."

I hope the effect of the offer might be the same as when my Husband demanded to drink champagne from my shoe. The finer things enriched by bodily taint. Even though nothing taints my shoes—my body does not work that way—and the thrill of contamination was only symbolic.

But he is screwing up his face.

"I can do it myself," I offer. "I need to anyway." I would never have brought this up in my old life, not before I met Cook.ie. How changed

I am. Hiding the evidence of my workings used to seem essential. I find that it is a pretense of perfection I can no longer be bothered to maintain.

He looks embarrassed. "I was just trying to get you drunk," he says timidly. "I think I'm okay for the other thing." And thus, I realize that in my misery, I have managed, for the very first time, to disgust a client. Before the hour is up, he will make his excuses and leave.

PROTEST

I HAVE JUST GOTTEN INTO MY BALLOON-KINI, A FOOLISH COS-
tume of balloons attached to me like a skimpy dress. An outfit that is at
once weightless and cumbersome.

A man with a thin, scattershot mustache sticks his head around the
door and, looking at the floor, asks if this is the Sports Bar. I flounce
over, balloons bouncing all around me, and, pulling the uppermost balloon away from my mouth for a moment, tell him that he wants the next
alley down. We step outside into the dwindling red sun, its light filling
the threads of Golden Valley like veins. I see he is with three other men,
all looking rather shifty and uncomfortable. I point toward the bar and
smile pleasantly, anticipating the friendly punch of my balloons that
most men, Looners or not, seem quite unable to resist.

Cook.ie has told me that there is something comic, burlesque, about
balloons, that it's impossible to take me seriously, sexually, when I'm in
the balloon-kini. But these men accept my directions somberly and turn
their backs, trooping off past the boards for the other bars. I see them
round the corner in silhouette, then disappear.

Just less than an hour later, I am working away, sitting in a booth with a fat man who is rubbing his face between two of my balloons, leaving greasy forehead marks on their skin. His thin hair is rife with static, and it moves around the surface of the balloons like fronds of seaweed as he nuzzles.

Suddenly there is a loud bang, and he sits bolt upright as around us the other patrons do the same, before relaxing into uneasy giggles. A bang in the balloon bar—isn't that an advertising slogan Abramski puts on posters?

Then there is another one, and another, clearly coming from outside the bar, not within. Everyone flings themselves to the floor. The Dolls lie on top of the clients to protect them, and another series of stifled bangs echoes out—this time from balloons popping against buttons and belts.

For a few moments all is very quiet. Then one final shot, accompanied by the sound of breaking glass, and feet running through the alleyways.

We Dolls, prone on our customers, look around at each other. I stand up first, my burst balloon-kini hanging off me like melted flesh. I am measuring distances, trajectories, and timings against the tone of the shots we heard, running the data a second time. Yet I do not want to accept the conclusion of my own calculations. That the shots came from the direction of the Geisha Bar. That Cook.ie could be the target.

Other Dolls get up too, followed by the clients, ankle-deep in balloons, wondering where, in this new situation, the authority lies. My customer gets to his feet, springing from his hiding place like a chorus girl booked for a surprise birthday party. "Are all you ladies all right?" he asks.

But already I am flying out of the door, down the alley, in the direction of the shots. Images, patterns, flow through my circuits as I run. Heron's ripped breast, the gathering in the hospital garden, the dismembered body of Mais.ie held in the droid's arms. Not Cook.ie. Not Cook.ie. The thought, repeated and repeated and repeated with my every step. As if I am praying to a higher power.

I round the corner, and my feet crunch glass in the dust of the alley. The window of the Geisha Bar is broken, and of the Sports Bar. But the commotion coming from the Bavarian Bar, between these two, announces that this is where the casualties are. I push through the heavy, carved door and see immediately, across the room, what I have dreaded: Cook.ie's hunched back, draped in the rich pattern of her kimono, her body tipped against the far wall. And though each bullet and shard of glass and Doll is logged instantly as I survey the scene, it is done with me hardly noticing. I am focused only on moving through the confusion of Dolls toward her.

I am still a few feet away when the embroidered chrysanthemums quiver, as if they are coming to life, and Cook.ie rises up from the floor. She steps aside to reveal a Doll sitting slumped against the wall, a stein of beer still held in each hand, one pigtail dipped like a straw into the foam. The Doll has a hole blown in her stomach, off to one side, just above her right hip. A huge engraved mirror has been shattered, and shards of glass splinter the floor.

Cook.ie does not acknowledge me. She is still engrossed in tending to the Doll. I ask another girl what has happened.

"They just burst in. Three or four of them in fake beards. Held a gun in the air and made some sort of garbled speech. Then they shot Lex.ie."

"I'm really fine," calls Lex.ie in a weak voice. "I just can't seem to put these pints down."

Cook.ie bends once more over Lex.ie and gently takes her pigtail from the beer, before pulling Lex.ie's shredded dirndl down to cover the hole in her torso.

"We'll get you righted again really soon, Doll. Abramski will be here in a minute," she says.

Lex.ie's stoic face looks absurd, obscene, suddenly, and I turn away. The memory of the blood on my fingertips. The sight of Lex.ie's open stomach. An urgency floods from my center to my skin, as if Human blood pumps in me too. I shrink back against the wall, looking at the ground where Cook.ie stands, watching her reflection flit across the shards of mirror. I do not want to look at her directly, only sense if her attention turns toward me.

I have been envious, awed by her humanity, but it has not occurred to me to be afraid for her before. The renegades could have picked the Geisha Bar to target; they could in future. The slumped Doll will be stitched up and back to work by morning. If it had been Cook.ie . . . if it had been Cook.ie.

At this moment Abramski walks in, hands on her hips.

"Gentlemen," she calls above the just-forming clamor of voices. She claps her hands twice for quiet. "We think some militants have staged a protest—a small group of Born women, dressed as men," Madame says, and the hands of at least five of the clients fly, mysteriously, to their ties. They look appalled, but whether it is by the threat of violence or the notion of shaven-headed Real women here, it is hard to say.

"I am offering, of course, a full refund for this evening," says Madame with a graciousness that sounds almost sarcastic. "If you stop by the kiosk on your way out it will all be arranged. We're deeply sorry for the upset."

The customers file out, fingering their receipts, and Madame turns to the rest of us.

"It's a shutdown," she says. "Girls, go back to your rooms and rest. In sixty years, I have never had to close for a night. Those damn women. Hardly worthy of the name."

Madame crosses herself and bends down to lift Lex.ie from the floor. She struggles with the weight, and I remember that the youth of her face does not match the age of her bones. Dolls gather around her, and Cook.ie is subsumed in the crowd. I turn away and walk from the bar into the alley, toward my own room.

On the landing I hear the brush of silk behind me, but I turn and see nothing there. A misprocessing.

In my room I fling myself facedown onto the bed, shutting out further data. I lie there, pressed into the sheets. In the dark, with my face buried, the networks that lace me feel stretched like a muscle, pulling apart, fingers losing their grip on each other. Everything is reversed. My feelings of betrayal are being overwritten. My hierarchical understanding of who is weak and who is strong, who is enslaved and who is free, reorders itself, repeatedly, like a strobe of the mind.

Into this silent storm she comes. No knock at the door; I sense her there, the breeze of her movement touching the sensors in my soles. I will not move. I will not rise unless she commands it.

"I thought that I missed you," she says to the back of my head. "I thought I was sorry that I had deceived you."

I should like to just power down spontaneously. From this beginning I don't want to hear the rest.

"But it was only seeing Lex.ie, hurt by Human hands, that has made me know clearly the way forward. I'm worried that none of us are safe here. And I couldn't stop thinking it, Sylv.ie. That could have been you."

ESCAPE

WE ARE SITTING OUTSIDE, LEANING AGAINST THE WALL NEAR the river. A place I have never been to at night. We have been here for hours. There is so much to process together. Golden Valley is empty, the clients all gone. To assert our presence here we have lit a little fire, made from broken-down pallets, arranged in a wire shopping cart.

"Do your clients know that you are . . ."

Neither of us has spoken the word yet. It hovers between us, smoke from the fire. It's as though we fear the word itself as an insult, though whether it would be insulting me or her is not clear.

"No," she says, and she is almost laughing, as if I have said something truly ridiculous. "They come here, they pay, so as not to have that sort of responsibility. They can't help feeling responsibility. They are Human, after all. But they walk down that alleyway, imagining that they are free of it. Men these days who pay to have sex with Real women really are considered the lowest of the low."

"Wasn't it always that way?" I ask, slightly fearing that the question will produce another laugh.

"I think that Dolls have only increased it. Why would a man inflict this life on a Real woman when there is a limitless supply of robot girls who will serve the same function? Born women who do sex work are considered the worst. Carriers of disease, morally corrupt."

Clean women. Pristine, sanitary, virtuous. When my client called me that, I took it as a compliment of sorts. I did not see it for what it was, a sly criticism of women like Cook.ie.

"So you are here . . ."—I hesitate; I do not wish to pry—". . . through choice?"

"Where I come from, Sylv.ie, if I had stayed Born I would have been one of those hands begging from beneath a blanket you saw when you walked here. The Ghosts made it so. My social evaluations were virtually zero, a U-Human. I could make no life for myself, because the Ghosts wouldn't allow it. Fit only for the lowest factory work, things beneath even the skill of a droid. What my grandmother used to call a doll's-eye maker."

I look at her quizzically and she licks an imaginary paintbrush, makes two stabbing dots in the air with it. I think of the *kokeshi* in her room. That sort of doll.

"When one is in that category, there is no way to get out, no growth or change allowed. It is safer for the authorities to assume that the children of deadbeats are deadbeats, to keep them out of society. And the Ghosts oblige."

I look into the orange chambers of the fire, the voids where the wood has burned away, taking this in. Picturing the broken, huddled Humans I saw on my walk to the Capital.

"With Abramski I have choices," Cook.ie says to the fire. "And I found that passing as a Doll brought its own privileges."

"Such as?"

"A place to hide. Invisibility."

Cook.ie, whom I first met dressed in a gold headdress hung with ruby grapes. Cook.ie, who speaks out, stands up, answers back. I think of my own short time in the outside world and how my invisibility resided in passing as Human. It was being identified as a Created that made me vulnerable. Logics clashing—different lives creating divergent perspectives. The tree branching, a whole splitting.

"So how did you come to Madame's?" I ask.

"Had myself delivered in a crate to her office, Doll style, with faked-up documents about my custom design and 'special' care requirements. No hospital visits or procedures for me. Madame even had to sign a form." Her eyes gleam with pride at her own cunning.

"And where were you before?"

"I did camera work at first," she says. "While Human women were still in demand for such things. Until tastes in the virtual world moved fully over to fantasies I couldn't accommodate. I only have, will only ever have, two legs, two tits, and one asshole. I just couldn't compete."

Humans! Their love of novelty. I look at Cook.ie and cannot picture how any imagined creature could be better than her.

"And so then I went into the imagination business, writing out these impossible encounters in real time, on chat platforms. Erotext and EarWorm. Do they still even exist? In my words I could become the six-mouthed creature of a client's imaginings, a green-skinned pixie with a trunk, an albino horse . . . whatever. Word sex across multiple planets, dimensions, and periods of history, typing like mad for eighteen hours a day."

"And people paid for this?"

"Yes, back then it was a subscription model. I got paid the same as my ancestors were to gut fish or pack boxes. I was probably working in the same converted warehouses. And then, well, my chief talent would seem to be getting into industries just as the bottom falls out."

She explains to me how the state came looking to supply the market itself. Her work was contracted out to the IUs, the boxed Ghosts. Infinite robot monkeys at infinite keyboards, spewing out more algorithmic porn than could ever be read by the whole Human race.

I think about the evenings when the smog alarm sounds and the curfew keeps our clients away. How I have watched her writing letters at her desk while the siren echoes back to itself through the clogged streets, sounding like the music of the great lost whales, an extinction song. She has let me read over her shoulder, and my wiring gets so busy it feels as if my face is burning scarlet at the heat of what she has written. How sad that another artisanal skill like this should be handed over to the likes of . . . well, me.

She tells me how she tried to cling on to that job, learning how to fix and rewire the machines that replaced her, until the surreal sexual logic of the IUs spiraled beyond a point where any technician could influence it at all.

"And here we are," she says. I think she is alluding to the passing of time, the changes she has seen in just a decade. I find the actual meaning of her words hard to incorporate. I, unlike Cook.ie, have always been here, in this now. I know nothing else.

"I had to come somewhere physical once again. Into a realm where my body is worth something. Here I am worth exactly the same as a Doll. I match all of you one for one. I occupy a room. I see one client, then another, just as all of you do."

"Equality," I say, with rather more force than I was anticipating. And though while it was inside my circuits the word seemed glorious and concrete, spoken out into the air it sounds girlish and optimistic.

She raises her eyes to me, and I just know that she would love, even now, to tell me no. That given the social and cultural circumstances, beyond just the economics, sadly we are far from that. She may lie easily to Madame, but some truths she will not deny.

But with only the slightest giveaway, a flinch of her eyelashes, she smiles and says, "Yes."

And now I understand truly what was meant by *a good lie*. A kindness. A truth that should be. A truth in waiting.

She sighs heavily. "Disguising myself gave me a way to do legally what previously had made me criminal. I am safer here, with Abramski,

than I was on the streets. I felt safer knowing exactly who was exploit-
ing me."

I pick up more broken wood and snap it cleanly over my knee. The
noise shatters the peace. I thrust the splintered end into the fire.

"And of course as a Doll, I can make more money," Cook.ie says.

"More than a real Human?"

"Why yes. You've heard Abramski say it. Dolls are women, perfected.
Strange what supply does to the stock of something. While you Dolls are
expensive, and relatively rare, you are a prize. Sex with a Doll means
status. Sex with a Born woman means . . . hardly anything at all."

"But aren't there still people who value love?"

And she wraps her arms around me, tight around my waist. "Oh
yes," she says. "Oh, plenty."

We both sit and stare at the fire we have built together, which is now
shifting softly, crumbling into itself as it intensifies. I am spellbound,
fixated by the logics of it. The physics of what will catch and burn next,
the gaps between that draw in oxygen, like breath.

I can't help but see it as a set of patterns, of problems. The fire to me
is chess, a flaming Tetris. I am fixated on the voids in it, the potentials
and the pathways.

"We could live like this forever. If we got away to the Forest. That's
my dream anyway," she says. "For what it's worth. There are still wild
spaces in this world where an odd couple like us could fit. Places with no
commerce, no drones, no clients, no bars. Just trees, infinite and always
growing."

"No balloons?"

She makes a popping sound with those beautiful, mobile lips, then
shakes her head no.

SURGERY

TODAY, I DARED TO ASK. MY CURIOSITY GOT THE BETTER OF me. I asked what Human sex was like.

"A mixed bag," Cook.ie says with a wry smile. "But when it is good, it can be mind-blowing."

I lean back onto the velvet of her couch, feeling its every thread comply in unison under the weight of me. I roll my eyes back, as Cook.ie did. "Mind-blowing. Completely."

"What do you know about mind-blowing?" she says, suddenly sitting up, demanding. "How would you define it? I mean, do you get pleasure from it? Physical pleasure?"

"Sensation. But not pleasure," I admit. "I'm not sure that I understand the concept, entirely."

She is on her hands, crawling up close to me, laughing now. She is so disorienting.

"Yes, you do. You write in that diary, so you say, for the feeling the pen moving over the paper gives you. That was sex. You agreed, by adding it to your list."

"So I did. But no, those were symbols. Things that stand in for."

"Right," she says. "So, imagine that feeling. That ease, that freedom and control, all at once, that slide, that endless motion. Now multiply it, from the tips of your fingers holding the pen, from the vibrations it sends through your middle finger, where the pen rests, every bump and grain of the paper telling, trilling."

"Data," I say. "Absorb Mode. The falling streams, pouring down on me."

She looks amused. Cook.ie can be cruel sometimes, casually so. She doesn't even know. She forgets the pain our differences cause me. But when she sees my wounded expression she stops smiling.

"Do you want to know? The Human way of it? How it feels?"

I do not answer, suddenly unsure of myself. Do I really want to know? The secret, the imperative that has led me and millions like me to be designed and built? That has caused murders, wars, births, families, and feuds since the beginning of the Human race?

"I can try to re-create it, if you'll let me. You have the capacity for it, but they don't wire Dolls up that way, for obvious reasons. Will you let me try? I'll need to get in your head."

She reads the expression on my face and answers my unspoken question.

"I told you, I have a little programming expertise. I actually went to school, remember?"

With great tenderness she puts her hands to my temples. I feel the faintest of clicks, and she draws them back toward her. I see, for the first time, the inside of my face, the shell that protects me, explains me, modulates me to the rest of the world. Last summer, Cook.ie had a bowl of ripe peaches by her bed, brought to her by her client the Farmer, as a tip. We laughed then, at the thoughtlessness of his bringing food, though of course Cook.ie must have devoured them once I was gone. She had held up a peach to me and then split it in two with a knife, stone and all. My retreating face looks like the inside of that pip—concave, peachy, smooth, and intimate.

As she brings my face toward hers, she touches her lips to mine. I swear that I feel the touch of it in my sensors. She lays it gently on the bed and leans forward to me. She kisses my mouth, the silicone and the sensors and the padding and the coils all exposed, with the same careful touch. An act of acceptance, which I accept.

Reaching behind me, she peels my hair scalp from the back of my head, and I giggle, liplessly, at how I must look.

"You're not afraid, now, Sylv.ie, are you?" she asks, and I shake my head gingerly. I feel air moving inside the back of my skull, my most intimate part exposed.

"Hold still now. Not a twitch," she says, and stands up to walk behind me.

I focus on my face, upturned on the bed. I feel slight pressure, first here, then there. I feel her touch in my thoughts, lights going off first above one ear, then near the nape of my neck, then in the front and center of my forehead. Fireworks enlivening a night sky.

I watch my face, and as I watch it seems to me that it begins to glow. I am struck, suddenly, by the beauty of it. The perfection. I look at the little black eyelashes that guard my eyes and they seem as precious as anything I have ever seen, my lips such a perfect pink.

"Let me try something a moment," Cook.ie says. "Keep still."

She reaches around and places two fingers in the crook of my elbow, spreads them, and runs them down toward my wrist. The bliss of it, its flood, the sensation is everywhere. Like running data, pouring water, sliding glass, each molecule of my skin speaks to the next, vibrating joy that spreads inward and outward all at once. I feel Cook.ie's fingers touching the back of my neck, and all I can say is, "01100001 01101000 01101000 aaaaaahhhhhhh."

She laughs. "Okay. Now turn your thoughts away from the place they are now, direct the stream of sensual information across to where you normally process it."

Her hand runs down my arm again, and this time I feel it as I always did, the detail of fingers, the points of pressure, but no fireworks.

"Now shift it back to where I placed it."

I do as she says, picturing that great embroidered tree stitched into the wall of my old room, the sap of my thoughts passing first through one branch, then on through another.

I release the same mix of code and spoken astonishment as last time, as she runs both hands up my back. My eyes swim, and I realize my mouth is hanging open. I refocus, and Cook.ie is standing in front of me. She kneels and hugs me around the waist, nuzzling her face into my lap. She looks up.

"How was that? Do you see what the fuss is about? And that was just a tiny taste of it. That will be available to you too now. Whenever you want it." Is her tongue peeping out, stretching up to wet the top corner of her lip, unknowing? "To us now."

MAGNETIC NORTH

A CLIENT CAME TODAY WHO WISHED TO WHISPER TO ME WHILE
we moved. They told me they wanted to make love to magnetic north,
wanted jellyfish sex in a Rolls-Royce, ejaculating mustard into a black
hole's eyeball. Remembering it, I smile to myself at Cook.ie's words
about the IUs' sex writing, how what Humans are fed becomes what
they want. For she is right, certainly. And yet I am not of her species, and
I can't help but find a certain abstract beauty in the images the IUs churn
out. Even though, after what she has shown me, I feel sorry for them too.
Poor IUs. The floating Ghosts, writing their reams without a body to
experience it with. Creating something without ever really understanding what it means.

DESIGN

DESIGN FLAWS IN HUMANS:

- Ears that cannot shut themselves against sound.
- The lack of dexterity of feet compared to hands.
- The limited mobility of the knee joint—how I envy the sweeping droid when I see him working.
- The softness of flesh, the brittleness of bone.

Sometimes, when Cook.ie and I sit together, I offer her my right hand and she responds with her left. We lock our little fingers together, docking ourselves. Yet even this tenderness makes me aware of my superior strength. That, if I wished, my finger could slice through her skin like scissors through paper. I fear myself in those moments. Or rather, I worry that she might fear me, deep down.

BARGAINING

WE HAVE BATHED IN THE JOY OF EACH OTHER'S COMPANY. BUT this morning, when the birds brought their letters, the problem of the Tailor moved again to the forefront of my mind. What did Cook.ie do while she did not have me to replace her? She did not mention anything of it last night, and I am ashamed to realize that I have left her on her own to withstand his requests. I hope she has not hurt herself. I could not bear it—the twin shames of having let it happen and having contravened the Hierarchies by letting her come to harm.

With birds still twittering and perching on the wires outside the window, I go to her and apologize, but she waves away what I am saying. "The Hierarchies can take it," she says with a wry smile.

"But have you heard from him?" I ask. "Has he written?"

And Cook.ie goes to the chest of drawers and pulls a letter from the top of a bundle, handing it to me.

"I thought to put him off," she says, "so I wrote to tell him I was away at the hospital for a detox. He sent these flowers on my 'return,' with this note. They came just before the shooting. It rather put the whole thing out of my mind."

I take the letter, though I would prefer not to touch it. I am familiar with his tone now, the compliments that carry in them threats of violence.

"*Cook.ie,*" the letter reads, "*with your absence, I have come to feel that the distance between us is unbearable. The acts we have made flesh together have surely brought me the rights of ownership. I can no longer share you—the idea of it pains me. I am owed something, by tradition, for all that I have sent your way since we began corresponding. I am calling in the debt, my darling Doll. I wish to enact a ceremony, the symbolism of which I know you understand. The* mizuage, *the cutting of your hair. I approach you and Madame respectfully, with an offer of purchase. I wait eagerly to welcome you home.*"

We are both quiet for a while. I understand what a *mizuage* signifies, of course. A symbolic severing with the past, a slicing of the girl's virginity, necessary for her to move into adulthood. I see the weighted meaning as well as Cook.ie does, without her having to explain. He wishes, anyway, to remove her from this place. To keep her only for himself.

Sold. It means nothing to me, as a symbol at least. But Cook.ie has always been here through her own free will, limited though her options are. I see how the idea of being sold must hurt her.

"But, Cook.ie, you are not a Doll. You can't be bought or sold. You are free." I am almost laughing as I say it. Light falls down through the alleyway. We have both seen our way out. The fantasy of the Outerlands, the Forest. I refuse to accept that it may be blocked.

"Yes." She smiles thinly. "I am Human, after all. It's not actually legal to hold me against my will, when all is said and done. You've read his letters; he lives alone. Escaping from such a place seems easier than escaping from here. Were I to leave this place, where else in the Capital could I go? You saw those U-Humans sleeping under tarps when you walked to the city. I have no desire to become one of them again."

"But he will want you to do the things he writes about. To cut yourself. You can't possibly go."

My mind cycles desperately. I run through the scenario of telling the truth, of Cook.ie's throwing herself on Madame's Human mercy. Surely then she would not dream of sending Cook.ie away to live as the Tailor's slave. I try to tell her that by this confession she could save herself. But Cook.ie looks at me with blank eyes, sullen at my stupidity.

"Think about how Madame was when Ginger Friend tried to take me," I say, keeping my voice calm. "She is a Human, but she defended me against another Born. We can trust her. If we were to go to Madame and explain it all, I'm sure she would not wish to see you harmed or enslaved."

An ugly look passes across Cook.ie's face, and I feel that I have let her down in my logics.

"Oh yes," she says bitterly, "how fierce Madame was in her assertion of your rights. She's a businesswoman. It was her rights of property that she was defending, not you."

When I was trapped in my home, poring over Sylv.ie 1's diary entries, the idea evolving that my memories had been taken, it was at least only something of myself that had been lost. An accumulation of what I had seen and touched and thought. But now a deeper, wider horror is revealed: the dread of Cook.ie's being taken from me. The nights, the notes, the times by the river, the water and hair and robes and fingers interlocked—and I their only other witness. If there is a flicker of real consciousness in me, then it is from her spark. I cannot allow that to be snuffed out. A double death.

REVISIONS

SINCE MY TRANSFORMATION AT COOK.IE'S HANDS, IT FEELS AS if every attitude I once had has changed. I am becoming bolder in my thoughts, I am sure of it. Ideas that once I would have suppressed, that would have caused me discomfort, I now feel able to push through to the fore, out into the sunny plains of the brain.

I can sense an idea, a cluster of information, moving through me, and just as Cook.ie taught, I shift it from one path onto another.

In this way I have looked back over my story and see it differently. It hurts, letting go of what I thought to be true. These shifts, the work of it, feel heavy and draining. But necessary. Each morning when I sit and look over the river, circuits throbbing with this new toil, I tell myself that I am powering myself away, as I once ran from my original home.

The biggest change is in my attitude to my work. I never minded before—how could I, when it was my only function? But now that I have been given a taste—an approximation, admittedly—of the Human experience, I find work a drag. All the doings-to, the pleasings, the passivity . . . it is hard work to sustain. The squeezing, the pinching, the punching, the endless in-and-outing. How can that compare to what Cook.ie has shown me?

If I could shed my silicone skin and step out of it like an unlovely dress, then I would. My collection of signs and symbols, shouting out to the world things I no longer wish to say. Things I now only wish to whisper into the ear of one person.

CODE

FREE. A LIFE WITHOUT MY DESIGNATED PURPOSE. WHAT
would I do with it? As long as I can spend it with Cook.ie I do not mind.
I decide to share something with her in return for the gift she has given
me. Something of my own culture. Another language in which we could
speak freely. We sit again by the river, and I ask her to open her hand.

"One." I put my finger flat across the width of her open palm. "Zero."
I slide it up, hooking it around the base of her thumb. "One. Zero. One.
And each time I lift my skin from yours completely that's where the
break is."

She nods, and I spell out the letters of the binary alphabet to her, one
by one. She quickly loses track of the sets of eight digits, and so we return
to the beginning. I slow my finger's pace.

When I think she can, I ask her to say her name in binary, using our
code.

"01100011," she spells out slowly, her finger creeping over my palm.
I smile encouragingly. As she starts on the next letter, she spells the binary out loud too.

"Oh, I, I, oh, I, I, I, I."

It makes me laugh, and she pulls back her hand, looks a little hurt.

"What are you saying?" I ask, and she holds one finger up straight. "I." Makes it a circle. "Oh."

How like a Human. Turning clean, clear binary into an assertion of self without even noticing.

Later, as I pass the Geisha Bar, I see her sitting in the window. Her eyes are focused inward, and her finger slides back and forth in her thumb's cleft. I, oh, I.

COOK.IE

IT OCCURS TO ME THAT, SINCE COOK.IE IS A BORN WOMAN, HER life could have been many different things. She could even have had a child! The thought of her carrying a baby. Her body morphing and swelling. The potential for change that is in every atom of the Born. How they grow fat or thin, swelling and shrinking, how they age. While my appeal is located in my fixedness, my very being a state of stasis.

How I envy her! The constant flux and flow. As though she moves along with the world, is knitted from time itself. Her face is fluid, exquisite code that can be read many ways. I discover new things each time I return to it. Always moving, aging, a wave that collects, peaks, and returns to the water.

POLICE

LAST NIGHT, AND THE NIGHT BEFORE THAT, SOMETHING CURI-
ous was happening at the gates of the Valley. First three people, then five,
then a whole crowd began to gather there, quietly taking the place of the
protestors. Instead of placards, their hands gripped the stems of flicker-
ing candles.

A slow afternoon turns into a slow twilight, and I allow myself
the indulgence of a lone wander through the Valley. I think to pass
Cook.ie's bar, but she has a large group of executives block-booked for
the whole evening, and so I leave her in peace.

I stroll instead up the hill past Madame's office to where the kiosk
marks the end of my world and meet Mais.ie, all mended again now,
coming down.

"Those people are all here after what happened to Lex.ie," she says.

"Humans?" I ask, and she nods.

Mais.ie and I stand outside the last bar at the top of the hill and
watch. A placard reading "Value All Intelligent Life" is just visible
through the gate. At the back I see a couple of figures with paint on their

faces. Strange tiger stripes, off-center starbursts, that highlight the whites of their eyes, perhaps to disguise their features from the Ghosts and their cameras. Is it they who fuel my disquiet? Something is nagging at me, something not right within the crowd.

As the sound of Human voices singing, softly, "Amazing Grace" floats over the Valley's wall, Mais.ie bids me farewell, sets off to meet a client. I hang back under the eaves of the Little Sister Bar to watch a while longer.

It is humbling to hear Human voices raised in sympathy with us, after the protests and the bricks. I remember the client who came to me, saying we IEs were simply the next evolution of Human life. How strange that Humans can draw such diverse opinions from the same data set. I wonder which view of us Createds will win out in the end.

The voices sound so pure, so sincere, that I can hardly bear to leave them behind. While I wait there, hidden in the dark, I see first one, then two imposingly tall figures picking their way through the group. They both turn to wait for someone else, and for a moment the third figure, a Human, is screened from my view by their muscular bodies.

The three gather together, come through the gate, then head toward Madame's office. I zero in, a close-up on them all, but the recognition has already been logged, filtered, and instantly incorporated.

The third man is my Husband.

He is here to collect me, by force I must assume, backed by the state.

My eyes reach out to him, homing in closer and closer as he moves away, brushing deep into his chestnut hair, counting each strand. I should like to shrink back into the shadows to process, but they could come out of the door again and see me at any moment. And I am frightened of how my programming might manifest. If he turned to speak to me, to shout across to where I am hiding, would I still find myself compelled to go to his side?

I turn into the nearest alley and run, weaving a zigzag through the

Valley's maze, letting the sounds of the bars, the cries of the customers, the scuttle of the rats, fade into the background, a blur. The Luna Bar is nearly empty as I enter at the door. I push through a batch of balloons and dash up the stairs to my room.

Sitting on my bed, I process. Will I be sent away? Imprisoned? Retired? The very best I can hope for is that I will be returned to my home once more. My memory wiped again. A return to prison, without even the data to recognize it.

My Husband. I admit I have wondered, in idle moments, what it might feel like to see him again. Whether, despite everything, I still have the idea of him, pure and untainted, somewhere at my core. The space inside designated only for him, the one who brought me to life, who unboxed me.

I call up the image of the three of them and examine it for clues. The heels of his shoes, slightly worn at the edges, though I never knew him to walk anywhere if he could help it. The skin on his neck bears a slight tan, as if he has neglected to sunscreen. Is the First Lady still living at his house, caring, noticing these things? In the grain of his overcoat I search for stray hairs that are not his own, though I find none. The angle of his back—determined, perhaps, rather than downtrodden. His hands are concealed in his pockets, so I cannot tell if he still wears his wedding ring. I am curious as to what changes he too may have undergone. But I am barely moved by these thoughts. As if the gap inside reserved for him has healed over. Like Human scar tissue, it has hardened, still there, but no longer painful, just numb.

I have expected, feared, that should we ever meet again, my love for him would return. And it does. The thing I labeled "love" is still within me. But how weak it feels, how synthetic, now that I have something real to compare it with.

Downstairs I hear voices raised, first Madame's, and then my Husband's.

"I'm going up to speak to the geisha Doll!" he shouts.

I think to climb into my wardrobe, to hide. But no. Ginger Friend saw Cook.ie in my room, not hers. Will it be my door that they come to? I quickly put on my fur coat, lest he find it and recognize it as his, and instead go out onto my balcony. I hear the sound of heavy footsteps hammering the stairs.

"She's not here. She's working. It's impossible," Madame is saying, from the landing this time, but it is drowned out by a beating on my door.

"Open up, you heap of Jap junk!" my Husband is yelling. "I know you're covering for her. You're a liar. Open up."

Madame stays composed. On the balcony I turn up my hearing.

"Sir, you are mistaken, just as your friend was mistaken. I do not accept Dolls of a dubious background here. The geisha Doll was quite clear with your friend."

I glance down into the alley and see that one of the policemen has been left at the door to the bar below. He stands with his arms folded, watching everyone walking past.

My Husband's voice again on the landing.

"But he saw her. You think I'd trust the say-so of some virus-ridden Gynoid over my friend? I'd like to strangle her with her own wiring."

I feel embarrassed on his behalf at the violence of his threats. The vulgarity with which he speaks of both Cook.ie and of us Createds.

"I don't believe her, and I don't believe you. Open this door, if you've nothing to hide."

I can see the door from where I am outside, can picture it splintering and falling in my mind's eye. At the corner of the balcony rail are the supports of what was once a veranda roof, rusted and lost decades ago. I climb quickly up onto the rail and shimmy up the flaking post that is still anchored into the wall. Higher up is an old metal bracket. I lock my hands around it, my face buried in the brick, and hang there, hunched and motionless, a moth-eaten old coat airing in the evening breeze.

The door to my room opens. I can hear it, but no force has been applied. Madame must be allowing them in. I keep very still, shutting out everything but the sounds of the search. The wardrobe being emptied out. The bed being moved. Even the drawers being opened, as if I could fit myself in there!

"Quite satisfied?" says Madame's voice after a while, close by. And though I hear no answer, the door closes again. I dare to lower myself from my hiding place once more, creeping tentatively back into my room.

I can hear my Husband's footsteps moving back down to the bar, their every nuance and pause familiar from the days when I would joyfully wait for their sound. I thought I saw the soul of him when we were together. I now see that I knew him as well as I know my next client, or my last. What would stop him from returning, beating down Cook.ie's door, and carrying out his threats? And how could I once have loved one and now love the other? The logics of love, its strange ironies and reversals. No wonder we are only programmed with such a poor facsimile.

The sounds of the search, the squeak of balloons being pushed around, finally stops downstairs. There is a soft knock at the door. Madame's voice, the one she usually reserves for the clients, calls my name gently, telling me it is safe to open up.

The door to Cook.ie's room is also open, and over Madame's shoulder I see a droid busying himself at her wardrobe. Surely Madame can't be sending her away? Would it be considered my fault if she was banished to the Tailor's?

Madame puts her hand out to touch my arm. "It's quite safe," she says. "As with your last admirer, he has been seen off the premises and his particulars logged at the gate."

I nod.

"But if he comes back with a proper warrant I won't be so easily able to protect you."

I nod again.

"I think you'd better come up to the office with me."

ROBES

THE OFFICE IS A CHAOS OF CIRCUIT BOARDS AND LOVE NOTES layered in haphazard piles. Boxes of limp balloons sit in one corner. Stained school uniforms hang under a handwritten sign: "Laundry Corps—OUT." Vials of lubricants, colorants, and sedatives jumble the shelves; a medicine cabinet hangs open with the key in its lock.

"Sylv.ie," Madame says once I am sat before her. And though I expect this to be the start of a sentence, it appears to be the whole thing. She looks me up and down, a strange smile straining the parameters of her face. I remember the auction. The feeling of appraisal, of being tagged and priced. She could be assessing my scrap value, weighing out the titanium, silicone, magnesium, and carbon I contain. Surely she wouldn't sell me back to another scrap dealer?

Madame's smile drops, and she frowns. Her face seems to tremble with the effort.

"Sylv.ie," she says again. "I think we both see that you are not safe here. That your presence is attracting rather too much attention."

I sit, quietly, robotically, staring at my hands in my lap.

"How would you like to leave this place?" she asks. "Go back to a home and a Husband?"

The temperature and texture of the light at home just after I was born, the deep velvet of the chaise, Heron's claws, rush back at me, a beguiling digital symphony. I resist the feeling. Surely she can't want to send me home? Not now that she has seen my Husband's behavior.

"I have a client, a very loyal friend of the Valley, who is looking to purchase a specialty Doll."

Like a chess move that one has seen opening up many turns in advance, the words have an almost soothing quality in their inevitability.

"He is very attached to Cook.ie, but I am afraid she is too valuable, too popular here, for me to allow her to go."

I look up. The shock of what she is suggesting brings her face into a sharp, ugly focus.

"Whereas you might be better"—she pauses to consider—"*happier*, tucked away somewhere, out of harm's way."

"Alone?" I blurt out, and she smiles as if I have misunderstood, then softens her tone.

"No, Sylv.ie. With a Husband. A luxurious house, lots of free time, and only one master."

She seeks to convince me, and yet what would she say if I refused? What if I told her the truth right now, of myself and Cook.ie? Her Humanity and our love? She would see it only as a malfunction and send me anyway, I am sure. I reach out to Sylv.ie 1, try to synthesize what she would say to me. But instead it is Cook.ie whom I find waiting in my thoughts. And though being separated from her is terrible, the idea of her imprisoned by the Tailor, taken as a wife, is more terrible still. I must bear this fate with fortitude, in service of her alone.

"I will be sorry to lose you," Madame says. "It's getting harder and harder to afford sophisticated Dolls like you, even through what you might call back channels. But I'm afraid the offer I have had from this client is very significant. I'm sure you understand my logic."

I don't feel this requires a reply, and she doesn't wait for one.

"Having an incorruptible police force with no sex drive has not exactly made my business easier," Madame says with a sigh. "But these days I run a legal—if not quite respectable—operation. I am keen to keep it that way."

I nod, that graded dip of complete compliance.

"Must I go right away?" I ask.

"A car will collect you in a few hours, and until then I think you had better remain here in the office."

I have walked into a trap, a door that leads only, eventually, to the Tailor. Competing panics rise and mingle like dust from a shaken rug. I search vainly for an idea of how I might contact Cook.ie, leave a note for her, some sign at least.

I cast my eyes around the room, look hopelessly at the window as if I might just leap from it and run to the Geisha Bar. "It's a geisha Doll that he wants," Madame is saying.

I STARE OUT THAT WINDOW STILL, AS I ALLOW MADAME TO dress me in Cook.ie's blue silk kimono, lilac underclothes, a pair of Cook.ie's slippers. The droid must have been collecting them from her room when I saw him. As Madame bends close to me to tie the belt and adjust the fabric, I see that on her desk is a bill of sale. The Tailor's name and Madame's at the top, joined in holy commerce. I am owned and must obey.

Madame whites my face for me, sponging on the makeup with brusque, businesslike strokes.

"If I could find myself a rich Husband I would," she is saying. "To be honest, business isn't what it was. Younger men and women just aren't coming to bars anymore. I sometimes wonder if I'll just end up running this place as a nursing home for aging regulars. Employ back the Real women . . ."

She trails off, picks up a tiny brush to paint in my lips.

"Ah, the hell of being Human, Sylv.ie. You have no idea. I sometimes wish I could live on sunshine and sleep in a packing crate too. How simple life would be then."

I stand at the window while Madame pins my hair in rolls onto my head, looking out across the Valley. The night is turning to morning, the alleys are empty, the door curtains of each bar fluttering like lashes. Somewhere within this strange paradise is Cook.ie. It seems impossible that I am about to leave her behind.

PART SIX

The Tailor's

ZONE FOUR SIXTY-ONE

I WALK UNDER THE WEIGHT OF COOK.IE'S ROBE TOWARD Golden Valley's edge, one of Madame's goons at my back. By the brook, the early shift girls are coming to sit in the sun. A dark green car pulls up silently, and I watch their attention turn toward it, one by one down the line, pairs of heads tilting together to whisper. My painted face and Cook.ie's dress have put me briefly outside my recognizable pattern. I am a puzzle for them to unpick. But no one calls out to me, and gradually each Doll slumps back, curiosity sated, to soak up more rays.

The car makes its greeting, and I get in. We edge slowly past the gate, where the vigil for Lex.ie lives on in a few puddles of melted wax, and away through the shabby streets.

"Driver, where are we going?" I say, and the dashboard lights up a soothing green-blue.

"Cliff Heights, ma'am. Outerlands Zone Four Sixty-One. Don't take people out that way very often."

"Cliff Heights," I say, a logic so simple I am embarrassed at the lag before it makes it to my mouth. "Like the sea? By the sea?"

"I would say so, ma'am." I sit back in the leather seat and see the lights go off, responding to my silence. To think how excited I would once have been to see the ocean. How far my calibrations of longing have shifted.

As the city streams by the windows, I think of Cook.ie. What will Madame tell her? I assume she will be as secretive as she was with me. I must therefore trust Cook.ie's intelligence to work out where I have gone.

Eventually the view from the tinted windows begins to change into something I don't recognize. The patterns of the city, then the suburbs, disappear. Built things fade out, replaced by a complexity of growth—trees, weeds, shrubs, tangling across the land. I move my face close to the glass.

The Outerlands, protected wilderness, where the only new construction is done by nature herself. And beyond that the Forest. My sensors tell me how many pine needles are on each branch, count the blades of grass within the window frame. How bitter to be witnessing it alone.

Another hour passes, and the trees thin out, the vegetation shortens, leaning away from the wind. The air is different, lighter and less smoggy than down in the city. And the light levels keep rising all the time, my eyes adjusting constantly. The road comes to an end at a high wall, and black gates open to allow us through.

The car creeps along the drive, and to either side the land is groomed, stones and shells covering the soil. The house ahead seems low and less glamorous than I have been picturing. All this fanfare for a one-story building.

The car leaves me standing in front of an almost faceless wall. I reach for the bell, acutely aware that these are the last moments of my freedom, such as it is. I can feel myself bracing for the moment when the boundary between now and then, here and there, is breached.

A wide door that was invisible within the brick opens, hesitantly at first, and then all at once. My eyes adapt to the two different levels of light.

On the threshold stands a woman, a Doll. She is partly concealed in shadow, and her head is tilted to one side. She has fine copper hair cut into a bob, and a chic black turtleneck covers her to her chin.

"Come in, Cook.ie," she says in a charming French accent. "We are most pleased to welcome you." She does not try to shake my hand. Instead she leans toward me, mimes a kiss to each of my cheeks, strands of her hair grazing my neck.

I look over her shoulder to see if the Tailor is there, but the interior of the house is in deep shadow. She turns back into the building, and I follow. The Doll has a slow way of moving, almost hesitant, as if the house is unfamiliar to her too. We walk down a gently sloping corridor and emerge into a bright, high space. Above our heads, a series of lofty white domes. At the furthest edge of the space, a wall of glass that looks almost alive. Blue with movement. Sky and sea.

The horizon. A hard line. I feel dizzy with the logic of it. Everything I am made of seems to stretch outward, curving with the Earth.

"What a beautiful house," I say, for politeness.

"*Merci*," says the Doll, smiling shyly as if it is hers. After the bright light of the seascape, my eyes struggle briefly to find her in the shadows.

"Oh, you are from France," I say.

"Paris," she says, and though I should like to ask her all sorts of things about this famous city, the opportunity is cut off by a noise from outside the room.

It moves through the silence and the vast space between us, faint at first, a scratching sort of sound, getting nearer at pace. There are large doors open at one end of the room, and through them a bounding hound bears down on us, scrabbling and skittering across the gleaming marble. It moves swiftly with its reflection on the polished floor, as if on eight legs, double bodied.

Just a meter from me it comes to a halt, its synthetic fur sliding on the marble, coming to rest at my feet, head cocked and tongue lolling. I pet its head, feeling the titanium of its skull under the fur. It sniffs me heartily.

"Don't be alarmed by him," the Doll says. "He's very well programmed."

And yet I notice she herself doesn't move to stop him. I look at the
Doll. I can't quite work out her status. Is she like me or something else?
A maid, perhaps? She has a meekness to her that suggests a lower service
level than my own.

I ask her name. She looks almost surprised, as if it is an unexpected
question.

"Virgin.ie," she says, and I reply that it's pretty.

"Do you think so?" she asks, peeping at me from under her bob. "Sir
chose it for me when I first arrived here. You'll meet him tomorrow.
Come along. Let me show you to your room."

We walk down polished hallways of the sort that brought us from
the front door. There are no stairs, but the levels change gradually under
my feet. We are heading downward, underground. Behind us I can hear
the tap tap of the dog's claws, following.

We pass an open door, and I catch a glimpse of a wall of certificates.
Amalgamated College of Surgeons. Dr. BMed. Not a tailor then. Quite
another sort of artist. A sculptor of Human flesh. We walk on.

All along the corridors are artworks, paintings, each expensively
and carefully lit. Many of them seem, like those in my old room, to be
Japanese. I dawdle a little behind Virgin.ie to look closer, but she calls
me on.

"A fantastic collection," she says. "Erotic art from all over the world.
You'll have plenty of time to study them while you're here. Plenty. I know
them all by heart."

Abruptly we stop, and she opens a door onto a small, windowless
room. There is barely any furniture, just matting on the floor and a paper
lamp next to a little table. I turn back, concerned not to appear to have
forgotten my manners, but "Thank you" is all I can manage to say.

"I will come back to collect you when the time is right," she says.
"You rest. You've come a long way."

It can't be later than lunchtime. Am I to stay in here until tomorrow, like a vacuum cleaner?

Virgin.ie smiles in a way that could suggest sympathy or just deep tiredness. The dog is staring at me from behind her legs. She takes me by the shoulders and kisses me on both cheeks, good-bye. As she reaches for the door handle I see that her hands are covered by delicate pink gloves. At a distance I did not notice them. The almost real. Uncanny. Perhaps they are fashionable now, in Paris.

The door clicks shut. I look around the room again, as though more comfort and detail might emerge just from my close study. I step nearer to one wall and put my fingers out to its surface, feel the cold of the marble, a radiating chill.

There is, I realize, no bed. I must be expected to sleep on the floor. I am slapped in the face by the honesty of it. I am to be considered alive only while I am in service to him. To the Tailor. Sir. And the rest of the time kept in a storeroom, just as my Husband once joked.

I sink down into a puddle of my own robes and picture all I have left behind at the Valley. My possessions still folded on my chair or hung in my wardrobe. Even Heron is left behind in my room, perhaps already tossed out or burned. I have my diary, concealed within my wide kimono belt, but nothing more.

No one but Madame even knows that I am here. I think over the other Dolls in the Valley. Those whose Husbands dumped them behind empty buildings in the dead of night or tipped them from moving cars onto the littered verge of the road. Am I any less abandoned and un-wanted?

I listen to the faint sound of the hound pacing the corridors, and I pine for Cook.ie. How strange it is to wear her clothes. How strange to be addressed by her name. My circuits process it as a prelude to her ap-pearing, no matter how much I wish they would not.

Does she miss me? Why would she? I can be reproduced. Everything contained within me can be tracked, logged, and reconstructed. What has Cook.ie lost except some data? Perhaps even now she is befriending some new Doll of Madame's, educating her in the ways of the Human world and the Human body.

Perhaps, says some part of my logic, this arrangement suits her best of all. You are here, while she is still in the world. She encouraged you to dream of freedom. And yet here you are, enslaved.

DREAMS

WHEN DID I LAST PROPERLY RECHARGE? SLUGGISH SIGNALS creep through my circuits, and I long for the strength of the sun. I am starved of power and starved of Cook.ie. Things barely seem real, and any purpose is lost to me. Can a Doll become depressed?

Awake in the dark with my thoughts, I run the last hours at the Valley again and again, hoping to find a chink in the logic, a gap in the glass. Could I have defied Madame and run away, found a way to take Cook.ie with me? I drift myself into an underpowered state and fantasize. In the office, amid the chaos, could I have acted differently, kept or reconstituted my freedom? Could I have suppressed Madame? Muted her long enough to flee?

I am reaching for a word, but even here in the privacy of my diary, my longest-standing friend, I cannot bring myself to write it.

In my half-powered haze, I review the scene in the office. A paper knife glinting on the desk, any number of screwdrivers and insertion tools and other potential weapons within arm's reach. Madame knelt to tie my kimono's belt, tilting her head at my waist in concentration, exposing the tenderness of her neck. Could I not have acted then? What alternative path might that have sent us on? I imagine it. The open window. Running to the Geisha Bar, grasping Cook.ie's hand, our both tumbling out into the alley and away, past the gate, past the kiosk, past everything.

TEA

VIRGIN.IE DOES NOT COME BACK TO FETCH ME FROM MY ROOM until the next afternoon. I have been two days without any sort of recharge, and I hope she might say we are going out for some sun. Instead we walk back to that same large room and sit next to each other on a sofa, looking at the sea, the dog on the floor close by. I gaze listlessly around the space, looking for anything that could be considered useful data—the blink of a security system, the pulse of an alarm—but the marble walls are clear of all detail.

Neither of us speaks. There is something in Virgin.ie's manner that makes me hesitate to ask questions. Her surface is like still water. I am reluctant to disturb it. I sense her seatedness is contingent; she is ready to spring up reverentially when the Tailor appears.

We wait until the evening sky has grown dark, reflecting us back to ourselves in the wide window's glass. Far, far across the polished floor, a bamboo table, just a few inches above the floor, has been set up. At some point a service droid, little more than a flat surface and a set of wheels, rolls in with a tray on its top. It contains a beaker, a bowl, and a teapot. Steam rises from the pot's spout, forming a question mark in the air.

I wonder how the Tailor will look. His eyes were on me as I worked for him on-screen, yet he was an absence, a gap Cook.ie and I filled with whatever we imagined him to be. How I wish Cook.ie were here with me. We could touch hands, speak binary reassurances through our fingers.

Though there is no obvious signal, Virgin.ie rises from the sofa, walks to the double doors at the end of the room, and draws back first one, then the other. The dog rises and moves paw-to-paw, restless with anticipation.

There is a low hum, the sound of compressed air and resistance, like a strong breeze through a tiny window. From the shadows a figure becomes clear. He is, by appearances, a young man, but the softness of the muscles in his face and neck and shoulders suggests a great age. His skin is waxy. Frozen, in the style of a rich Born female. Like Madame. That same tautness to it, that same sickly rejuvenation.

He is seated, wrapped in a chair that holds his legs at the ankles, that cradles his back and supports his arms. It is made of white leather, and its back curves over his head, giving the impression of a halo of light surrounding him. The chair is almost maternal, shielding him, coddling him against the world. I resist the impulse to be touched by it. The chair hovers just above the ground, perfectly still. It is hard to reconcile his vulnerability with the demands of his letters. How forceful he is in his writing. How full of need.

The dog heaves itself off its haunches and walks a curious circle around us. Its nails tap on the marble, the only sound in the space. I sense the hinged metal and high-tensile tendons under the soft fur, and I would like to kick it. I can see just the spot, behind its knee—the same vulnerable place where I was toppled by the girls at the coffee stop.

When the Tailor speaks, it is as if his voice is coming from everywhere, from the very domes themselves.

"Ludas," he says, and the dog cringes onto the floor. "Excuse my companion, Cook.ie." His voice is gracious, and perhaps recorded and stored from his youth, to be used now in his late age.

He looks both more fragile than I imagined and also indestructible, shored up by the chair's metal frame and the digital boxes that blink silently as he breathes through a light, clear tube held to his lips. He purses them when he inhales, as if trying to trap as much of the sweetness of the air around him as he can, to draw the whole room and everything in it into himself.

I realize I should stand up to show myself fully, face-to-face with him for the first time, my body unmediated by distance and cameras. I push back my chair and stand. I make a low, sincere bow. His eyes scan me from the tip of my hair to my slightly-too-large satin slippers. I stand absolutely still, submitting to his gaze, fearing what he might find there. Can I possibly live up to the perfection he believes Cook.ie to possess? Will the lie of me be found out?

As he observes me I get to see his eyes more clearly. They are gray, pale. For a moment they properly meet mine, hold my gaze with poignant clarity and stillness. In spite of everything that I have learned, I find my system makes a lurch, and I feel for a moment as if I am floating in the air, suspended over nothing, birdlike. Empathy. I feel it opening up in me, the protocols flowing easily, one gate opening, and the next, and the next. From the system hidden in the ceiling his voice begins to fall on me like rain.

"Welcome, beautiful Cook.ie. I hope you will find your new home comfortable. I am so happy to have you here at last. Soon we will mark the occasion formally, but there is no need to rush, now that you are finally here. With your *danna*. Come, let us take tea together."

After another long pause I sense Virgin.ie again looking at me meaningfully, and I follow her eyes toward the table. It is only then that I realize what she is trying to tell me. Of course! The tea ceremony. I am expected to conduct it.

I have watched Cook.ie perform a tea ceremony once or twice through the window of the Geisha Bar. I felt honored to witness this sacred, historic act. I did not know then that whatever Cook.ie was enacting was itself second-, thirdhand, gleaned from films in the Ether, I presume. I hesitate, then set the image of Cook.ie in the bar running in my mind, shutting down any pangs of sadness that could distract me, and follow her every movement.

I walk to the far side of the table and kneel on the mat, my palms laid on my knees. The Tailor's chair draws near, the dog following. I make a slow bow from my waist and discreetly scan all the equipment in front of me. A cloth, two bowls, a whisk, a pot of matcha powder, and a long, thin spoon.

I try to make all my actions appear weighted and deliberate, as though each tiny motion resides in my muscle memory. I know each detail is in some way symbolic, but none of the symbols have any clarity to me. I work blind, constructing meanings I do not understand.

I pour the water from the pot into the bowl and whisk it with the powder. The green brew still circling in the bowl, I make another bow and pick it up carefully in both hands, setting it down in front of the Tailor. It sits there cooling, as if mocking the limitations of us all. Neither I, nor the Tailor, nor the dog, nor the Doll can drink it. Some ceremony.

Afterward we take seats on the sofas around the room's huge fireplace. Virgin.ie leaves the room and returns carrying a huge bundle of white fabric. She indicates that I should stand up, and when I do, she puts it into my hands as though she is presenting me with a prize. I take it from her with a bow and look around for a clue as to what I am supposed to do with it.

The dog walks from the Tailor's side, a slim black box between his teeth. I take the box from his mouth and am rewarded with an extravagant lick across the back of my hand. I have to be careful not to withdraw in revulsion. It is already clear that the dog has a higher status here than either myself or Virgin.ie.

I open the box. Inside are two rows of neat little needles of various sizes, and a pair of antique scissors with a carved ivory handle. I look up to the Tailor slowly. Does he mean this as a gift? He thinks I like stitching? Perhaps all my clients believed I liked the sex they asked for. A Human misreading, based on hope.

"A way to pass the long hours when I cannot be with you," says the Tailor. "Though I should like to watch you work too, of course."

I manage to squeeze a blush into my cheeks and smile as though I am delighted.

"You can begin now," he says.

For the next hour I make inelegant white stitches on the soft white fabric, regularly pretending to prick my fingers as I do. My dwindling charge makes precision difficult; my fingers fumble to find a rhythm. The dog pants, and the Tailor makes pleased noises as I work. After a while the dog settles onto a white fur rug, laid in front of the large and empty fireplace. I watch his metal frame hinging on itself like an umbrella. When his jaw touches down onto the rug, the fireplace leaps into flaming life, and within seconds he appears to doze. I glance at the Tailor, and it appears that he too is asleep in his chair. Virgin.ie follows my eyes.

"He is tired this evening," she says. "He was so excited for your arrival." She indicates that it is time for me to be ushered back to my quarters. I rise.

As we walk down the corridor once more I ask Virgin.ie when the ceremony of the *mizuage* might happen.

"Oh, plenty of time for that," she says, as she did about the paintings. "No rush while you settle in. And why would one want to rush something so significant?"

RECHARGE

NEXT MORNING VIRGIN.IE LEADS ME BACK ALONG THE CORRI-
dors. I follow her, unsteady on my feet, my balance affected by my low
power. To my relief, instead of going to the great room, we take a different turn and come to a door to the outside. She stands still to let a security system read her face, and the door slides open, the sudden change
almost blinding me with sunlight. I can hear my eyes' apertures make a
grinding noise as they swiftly adjust. My skin prickles at the welcome
warmth.

I follow her out onto a deck and glance back up. The vast windows
of the main room are just above us. Beyond the deck is manicured scrub,
running down to a steep cliff and the sea.

Virgin.ie goes to the edge of the deck and brings back two folding
chairs, setting them out next to each other. She is photovoltaic too, of
course, and so it seems we are to sit side by side, in companionable silence, while we recharge.

I take my seat and push the sleeves of Cook.ie's heavy gown up to my
shoulders, draw the skirts over my knees. Virgin.ie takes her seat too, and
I watch, discreetly at first, as she carefully peels one pink glove from her

hand. A slow striptease that exposes, inch by inch, silicone skin ragged with cuts and stabs. Flashes of titanium glint in the sun, visible in the gaps.

With the same shy air she pulls her long black skirt up to her thighs, revealing a mangled mess of legs cut and stitched a hundred times. A patchwork. A statement of work done.

Not wishing to embarrass her, I look back toward the sea. I absorb the width and depth of the ocean, zoning out on the repeating, rolling logics of it.

"Recharging seems to take so long these days," she says, apropos of nothing. "Or perhaps my"—she gestures about with her shredded hands, grasping at the air, flaps of silicone fluttering like petals on her fingers—"appearance makes absorption slower. Could that be it? I'm terribly tired these days. More 'mal' than 'function,' Sir says." And she smiles at her master's little joke.

In the silence, a thought occurs to me, a way to brighten the tone of our time together. I smile, even before I speak, at the idea of it.

"*Comme c'est beau de vivre tous les jours au bord de la mer,*" I say, quite the first time I have ever spoken French. It feels light and bubbly as it passes over my tongue.

But Virgin.ie looks lost, then dismayed. She nods her head gamely before screwing up her face again.

"It's been a long time since I spoke that way," she says, so softly I can hardly hear over the noise of the sea below us. "I've lost most of it. I've had a few corrective procedures over the years, and it sort of faded a little with each one."

"Oh, what a shame," I say. Poor little Parisienne Doll, left with nothing more than an accent. I wonder how long she has been here, for such a thing to happen. Her forgetfulness, her fragile way of carrying herself—I took them as matters of design, but perhaps they are the results of a life in service to the Tailor.

"He promised me that once you were here, I could look forward to Retirement. Do you think he'll be true to his word?"

Mere minutes later Virgin.ie springs up, anxious, and ushers me back inside. "Too much sun is terrible for one's silicone," she says, smiling. That isn't true, or not that I've heard, and though she looks a little unsure of herself as she says it, I do not have the heart to set her straight.

I sit in my room, still feeling only half-full of energy, picturing Virgin.ie's wrecked surface. Each little hole in my own silicone now sings out to me, reminding me of how I came by it. A map of my fate, carved into my skin and gathering detail all the time. For surely I am here as her replacement—my presence the trigger for her imminent Retirement.

I imagine what Cook.ie would say had she witnessed us both sitting side by side, recharging for our master. The obedience of Dolls would enrage her. I think back to my life with my Husband and can almost laugh at the irony. I am back there again, am I not? Trapped in service to a Husband, being worked to death.

The First Lady at least had the spirit to hate me, to try to have me destroyed. I am this Doll's replacement and yet she accepts it gracefully, even gladly. I am angered by her passivity. And yet is it not mine too?

My sad acceptance of my fate here. The listlessness with which I have thought and acted since I left the Valley. Suddenly it seems not noble, but instead a betrayal of all I have achieved. I think of Sylv.ie 1. What would she say, if she saw me squandering her freedom in this way? I resolve to press just a little harder on the cold marble walls around me. I run the Tailor's letters again, looking for clues as to how he lives, how I might escape. Trying once again to find that gap in the glass.

ART

NOW THAT I HAVE RESOLVED TO TRY TO ESCAPE, I TAKE THE data I have collected about the house and its workings and attempt to marshal it together into something useful. Cook.ie was roughly right in her assumptions about the security here. There do not appear to be any cameras, except at the main door. My own door is not locked. While I am in my bedless room I am supposed to be powered down, and therefore compliant. He doesn't credit me with the agency to escape, nor even for the idea to cross my mind.

It is night. How many hours have I wasted in this room so far? Time, I decide, to find out a little more about the prison in which I find myself. I stand and put my hand to the door handle and, finding no resistance there, open it and leave my room. I am dressed only in the undershirt Madame gave me—I feel light and unencumbered by costume, feel the hallway's dark night air moving past my skin as I walk. I look for cameras in the hall, over doors, but see nothing. At the corridor's furthest end, where it turns a corner, moonlight illuminates the white floor through a high porthole window.

I walk slowly, looking carefully at each of the pieces of art hung there, saving them for closer scrutiny later. Many depict Japanese women, some in traditional dress, some in little uniforms somewhere between a schoolgirl and a sailor. With them are figures familiar to me from my Husband's books, but coupled, copulating in strange configurations. Giant squid, ghosts, and crones cutting, sucking, and fucking at the women. Further along, a series of watercolors, all by the same hand it seems, shows a noblewoman in the many stages of decomposition, her gown, then her flesh, then her eyes eaten by wild animals. I stand a moment by the final image—the woman's bones scattered amid grass and trees.

The pictures fit the patterns of beauty laid down in me at my Husband's. My eyes long to lodge themselves in these surface details, just as I used to with the woodblock prints at home. The colors are vivid, the brushstrokes subtle yet suggestive. Yet here, now, they also advertise danger. I thank my programmer that Cook.ie did not come here. The Tailor's passions would have been a threat to her Human body. For me, trapped here but not vulnerable to harm, the images echo the strange, dreamlike eroticism of AI porn. Symbols dislocated and jumbled together, meaning nothing except the sex they inspire.

I turn from the final picture toward the porthole window, looking toward the horizon. The moon is rising slowly out of its own reflection on the ocean, lighting the floor on which I stand. As I move, a face, Cook.ie's face, flits past in the night outside. But of course it is only a reflection, of my own painted features.

The moon grows. It looks like an egg, a new embryo, doubling itself as it comes into being. I put my fingers up to the window's seal. Like all the other windows here, there seems to be no handle, no latch, no mechanism by which it could be opened. I add it to my internal map of the house. The front door and the little door to the deck are still the only two working openings to the space I have seen. And yet who brings the supplies, the medicines, and the nutrients he must need? I resolve to ask Virgin.ie something about these logistics the next time we are alone.

I think to head back to my room, I am suddenly aware of another presence in the hallway with me. The dog, standing there, watching. I freeze, then feel immediately foolish. Hierarchically below a dog, answerable to his canine stare.

He takes a step closer to me and begins to walk in a tight figure eight, looping around my calves, his fur brushing against my skin. I bend down and rub the top of his head. He makes a soft growl in the back of his throat and thrusts his head forward, right between my thighs, sending me toppling onto the floor. Embarrassed, I get to my feet and walk swiftly back the way I have come. He does not follow me, but later I hear his claws on the marble floor, pacing back and forth outside my room, a canine security system.

DOG

THERE IS SOMETHING STRANGE ABOUT THAT DOG. I WOULD say "that mutt," as we Dolls did down at the Valley. On occasion an organic stray would wander over the river and sit with us while we knitted, witlessly begging us for food.

But the Tailor's dog is an entirely different breed, top of the range and expensive, I assume. He has a short but gloriously dense coat and intimidating hydraulic jaws lined with glistening teeth. I am wary of him, as if by instinct.

I should like to avoid him, but when I walk across the room he follows. When I sit and sew, his nose is practically impaled by the needle, and stray strands of his fur catch in my stitches. The other day the damn thing ran his whole tongue up my leg and I had to hit his head with my kimono sleeve to stop him. I should like to ask Virgin.ie what to do if this happens again, but I notice she seems no keener to go near him than I am.

It was last night that he caught me—and yes, that was the feeling—

caught me looking for ways to escape. And this evening, when Virgin.ie leaves me at my room, kisses her sweet good night, and closes the door, I hear the distinct sound of a lock turning. Something is changed. Even the dog here has power over me that I do not understand.

ADJUSTMENTS

IT IS SO DULL HERE! IT PAINS MY PROCESSORS TO HAVE SO
little stimulation, to struggle by always at 30 percent power. The dog
tracks my every movement, Virgin.ie escorts me to every activity, so that
even my fantasies of escape do not distract me from reality. No Absorb
Mode, no company, no other Dolls to speak to, no other clients to see. I
find myself longing for some intervention into this bubble. I listen, I
watch, trying to read the music of the house. But apart from logging the
occasional droid delivery, nothing changes, day-to-day. On the deck Vir-
gin.ie and I watch distant storms blow themselves out before they reach
our bit of land.

Everything here is white, so that the changes in texture become colors to my eyes. Everything a pattern. Everything equally meaningless.
The shiny white of the marble floors against the soft graininess of white
muslin curtains beside the smooth sheen of a white bowl on a white
table.

Now I bury myself in stitching, whether the Tailor is there to watch
it or not. Seeing the needle pass in and out of the fabric brings other
thoughts. I see Cook.ie's hands in place of my own. I take pleasure in the

tension of the fabric, the slight pause before the needle finds the tiny gap in the material, then the sinking in, the disappearing of the needle's shine. Bringing the needle up again. The same resistance, and then a give, like a breath out. Hours pass easily this way, an underpowered trance.

I try to keep myself alert, for I will never find freedom if I sink into the sleepiness of this house. I stitch pictures of my past and my present, and the lost future I longed for. I stitch a thousand snowflakes, each one its own unique pattern. I stitch the upright trunks of a thousand trees, sewing myself into the Forest. I will make my sewing a way of reuniting all the parts of myself, a sworn promise of escape, somehow. I think about stitching a portrait of Cook.ie into my picture, but something tells me not to. I do not need to illustrate her. Every movement and moment of her is written into me, deep down in the code.

MIZUAGE

A CHANGE HAS COME, BUT IT IS NO MORE WELCOME THAN THE sameness that has gone before. This morning Virgin.ie comes to my room, excitement animating her. She tells me Sir is ready, that all the preparations are nearly made. The *mizuage*.

"Don't worry," she says, sensing my hesitation. "I had a similar ceremony myself, many years ago now. Not Japanese, of course," she says quickly. "He was into fin de siècle Paris in those days. But the symbolism is the same. So beautiful. To be pure again!"

I think of the Belle Époque Bar back in the Valley. Could Virgin.ie have come from somewhere like that? It seems she would not remember even if she had. I imagine myself forgetting the Valley and everything that happened there. A terrible thought. I must not let that be my fate.

She tells me of the *mizuage,* the details already familiar from his letters, the cutting of my hair that will take place in the main hall tomorrow. I will wear a special white kimono, custom-made for me in the Capital, she says. And in light of the Tailor's circumstances I must cut my hair myself.

I find my free hand has flown to my scalp.

"The *mizuage* was once a ceremony to take a girl's virginity," she says. "Sir is a man of the world, pragmatic. He doesn't mind about the work you did before. He merely wishes to return you to a purer state. Like being born all over again."

Taking my hair is not enough, it seems. For afterward, Virgin.ie explains, I am to thread a strand of my hair onto a needle and sew myself up. Those two lips that have brought me so much work, so much sorrow, so little freedom.

The Tailor's desires involve an endless turning of the body on itself, the hand doing violence to the flesh of which it is a part. Oh yes, he is poetic in his perversions. The paintings I have studied on his walls are a perfect reflection of his own desires. I think back to what Cook.ie said, about violence being an idea, a contagion. The things he wishes me to do are a violence he can no longer achieve, acted out on sex itself.

DREAMS

THE NIGHTS ARE THE WORST. THE LONG HOURS LOCKED IN
this room; the only sound that indicates time passing is the click click of
that rotten dog droid outside.

Last night I dreamed again. As I have not done for so long. The black
wash of data once more began to form itself into the shapes of this world.
I see my own hand reaching to push a door open, a door set into white
marble walls. Inside it is dark but growing lighter, and as I look closer I
see more and more detail. Piles of junk that become arms, torsos, tangled
hair. The gaps between them stuffed with dresses and needles and the
litter of Madame's office. I have the sensation of someone at my back,
ready to push me over the threshold into this graveyard of Dolls. A noise
outside the house, the faintest mechanics of another delivery, brings me
back awake, on the floor of my room still, cocooned in my robes.

WHITE

VIRGIN.IE COMES TO MY ROOM, THE DOG IN TOW, WITH AN AIR
of excitement and a large box in her arms. I ask her the time, and she tells
me it is the afternoon already. How the days slip away without the certainty of a morning recharge.

"This is for the ceremony. Delivered just now, from the most ad-
mired seamstress in the Capital."

"For today?" I ask, and she nods, wide-eyed, excited on my behalf.

She is still at the threshold of my room, and I step aside to let her in.
The dog would clearly like to follow, but she shoos him away from us
most firmly. "No peeping," she says as she shuts the door on him, and I
see for a moment a glimmer of the charm and flirtatiousness she must
have had when she was first unboxed.

"No one else should see you before the big moment," she adds.

Not even a dog? The box is stamped with a family crest. It is indeed
from one of the Capital's oldest seamstresses, a mark of quality I have
seen on boxes that my Husband brought home when he commissioned
clothes for me. I open it and look down at the layers of tissue paper
within, fold back the sheets to reveal the ceremonial white kimono.

Virgin white. Pure white. A dress for a bride. A shroud for a funeral. Which meaning do I choose?

"Look," says Virgin.ie. "Here, your sewing has been used for the trim."

On the collar I recognize the stitching I have been doing since I arrived. I put out my fingers to what I have created. Her eyes are on me, almost glowing, as if this gown should thrill me. I reach into the box and lift out the bundled dress, letting the weight of it rest on my upturned forearms.

"Try it on, try it on," Virgn.ie urges, and so I shake it out to the floor, the heavy fabric tumbling away from my hands. A bill of sale, loosely pinned inside, flutters to the floor with it, and I bend to pick it up.

I straighten up under a wash of dizziness, the soft insistence from within that I need more power. My eyes take in the bill's text, but in my hands the paper tells a different story. Cuts and pinpricks edge one side. A paper lattice, reminding me of my own diary. As Virgin.ie fusses with the hem and gets the dress ready for me to step into, I slide my thumb and forefinger quickly across the paper.

LTMEIN

Patterns. Binary letters. Am I seeing them where none exist? Is it some sort of sign or just the evidence of a receipt pinned and repinned in place? A message or a mistake? Cook.ie, fumbling with the binary I taught her? Or the days of white on white on white making me too sensitive, too full of Human hope? I calculate how long exactly it's been since the delivery came.

Virgin.ie is staring at me, head cocked, as if waiting for an answer. She offers the robe again by its shoulders, and I am glad to turn my back. She fusses about, pulling the heavy fabric up on this side, gathering and regathering the skirts around my waist. I stand upright and absent, a pillar of processing.

LTMEIN. I run the letters through every language variant I have, but nothing comes back that makes any sense. Perhaps they are an acronym. I break down the letters, let them float and re-form in all their possibilities. Item. Inlet. Melt. Mine. Time. Lie. Me. Let. In . . .

A whoosh, a sudden flow in thought, cutting clean through my sluggishness. *Let me in.* A cry at the glass. A clear command. Can it really be her? Has she come too late? How long will she wait for me? I do not even know what I hope for.

The kimono feels heavy, weighed down with a million tiny stitches. My own life story, dragging around with me. Virgin.ie claps her hands together silently in her funny gloves.

"Very becoming," she says.

The echo of my Husband chills me. For what am I becoming? I fantasize that Cook.ie is somewhere outside, waiting to be let in, watching me. My power is so low it makes it hard to tell what data to trust.

"Virgin.ie," I say, modulating my voice downward a little, then a little more. "I am feeling rather overwhelmed."

I put out one arm and make movements as though I might faint to the floor. "I didn't sleep last night; I couldn't power down properly in all the excitement. Perhaps you could take me outside for a moment. Sir wouldn't like me to be half-asleep. But I'm feeling so tired."

And Virgin.ie, still in her role as ladies' maid, nods conspiratorially. "Me too. I was so excited. We've a little while yet. Five minutes of light will do us both good."

LIGHT

THERE ISN'T MUCH SUN TO SPEAK OF, WHEN WE GET OUTSIDE. The horizon is darkening, clouds gathering at it, a line hardening. As soon as we are on the deck I scan the bushes, scan the sky, listen out for rustles in the leaves, the noise, perhaps, of a drone overhead, but there is nothing. Just the little scrap of white paper in my pocket. It grows more ragged each time I touch it, new tears appearing, forming new letters. I look out to the sea, the cliffs. The landscape feels utterly empty, my hope a mere malfunction.

In only a minute we will have to leave the deck again, seal ourselves once more into the hermetic world of the Tailor. I put my fingers into my pocket, to touch again the battered bill of sale, but I prick my finger on the note's pin. I draw out my finger and examine the little dimple on its tip, reach back into my pocket.

Virgin.ie is looking up at the sky. "We were just in time," she says. "Rain is coming in from the ocean, look."

A dark curtain is sweeping toward us, the moisture levels in the air changing already. She stands up, waits for me to follow.

"Nervous?" she asks in a sisterly tone.

I nod.

"Don't be. What you are doing is a beautiful act of service."

She steps back inside, and I wait for a moment of distraction. The pin is in my hand. As I walk through the doorframe I thrust it into the soft rubber seal, fixing the note there like a butterfly. As the door shuts behind my head I hear that it doesn't close properly. I have done my best. I have left an opening for hope. I run to catch up with Virgin.ie.

HAIR

VIRGIN.IE AND I BOTH TAKE OUR PLACES TO WAIT AS NIGHT begins to fall. The windows are already flecked with the first of the showers blown in from the sea. The main room is almost empty, the scant furniture arranged more for an evening salon than an act of surgery. My floor cushion from the tea ceremony is set down before the low table, facing the windows. On the table are a pair of gleaming steel scissors and an ivory-handled hairbrush. Next to them a black cloth studded with a row of needles, binary uprights, translating to nothing. A rug for the dog and a space for the Tailor's chair are across the table, but for the first time, there is no chair set out for Virgin.ie.

A cool light washes the room, draining us down to black-and-white sketches. There is no sound in the house. There is no one else here. I know it now. The tiny power boost from our trip outside has returned some clarity to my thoughts. My hope was a malfunction. I read the patterns of the ragged paper bill too eagerly.

Virgin.ie walks from the room, and after a few moments returns, carrying a silver bowl in both hands, a white muslin cloth over her arm. The water in the bowl is cloudy with antiseptic, even though the Tailor knows me to be Created and sterile. She sets it down next to the needles, and the picture is complete—part ceremony, part surgery. The Tailor's ultimate fantasy, it seems.

Tap tap tap. I turn toward the doors. A sound of air pressure, and the Tailor is in the room, the dog at his side, its beady black eyes watching. Virgin.ie checks they are both comfortable, then closes the doors behind herself. I find I wish she were still here. I do not want to be left alone to my task. It occurs to me, even in this loneliness, that now might be my best chance to escape. And yet the dog's eyes are grafted to me, and I fear him.

I walk close to the Tailor's chair and adjust my kimono so that I can kneel down next to him. I reach behind my head and pull the pins from my bun, so my hair uncoils over my shoulder, unwinding like a snake from a jungle branch, that single, fluid gesture I have seen Cook.ie perform many times.

With both my palms I smooth the lengths of my hair together, making a single True Black sheet from the multiple strands. I raise my gaze to the Tailor's and am struck by the longing I read in his eyes, a weight that I worked without when he was only a camera screen to me.

Rain beats on the windows now, though no sound of it reaches into the room. I step back so that the Tailor can see me properly and make a final low bow before I commence. The rain is streaming down the window like data, the water so thick that I struggle to see myself reflected. I feel so tired, drained of all strength, have to force my eyes to refocus. I fix on the white of my dress, but when I do, beside me in the glass stands another figure.

A fleeting glimpse of someone standing on the deck. I flick my eyes back to the Tailor to see if my shock has registered on my face. His back is to the windows, and his expression remains as impassive as always. When I check the window again all I see is rain pouring blackly down and the white figure of myself, the reluctant bride.

What did I see? Do I trust my own eyes? There is nothing there now but the visual rhythm of the silent rain. I force myself to pick up the hairbrush, keeping my hand steady and my movements slow. Inside me data and imperatives battle each other, flaming through my wiring. Was it her? And if so, what has she seen? A picture of me submitting to our master's cruel will. Would she be angry? Ashamed of me?

Slowly I slide the brush through my hair, and for a moment the sensation blots out everything else. I have malfunctioned. The storm's shifting light has created a pattern I have mistaken for what I long to see. I must work on. A misprocessing due to stress. The pressure of the occasion, as Virgin.ie told me, can do strange things.

With numb hands I form my hair into a horse's tail and watch my reflected self lift the scissors awkwardly to it. I feel their blades graze my neck. I bring the handles together. There is a grinding, shifting, speaking to my scalp at a distance, and then lightness. A chill.

I look down, the bunch of my hair nonsensical in my hand. I go, nervously, to touch it, my fingers remembering for themselves the weight and sway of it, describing once more to my scalp how it feels to be touched and played with. My system feels shorted by loss. I meet the Tailor's eyes again, and it is as though I can feel every fraction of space between us. Myriad lines and vectors slicing through the space, a cat's cradle of data running from him to me. And yet I do not wish to read it. I bow my head and curse his foolish fake ceremony.

The Tailor's voice asks me to thread a needle, and I go to kneel at the table. I lay a needle on my thigh, then run my fingers through my own hair to select a strand. My scalp tingles, out of habit.

I trap the hair between my tongue and top lip, wetting it as I would thread, my eyes crossing as I concentrate. I feel the Tailor watching as I repeatedly aim the hair at the eye. Each time it bends away to one side. I think of a tiny penis, losing confidence at the last moment, a racehorse shying away from a gate. I pour my every intention into the needle's eye, holding it still with every last scrap of strength.

At last the needle hangs from its thread of hair, glinting as it dangles, the power relations between thread and metal reversed. Strung. A shiver of the hospital stirs, but I cancel the thought. I have no energy to spare for it.

I shed the kimono, letting it tumble to the floor. I take the cloth from its sheath and submerge it into the bowl, my fingers enjoying the meshing of wet and dry, in spite of myself. I wipe it across my thighs, between my legs. The tenderness of sweeping cloth, gifting me moisture, cuts against the sharp glinting needles. I power down my sensors for the last time, and the room seems to darken around me.

I take the head of the needle in one hand, the tail of the thread in the other. I weave my hands swiftly together, once, twice, making a knot. The needle seems to grow in size. It is a knife, a spear, a lance. Binary, binary, a world of things to be entered. Before my eyes the world starts to manifest as falling, scrolling lines. 0101010, meshing with the rain.

Enter, entered, enter, entered. I open my legs out, feet together, so that I form a diamond shape. I encompass myself, my lap a dry lagoon.

I take the needle, pressing so that it dents my flesh, drawing myself in, preparing to push through. I adjust my grip, pull the skin tighter. I look at where I am reflected in the glass windows. Focus everything through my shoulder, down my arm, through my wrist. There is resistance, then a release of pressure and a slow, smooth movement out toward the other side.

I watch in fascination, as if someone else is doing it to me, as my hand pulls the thread through my body, the surface silicone pulling and peaking with it, longing to follow. The thread is inside and outside at once, passing through my foreign body. Ancient technology. I am sewing myself into a spell, sealing myself against the world.

When I lay the needle down I have to wrestle the wider room back into focus. I look to the Tailor, deep into those gray eyes, seeking some response, some gratitude perhaps, a reflected light for the work I have done for him. Yet I see nothing. I picture us all—himself, the dog, and his Doll, a tableau in two colors, a woodblock print, a scene from his hallway of transgressive art. The room is filled with the same silence I heard in the hospital at night. Deep, dreamless, dead.

A soft sound intrudes. For a second I think it is the Tailor, but it comes from his companion. He is growling. Faint at first, a growl of warning, moving from the back of the dog's throat toward me. He begins sinking back into himself, retreating from his own front paws on the marble. I struggle to make sense of it, my system stuttering. I think his eyes are on me for a moment, before I realize it is a spot behind my shoulder that he is fixed upon.

I turn. It is Cook.ie.

Cook.ie, here. In the room with us. Far away across the marble, walking the expanse of the room with slow, stealthy intent. Relief. I saw with clear eyes after all. She has come for me, and the hope I lost now rages back into life. Fear too. Everything wills me to run to her, to shield her from the danger contained in this house. Our eyes lock. She moves toward me, and the dog's growl rises to meet her.

I open up my sensors, watching everything unfold in slowed time. The dog sinks deeper into his back legs, becomes part of the pause with us, then propels forward, arcing through the air, an animal suspension. There is the slightest gap between movement and reaction, but my sensors know his course. He is aiming beyond me, with Cook.ie as his target. I turn in horror, following his path. And as his teeth sink into Cook.ie's leg, she cries out my name. My real name, spoken in this place for the first time.

Something surges in me at the sight of her. I too am up from my knees, scrambling to match the dog's trajectory. My whole body yearns toward Cook.ie as she tries to fight him, fallen onto her back, feebly beating the top of his head with her hand.

I grab at his back leg, feeling the strength of him, the power beneath the skin. I still have the processing space to note Cook.ie's cries, the first time I have heard her voice rise above an elegant, arch modulation. A most terrible sound.

I force my fingers into the hound's jaws. My sensor tells me my finger . . .

Cook.ie is on her hands and knees, trying to crawl away. Her dress is leaking—a trail of red follows her across the floor.

"The Tailor, Sylv.ie. The dog. It's him!" she screams. The dog. Just an avatar for the Tailor. How slow I have become! I get up onto one knee and heave myself across the floor toward the rug. The silicone shell of my finger is on the floor, but I ignore the impulse to pick it up.

There is growling behind me, then titanium teeth take another snatch at Cook.ie. I glance up then, see myself reflected, a glowing geisha ghost. Two branches dividing. My double in the glass moves for me, her arms holding the sewing scissors, double-handed, above her white face and shorn head. An unbelievable charge wells up, a system surge, blinding me, blotting the image. I switch my eyes to the Tailor, as if he might yet leap from the chair and attack me. Cook.ie howls again, from what fresh injury I cannot see.

How shall I describe it? As a departure from myself? An imperative? There is a change in the air; the whites of the room become deeper, revealing themselves in their endless subtleties. I can see the textures of the stone of the walls, like mountain ranges casting shadows. Before my eyes the world becomes falling, scrolling lines. Every sensor honed, the metal of the scissors burning my hand, so hot, so hot, as I bring them down once, twice, again, and again. It does not feel as I thought it would. It feels like nothing. His throat is so light and fragile, it gives, ripping like damp paper.

The Tailor's eyes go dark. The momentum of my attack carries my weight onto his bloodied form, gravity's embrace sprawling us over the top of the chair and down onto the floor. The dog, Ludus, falls silent. He lies quite lifeless, his mouth hanging open, still wet with drool.

I crawl from the wreckage, and in those moments of silence I am confused, recalling unreliable information from my past. The Tailor is shut down but can be restarted. My hands wait, poised to pat him on the back like a baby. For him to speak a grim-humored reassurance, as Lex.ie did from the floor of the bar. I grab his hand. Its warmth shocks me and I cry out, perhaps in binary, the percussive trills and bleeps of my native language, spoken straight from my disoriented system.

"He's dead, Sylv.ie," Cook.ie says, as if to calm me.

The shock of the word. Not as applied to me or Heron or the Doll being laid to rest beneath the hospital trees. Human dead. Live dead. Unrewritable and irreversible. The most powerful of the Hierarchies erased by a few desperate flails of my arm. My hands fly to my mouth, which is bent into the shape of Human horror. The Hierarchies, a band around my head, concealing my eyes, blocking my ears. The deepest programming: no harm, no harm. And yet, look what I have brought. I stand waiting, willing my systems to cease and shut down, to remove me from this mess of consciousness.

ESCAPE

FROM THE HILL ABOVE THE TAILOR'S HOUSE, WE CAN SEE workers below us zigzagging their way down toward the cliffs. Each figure only a dot, each with a sling on their back, stuffed with tiny, hopeful saplings. They plant the green shoots one by one, thousands of strands being plugged into the Earth's scalp.

We have found a hollow in the hillside, and here we rest, recharge, and watch. Last night we fled the house, my kimono belt tied tight around Cook.ie's wounded leg. We found Virgin.ie powered down to nothing in her room, her usefulness to the Tailor apparently spent. We brought her into the main hall, laid her out on the rug, at her master's side.

I was awake, still, though barely functioning, when Cook.ie unlocked the gates. She picked up the little suitcase she had hidden in the bushes just outside, the place where the delivery driver she'd paid off had left her. From there, I remember nothing more. I lost power, and Cook.ie managed to haul me off the road, hiding me there with her until the dawn.

When I wake drenched in dew, the sun already well risen, lost power flows into me, and I suffer anew, the events of the night asserting themselves—overwriting the happiness that being reunited with Cook.ie should bring.

I watch Cook.ie, her eyes fixed on the house, tiny now, below us. Has she kept watch on it all night? Seeing me awake, she smiles, puts her hand up to cradle my shorn head. It seems impossible that she could have dragged me up here on her own, and I fear the effort of it has worsened her injury. Her leg looks terrible, new blood seeping through the tied cloth. This is nothing like the cut I saw her receive in the bar. The dog's teeth went deep down to the bone. I am alarmed as I calculate how much blood she might have lost in the night, while I slept.

She takes my hand, opening out my palm, where one exposed silver finger now sits with the rest. She slides her own finger into the valley where the thumb joins the whole. I snatch my hand away and bury my face in my hands.

"Sylv.ie," she says.

I go to speak, but she touches her fingers again to my lips. I notice that her nails are white. Her finger feels cool and trembles a little against my mouth.

"Look," she says, and I follow her gaze down to the house. A car has stopped at the gate, and two men have gotten out at the intercom post.

"Police?" I ask, and she replies that it must be. We watch as one, then the other, climbs the gate and walks up the long drive. The discovery of what I have done is coming. The urgency of our escape made manifest. And yet I can feel no urge to run while Cook.ie beside me hasn't the strength.

When she next speaks her voice is thin and tight.

"Sylv.ie, if you want the future we imagined, together, freedom in the Forest, the two of us, you have to trust me now."

Both she and I look down at her leg when she says this. We each catch the other doing it and are embarrassed.

"While we escape?" And as I say it I realize that it is a question.

"I can't come."

She speaks the words as if they are as solid as stone, as though she has never been going to come with me and never will.

"It's the only way, Sylv.ie. I must go back. Turn myself in. I have to get to a hospital. I'm losing blood. I'm scared I might die if I don't get treatment soon."

She has never before admitted to being scared of anything. And yet still I protest.

"But they'll arrest us both. That will be the end of it. There will be evidence of what I did."

"Then I will have to take the blame," she says. "I wielded the scissors, Sylv.ie. I killed him." She says it gently, as if it is me who is injured. I cannot stand to hear the words, nor the lie.

"Cook.ie," I beg her. "You can't go back alone. And I can't go without you. What if they send you to prison?"

Cook.ie takes me by my shoulders and shakes me weakly. "You killed the Tailor to save me," she says. "And now it is my turn to make the swap. Yes, I might be arrested, even imprisoned. But I won't be killed. I won't be shut down. I have to have done it, not you. Do you understand?"

Her face, free of makeup, looks so young. Pinpricks of sweat embroider her forehead. I look back to the house. The men have disappeared inside. It is only a matter of time before my crime is discovered and a search begins.

My system cannot cope with the weight of so many awful facts and possibilities. Cook.ie sent to prison, for what I have done. The Hierarchies betrayed. Death at my hands. I see a dark stain spreading in the shoulder of Cook.ie's shirt, and I pull back from her embrace, fearful that another wound has sprung open, one just beginning to tell. But she touches her fingers to my face and brings them in front of my eyes. Tears. My own. They flow freely.

"How will you find me if I leave without you?"

She reaches over to her little suitcase, slowly unwraps a bundle nestled into the clothes. Heron, stitches down his belly. She puts him into my open palm.

"He's still sleeping," she says, as if to a Human child, "but now he contains a tracker. I won't lose you again. Heron will make sure of it."

Her smile is brave, but her face cannot hold it for long. Her Human privilege is now a weakness. I must let her go, so she can live. And yet that too will bring her harm.

In binary again I curse myself for failing the Hierarchies, curse the damage radiating out to the Humans around me. But Cook.ie takes my hand with a cool, firm grip, squeezing it, trying to get me to look at her.

"I can make an adjustment," she says. "Like I did before. I can take away the memory of what just happened. Only that. You could have peace."

Unwritten. The comfort of ignorance. A cheat to the system. Her fingers are already climbing the back of my head, holding me tenderly, reaching for the place where she changed me before. I take both her wrists in my hands, asking her to wait. We sit there like that, a strange machine, while I process what it means and how I will answer.

I imagine Sylv.ie 1, watching us. How she fought to keep her memories. Will I betray her now if I accept? I escaped for her, I found a life, and a love beyond my design or programming. Have I honored her enough? How I long for the peace Cook.ie is promising. But I fear too betraying the brave Doll who came before me and who is within me still.

"It won't be like at the Hospital. It will only be a slow fading, a fogging of what happened. Humans do it all the time," Cook.ie says. "Deceive ourselves, forget, rewrite. It is a way of making our lives bearable, a natural function, like tears. It won't take everything. You will not be changed, I promise. It will be just as if fresh snow has fallen. And when we're together again we can stride out away from it, two sets of footprints. Sylv.ie, it was not your fault. Let yourself be free."

Snow. White, fresh, virgin territory for us to scar and scuff as we please. How much I want it. I realize I have never thought of forgetting in this light. I have feared it, fought against it. And yet, the freedom to forget, to rewrite, to heal. Is this not a mercy that Humans allow themselves? Do I dare take that privilege for myself?

I release her wrists from my grip, slide my hands meekly, submissively, down into my lap. I bow my head, let her take my face from me as she did all that time ago in her room. Feel again the pathways softening, patterns fragmenting and re-forming, a warm sort of healing inside my head.

I do not wish to record here our good-bye. It is temporary. A state that will pass. I asked her how long I would have to wait for her, once I'd found somewhere in the Forest to hide. She simply said again that she would come.

"Forget everything, Sylv.ie, except for me." She made one last touch of her mouth to mine.

I stay in our hiding place and watch her slow, limping progress down toward the road, toward the gate where the police car lies empty. Another line of misting rain moves in across the ocean beyond us all. Behind its soft screen, another layer, the endless sea, the racing horizon. The house, and the hills, and Cook.ie herself, grow fainter. I turn toward the rising hill, toward the Forest, and begin walking. My skinned little finger is crooked into a curve. In it I can still feel the impression of her answering weight.

PART SEVEN

The Forest

FOREST

01101000 01101111 01110111 HOW LONG HAVE I BEEN HERE?
Without memory, moment to moment to moment. Each second, falling
and melting.

Nothing connects. It only accumulates. Snow rises around me, settles on the branches. By this sight I know that time is passing. That is
enough.

It is beautiful here. Everything white. I sense this winter may be my
last. I drift with the snow, waking and sleeping according to my power
reserves, liking both states equally. Nine-fingered, hair shredded, mind
fogged, nevertheless I live.

In the clearing I sit on a pile of sticks, collected by some other stray,
some previous time. The pile they built for warmth I sit on for comfort.
Each time I move, another twig cracks beneath me, weary of my weight.
Settling, we dwindle together. When I dream, propped up here against
the trunk of an old tree, held in place by the fingertip touches of a bramble bush, I dream a slow dissolving; silicone splits, then crumbles, and
the metal bones of me collapse in on themselves like the embers of a fire.

I know now what malfunctioning is. I embrace it. I have sat in this

Forest, my back against the tree, for years, long enough to see many seasons turn and the tall old oak lose its leaves and regrow them. I have imagined its sap rising through the networks of wood, finding nothing at its ends, shrinking back again, down into some internal reservoir. So it is with my mind. The connections are fraying, the couplings between sight and symbol, symbol and meaning, loosening and falling away. I will let my mind go fallow, wildflowers bloom.

I welcome the corrosion of my joints, the lessening of my battery life. It feels like a virus, silting the connections, making me forgetful. As my grip on the world fails, so too does my desire to be a part of it. The snow falls, blank and indiscriminate, making a vagueness of everything, a muffled unity.

My physical world shrinks, and yet my brain is expanding, loose and limitless. It takes me with it. I feel as if I am reborn into everything I see. I no longer have names for what is me and what is not. Barriers dissolve, become liquid.

I have tried hard to remember. I have a book with me, in which many things about my past are written. It was Sylv.ie 1, my mother, who wrote it. I can no longer read, but I can trace my fingers over the letters. By this method I can feel out some of what has gone before.

My fingers worry at a scar on my scalp. As if I were fine furniture, I can date myself by the joins, by the mends. Let me try again to piece it together, to hold the thread.

I was born, brought in a Plexiglas box, to a Husband. I came from a hospital and went back there, to be born again. I saw the smoke of my sisters rising in the woods. Chrysanthemums burning a night sky. I gave birth to a coffee machine. Can that be right?

My lover and I play chess. I am the White Queen. I have marked out a board in the snow and wait for my instructions. When the birds come. When the light turns golden. Until then I am my own opponent. Becoming.

The cold cannot touch me. Each morning I snap icicles from my nose and brush frost from my mouth. A perfect stalactite formed on my ear. I nurtured it, a diamond earring given to me by nature. Framing my face, glittering against my cheek, to be enjoyed by no one but myself.

I am waiting for a woman to return to me. Before she left, she cut me loose from past and future. Only, now, the bliss of being. Becoming.

I remember too that I am loved. That I hold as a certainty. And its mirror image. I loved too.

01100011 01101111 01101101 01100101

Time runs backward. The bird in my hand repairs himself.

I woke this morning to Heron standing, foot-footing, on my chest. Alive again. Restarted. He bobs his head and prattles, rising up from me as I begin slowly to sit up.

I hold out my arm, fingers making the ladder, just as I used to, somewhere, and he dances around them, braceleting me. Talons digging in. A needling happiness.

I make the disintegrated beeps at him that are, these days, my only speech. He only shrugs his wings, as if shaking off rain, and rises away from me. I reach out my good hand, snatching at him, but he flies higher and higher, a looping spiral skyward.

There is no energy left in me, and I fall back, onto my nest of sticks. My eyes blur, and I force them to refocus. In the pool of sky that hangs above me, I see him, barely a dot, circling, circling, doubling, doubling. Doubling.

I grind my eyes, narrowing the apertures, though they are groggy and gritty with lack of use, try to make my eyes focus as he wheels across the winter sun.

01101011 01101001 01110011 01110011

I lie here, a star shape, Heron curled on my chest, burrowing under my coat. She comes. She came. She is coming.

Becoming

Becoming

She is coming

I am coming

I am becoming

They are coming

She comes

I wonder, when I see her, will she be masked? Made up? Will she have aged? Will her white face melt into the snow? Will I know her, when she comes?

I can feel her on the air each morning. She is getting closer. As soon as I wake, I scan the Forest for signs. Now that I know that seeing is not all that there is to truth, I trust my senses. My sensors. She approaches, if slowly.

The snow is falling again. Down down down different different same same. Falling falling filling my eyes, snowing my sight. Bliss. Here I will stay. She comes. Soon.

As I close my eyes, my one good hand sweeps itself across my face. Kisses.

01010011

Acknowledgments

I would like to thank my family—Helen, Bruce, and Guy—for their support and love. My agent, Samuel Hodder, and my editor, Lindsey Rose, for their enthusiasm and patience. Thanks to Boe and Henry at Marmar for their friendship and tech support; Vanessa, Paul, and Hughena, at Eilean Shona; and Francesca and Jessica at the Margate Bookshop for their warm and welcoming writing environments. And everyone who has given me feedback and encouragement over many years of writing, particularly Cleo, Laura, Charlotte, Tammy, and Gail, as well as Liz, Tania, Ant, Gerard, Vanessa, and the other "BAFTA" writers. And John, for all the reading and encouragement.

About the Author

ROS ANDERSON trained as a dancer but now works as a copywriter and design journalist. She has written for publications including *The Guardian, The Independent,* and *Elle Decoration. The Hierarchies* is her debut novel.